Praise for Tracy Brogan

My Kind of You

"In this relaxed contemporary, Brogan (*Love Me Sweet*) creates a charming small town where even the scandals and secrets are relatively wholesome. Events sweep readers along, making them long for the idealized community Brogan portrays."

—*Publishers Weekly*

"Recommend this romantic story to fans of women's fiction."

—*Booklist*

"This story is filled with lively characters who jump off the page. The author knows how to capture her readers' attention. The scene where the hero tells the heroine that she's 'the kind of woman a man wants to make promises to' was romantic and sweet."

—*RT Book Reviews*, 4 Stars

Crazy Little Thing

WALL STREET JOURNAL BESTSELLER

RWA RITA® FINALIST, 2013, BEST FIRST BOOK

"Heart, humor, and characters you'll love—Tracy Brogan is the next great voice in contemporary romance."

—Kristan Higgins, *New York Times* bestselling author

Love Me Sweet

RWA RITA® FINALIST, 2016,
BEST CONTEMPORARY ROMANCE

"An upbeat, generous message about finding yourself, standing up for yourself, and living an authentic life . . . A sexy, slightly kooky romance that should please Bell Harbor fans."

—*Kirkus Reviews*

Jingle Bell Harbor: A Novella

"Brogan's hilarious voice and wordplay will immediately ensnare readers in this quick but satisfying small-town romance."

—Adrian Liang, Amazon Book Review

"*Jingle Bell Harbor* is a fun, funny, laugh-out-loud Christmas read that will surely put you right in the mood for the season."

— *The Romance Reviews*, 5 Stars

"This was an incredible read! I was definitely surprised by this book and in a great way."

—*My Slanted Bookish Ramblings*, 4.5 Stars

"*Jingle Bell Harbor* by Tracy Brogan is about discovering what you want, deciding what you need to finally be happy, and rediscovering a love of the holidays. It's a quick, easy read filled with laughter and enjoyable quirky characters. If you're in the mood for something light and funny, I would recommend *Jingle Bell Harbor* by Tracy Brogan."

—*Harlequin Junkie*, 4 Stars

"This is a really cute, uplifting Christmas novella. It's quick, light, and gives you warm fuzzies just in time for the upcoming holidays. There is plenty of humor to keep you entertained, and the quirky residents of Bell Harbor will keep you reading to see what else is in store."

—*Rainy Day Reading Blog*, 4 Stars

Hold on My Heart

"Successfully blends a sassy heroine and humor with deep emotional issues and a traditional romance . . . The well-developed characters and the sweet story with just a touch of heat will please readers looking for a creative take on romance."

—*Publishers Weekly*

"Launched in hilarious style by an embarrassingly cute meet, this delightful romantic comedy will keep the smiles coming."

—*Library Journal*

Highland Surrender

"*Highland Surrender* features plenty of action, romance, and sex with well-drawn individuals—a strong, yet young heroine and a delectable hero—who don't act out of character. The story imparts a nice feeling of 'you are there,' with a well-presented look at the turbulent life in sixteenth-century Scotland."

—RT Book Reviews, 4 Stars

"Treachery and political intrigue provide a well-textured backdrop for a poignant romance in which a young girl, well out of her depths, struggles to reconcile what she thinks she knows with what her heart tells her. *Highland Surrender* is a classic sweep-me-away tale of romance and derring-do!"

—Connie Brockway, *New York Times* bestselling author

The New Normal

Books by Tracy Brogan

The Trillium Bay Series

My Kind of You
My Kind of Forever

The Bell Harbor Series

Crazy Little Thing
The Best Medicine
Love Me Sweet
Jingle Bell Harbor: A Novella

Novellas and Stand-Alone Titles

Highland Surrender
Hold on My Heart
Weather or Knot

The New Normal

TRACY BROGAN

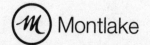 Montlake

Published by Montlake, Seattle

www.apub.com

Amazon, the Amazon logo, and Montlake are trademarks of Amazon.com, Inc., or its affiliates.

ISBN-13: 9781503905238
ISBN-10: 1503905233

Cover design by Laura Klynstra

Printed in the United States of America

For Jane,
who has been with me through every rendition
of every story.

Chapter 1

Carli Lancaster knew mistakes came in all shapes and sizes. Some were minuscule, insignificant, and easily overcome, like forgetting to move the laundry from the washer to the dryer or setting down your latte too hard and having a sploosh of foam splash out the side of the cup, while other mistakes were far more vast, tangible, and impossible to ignore, like the one currently staring her down in the middle of her own front yard.

"Gus," she said firmly, "drop it."

Her oversize puppy with his undersize motivation to comply did not, in fact, drop it. He didn't even blink. Instead, the black-and-white Bernedoodle just stood there in the grass, wagging his floofy tail with a raggedy stuffed panda dangling from his mouth and a mischievous *come near me and I'll bolt* expression on his sweet, fuzzy face. It was a standoff and one Carli was certain to lose. Just like she'd lost the emotionally charged negotiations with her daughters when agreeing to get them a puppy. Carli had assumed they'd want something pocket-size and portable, like the kind celebrities dressed in pointless argyle sweater-vests and carried around in their purses, but Mia and Tess had outnumbered and outmaneuvered her until she'd agreed to this Clydesdale of a dog. At six months old, Gus weighed almost seventy pounds, and his growth spurt was more like a growth eruption that showed no signs of slowing. Just as *he* showed no signs of letting go of that panda.

"Don't slouch. Stand up straight. Say it like you mean it," said the aptly named Mrs. Stern. The dog-obedience trainer stood next to Carli, looking both superior and annoyed. If the woman had been holding a whip, she most certainly would've cracked it. At Carli, not the dog. Mrs. Stern's philosophy was that there were no bad dogs, only incompetent humans. She wore a tweed jacket in spite of the warm August evening and chunky, serviceable shoes. Carli was both fascinated and intimidated by her abrupt, humorless demeanor, but the trainer had come highly recommended by several of the neighbors. Probably because they were all equally invested in making sure this behemoth of a hound learned some manners. Nervous joggers, stroller-pushing moms, and even the other neighborhood dogs crossed to the other side of the street when they saw Gus bounding across the yard, and more than once Carli had lost her grip on the leash and had to chase after him.

"Drop it, Gus. I *mean* it," Carli said, and wow, did she mean it. With all her heart she meant it, because she'd grown to love him in spite of herself—and in spite of *him*—and if she couldn't get this wildebeest tamed, she'd have to find someplace else for him to live, and her kids would never forgive her. And she'd never forgive herself. They'd all lost enough over the past year, and no one wanted to face another goodbye.

"Drop it," Carli murmured under her breath one more time, mentally willing him to understand. He didn't. Or if he did, he just didn't care. He wasn't a bad dog, of course. Carli understood that he was just young and impulsive. And big. Goodness, he was so big, with silky black fur dotted with patches of white and feet the size of catcher's mitts. He already took up half of her bed. And yes, she knew she should probably make him sleep in his crate at night, but they liked to watch *The Late Show* together, and then she was always too tired to take him back downstairs. Besides, she liked the company.

Mrs. Stern paused before finally making a gruff little sound from deep in her throat, and Gus, that traitor, instantly dropped the panda.

It landed softly on the ground as he sat down, his pink tongue lolling from his mouth.

"I think that's all for today," the dog trainer said with an audible tone of exasperation and a not remotely subtle frown at Carli, indicating it was definitely *she* who was being judged, not the dog. And maybe it *was* her fault. Maybe she was too lenient with him. Or too inconsistent. Or too unclear with her expectations. Or maybe she was just bad at relationships, even with her pets. She'd never been any good at setting boundaries and sticking to them, and dogs were intuitive about stuff like that. Maybe Gus was onto her. Maybe she *should* put him in his crate at night . . .

"Are you sure we should stop? I've got more time," Carli said.

"I'm quite sure," Mrs. Stern answered. "After all those liver treats, the urge to defecate will start to distract him."

A grown woman shouldn't chuckle at the word *defecate*, but the stress of training was making her emotional, and she needed a release valve after forty-five minutes of obedience work. Laughing at the dog trainer's word choice would not earn her any points for maturity, though, so she held it in, even while feeling as if Mrs. Stern could read the imaginary thought bubble above her head that said *ha-ha-ha-ha-ha!*

"I'll work with him again tonight, after he's had some time to rest, and . . . do whatever else he needs to do," she said with forced solemnity.

"That's fine. I can come back on Friday afternoon. I think you'd both benefit from twice-weekly lessons."

Yep, there it was. Confirmation that all the dog's misbehavior lay squarely on Carli's ineffectual shoulders. Well, at least she knew where she stood.

"Thank you, Mrs. Stern. That would be very helpful."

Mrs. Stern scratched Gus behind the ears, and he gazed up at her lovingly, sighing and leaning into her hand, proving there must be some sweetness somewhere inside the boxy, matronly woman. Something that dogs could sense but was totally invisible to humans. "Very well, then. I'll see you Friday at three o'clock," she said crisply, then climbed into her Subaru hatchback and slowly eased the car out of the driveway.

Gus sniffed at the grass and meandered around the yard, looking for just the right spot to defile as Carli looked away and wondered how she could care about him so very much and yet be so frustrated with him at the same time. If only he understood what she was asking him to do, maybe he'd do it. Maybe she could somehow find just the right method to encourage him. Then again, that's kind of how her eighteen-year marriage to Steve had been, too. A merciless combination of love and agitation and unmet expectations until finally, eight months ago, he'd moved out of their family home into a luxury condo and filed for divorce. It hadn't been a shock to Carli, exactly. Over the past few years, they'd gone to marriage counseling more often than they'd gone out on dates, and each time they seemed to resolve less and dig in more.

"What's your goal for this counseling session?" the last therapist had asked.

"I'd like to be able to communicate with Steve in a way that helps him understand how he's hurting my feelings," Carli had answered. "So that he might choose to do things differently."

Steve had looked smugly impatient, his six-four frame stretched out so that his legs took up virtually all the floor space of the tiny office. "And I'd like Carli to realize she's clinically depressed and should probably go on medication," he'd replied. "She always gets grumpy like this whenever she gains weight, and then she hauls me into counseling until she feels better."

That was the first and last meeting with that particular counselor. But Carli wasn't depressed. She was resigned. Living with Steve was like pushing a boulder up a mountain every single day, and she was exhausted. Now that he was gone, she couldn't decide if she was sad, angry, or just relieved. Maybe she was all three. And she was still exhausted, because being a single mom of two teenage girls was not an easy road—but it was a different kind of fatigue. She was lighter, somehow. Decisions were easier to make because she didn't have to run them past Steve. And if she made mistakes—like getting a puppy when she probably should have gotten a goldfish—well, they were her mistakes to own. And her mistakes to fix. So if Mrs. Stern had to come to her house every damn day, Carli was going to turn Gus into the most loyal, obedient companion of any dog in any family in any neighborhood in any town. On any planet.

The rumble of a modest-size moving van pulling into the driveway next door caught her attention just as she and Gus headed inside Carli's traditional, two-story house. The geriatric Mortons, who'd been Carli's neighbors since the day she and Steve moved in as newlyweds, had just sold their home to relocate to a retirement community in Boca Raton, and from the looks of it, Carli's new neighbors were about to move in. She hoped they were a bit younger than the Mortons, by about three decades. And she sure as heck hoped they didn't mind dogs.

Within minutes, Carli's phone began to ping with messages as word quickly spread that the new occupants of 2525 Monroe Circle had arrived. This neighborhood was small and incestuously close-knit, with rarely a happening, foible, shenanigan, occurrence, event, or incident going by unnoticed or undiscussed. Lynette Barker from across the street prided herself on being the first to report the latest news, gossip, whisper, or scandal, and it was generally well-known that she was not above fabricating details if reality didn't sufficiently titillate.

That was fast! The Mortons only left last week. Did you know the new buyer was coming? Lynette texted.

Carli gave Gus some water and led him to his crate, which, thankfully, he had no aversion to spending time in during the day, and then tapped out a response as she peeked out her window to see whatever there might be to see.

I didn't know. It's not a very big van. Maybe they're just dropping a few things off.

Carli watched the three dots wavering on her screen before Lynette's response popped up.

> Single dad. Middivorce. How much do you want to bet there's nothing inside that van but clothes and electronics?

Carli chuckled, since that was exactly what Steve had taken when he moved out. He'd left behind all the furniture and family photos and yard equipment. All the holiday decorations and trinkets they'd collected over the years. He hadn't even taken the stuff given to them by his own parents and grandparents. When he and Carli had calmly sat down to discuss the division of their assets, all he'd wanted was their fifty-two-inch television and as much cash as he could squeeze from the situation, and since all she wanted was the house, it seemed like a fair trade. Now that she was eight months into taking care of this place on her own, she wondered if he'd gotten the better end of the deal, because the air conditioner had recently started making a scraping, wheezing sort of sound, and the garage door had a new rattle to it as well. A birch tree they'd been keeping their eyes on for years now had a branch leaning dangerously close to the roof, just waiting for a windstorm to send it crashing down. The deck needed a fresh coat of stain, and everything in the yard needed pruning, thinning, or weeding, except for her hosta plants, which had been thoroughly and relentlessly snacked on by bunnies. How Steve had managed to keep them at bay, she had no idea. She could ask him . . . but she'd rather figure it out for herself. Asking him a question always resulted in too long of an answer.

LOL. UR probably right, Carli replied to Lynette before slipping her phone into her pocket and opening the refrigerator door. Her kids were both out with friends (funny how that always seemed to happen during dog-training sessions), and since Carli still found it strange to cook for one, she grabbed a yogurt and some leftover pizza and went upstairs to peek out her bedroom window. The vantage point from there was superior, giving her a full view of whatever might be happening next door. If she were Lynette, she'd probably get out her binoculars. But she wasn't Lynette. Carli loved the random tidbit of gossip as much as the next person, but going through a divorce had made her a bit more respectful of other people's privacy. Still, looking out her own window, well, that wasn't spying exactly. It was just . . . gazing.

She nudged the curtain aside with her pizza-free hand and observed as a handful of guys wearing baseball hats and sunglasses moved boxes into the house. There was talking and laughter as they worked, leading her to think they were friends rather than just hired movers, and a short time later, when one of them started playing basketball in the space of the driveway not occupied by the van, the rest joined in. The hats stayed on, but the sunglasses and shirts came off, and she reconsidered finding her binoculars.

∞

"Five guys, all in pretty good shape," she told her neighbor Erin the next morning.

"Why didn't you go introduce yourself?" Erin replied, handing her a perfectly crafted organic, free-trade vanilla latte, compliments of Erin's state-of-the-art La Spaziale Vivaldi espresso machine. Carli took a grateful sip as Erin sat down on the ivory velvet barstool at her generously proportioned kitchen island. As always, Carli found it difficult to believe their houses shared the same floor plan, because Erin's place had trendy, newly remodeled everything. Oversize crown molding, plush rugs, burnished gold fixtures. Everyone always said that Erin had the nicest house in the neighborhood, including Erin. She didn't mind mentioning it. She wasn't a snob, per se. She didn't judge anyone for what they had or didn't have. She just liked really nice stuff and worked hard as a real estate agent to pay for it. She also had a housekeeper, a nanny, a landscaper, and a handy fix-it kind of husband. Carli would like to live Erin's life for just one day. Or maybe just borrow her staff. Except the husband. She wasn't currently interested in one of those. She was taking a well-deserved and much-needed testosterone break. Although seeing the shirtless guys from next door had given her a mild thrill. Good to know she wasn't entirely numb from the waist down.

"They seemed pretty busy moving stuff inside, and by the time they started playing basketball, I was already in my pajamas," Carli answered.

"You're always in your pajamas," Erin said, smiling. Her brunette hair was salon shiny and pulled up into a basic ponytail that somehow, on Erin, looked chic and polished. Carli's wavy, dark hair was also in a ponytail, but hers was more of the *I'm cleaning out my garage and didn't expect to see anyone* variety.

"I put on real clothes when I go to work," Carli responded, not bothering to take offense. "It's one of the perks of single life—wearing whatever is the most comfortable—and pajama pants are my jam. My pajama jam."

Erin chuckled. "Speaking of work, please tell me you're going to apply for that on-air job. Or better yet, tell me you've already done it."

Carli was a part-time receptionist at Channel 7 News in downtown Glenville and had been for the past four years, working ten to three, Monday through Thursday. It was basically the perfect schedule, allowing her to be home when her daughters left for school and then be available again in the late afternoon to attend their various sporting events, get them to their doctor and dental checkups, and treat them to spontaneous trips to the salon for pedicures. She loved that girl time with them, especially since Steve had moved out. It made her feel like they were a team, the three of them. More often than not, they'd go out for ice cream afterward, and the girls would tell her about their day and their friends and their homework. They'd talk about the divorce and how life was different now, the ways it was harder but also the ways it was a little easier. Steve had never been the best when it came to dealing with the emotional component of girls, and Carli often found herself trying to overcompensate for that. She still was, actually. Cue the big, messy dog.

"I'm not sure about that job," Carli answered in response to Erin's question. "I haven't been in front of the camera since college. Not sure I have what it takes."

"But you have a degree in broadcast journalism, right? You are qualified." Erin's gaze was direct. She was a no-fear, no-regret kind of person and liked to nudge other people to be the same. And if her nudges didn't work, she'd sometimes shove.

"Technically I guess I'm qualified, but honestly, a lot has changed in the industry. And they all see me as the receptionist. Jumping from that to doing on-air segments would be quite a leap."

"But the only one stopping you from making that leap is you. Sure, maybe they see you as the receptionist now because that's what you've been doing, but maybe this is a good time to show them there's more to you than that. Life begins outside your comfort zone, you know. And the pay has got to be better than what you're getting."

Erin never shied away from discussing money and thought all her female friends should be earning more than they were. She also thought they should maintain their own bank accounts and have kept their own names. A brief marriage at nineteen that had lasted just long enough for her derelict musician husband to open up an assortment of credit card accounts and max them out in a matter of months had left Erin with a sizable, and logical, chip on her shoulder when it came to women and their financial independence.

"The pay would definitely be more, but the hours would suck. I'd have to be at the station by seven o'clock every morning, not to mention the weekend and evening stuff. I'd be doing segment work along with cohosting the new morning program."

"Seems like a pretty good opportunity to me. The early mornings might be kind of a drag, but it's not like your kids need you home to make them breakfast before school."

Carli felt a blush steal over her cheeks.

"Oh my gosh. Tell me you're not still making them breakfast. They're in high school." Erin was smiling again, her tone more amused than accusatory.

"I like to see them in the mornings," Carli said, hiding behind her coffee cup. "It starts their day off on the right note."

Erin nodded. "Sure. Okay. But do you know what starts the day off on an even better note? Having more money in your bank account. Having a career instead of just a job. They'll both be off at college soon, and you're going to need something to do with your time. Something besides cleaning up muddy paw prints from your kitchen floor."

From some this might seem like an insult, but Carli had known Erin for a very long time and was quite accustomed to this particular soapbox. She knew it was well intentioned and not personal. Well, it *was* personal, but in an *I just want the best for you* kind of way. Not a *why can't you do better* kind of way. She knew the difference, because Steve's *advice* had always been the latter.

"I'm too old to start a television career now," Carli said, staring at the foam in her cup. "I'm forty-two, and since TV age for women is like dog years, I may as well be a hundred."

"Ridiculous. You look thirty-five, and besides, wouldn't it be just a little bit fun to suddenly become a local celebrity and have Steve be all like, 'Wuuut? I was married to that and I walked away?'"

Carli smiled at the notion, although she had no illusions she'd become a celebrity even if she did get the job. The new *Glenville in the Morning* show would air locally at eight o'clock while most people were either rushing to work or rushing to get their kids off to school. She'd be background noise to much of their audience while delivering stories about apple orchards and craft shows—not exactly hard-hitting stuff. Still, she *had* thought about it, and maybe it wouldn't be that dumb to at least try. But what if she was awful? What if she walked into that audition room and the news director said, "Um, aren't you our front-desk receptionist? Did you bring us coffee before the next talent shows up?"

Carli's degree from Michigan State was literally decades old, and other than a few brief internships, she'd never actually worked in front of the camera. She'd planned to, but a surprise proposal from Steve, followed by an even bigger surprise pregnancy, curtailed her journalism aspirations. She'd gone from college grad with a backpack to tired mom with a diaper bag in the span of a few months, with just a bit of time in the middle to also be a round-bellied bride. Her own mother had cried through most of the wedding ceremony, and Carli hadn't had the courage to ask if those were tears of joy or sobs of disappointment. Then her mother went and died a few years later, and she still hadn't asked. She'd never asked her father, either, and since he'd remarried about fifteen minutes after her mother's funeral and moved to Pebble Beach to play golf with his new bride, she probably never would. Although there were some hints as to his opinion on the matter.

"It lasted longer than I thought it would, kid. You had a decent run," her father had replied when she'd emailed him about her divorce. That was the depth and nature of their relationship now—emails, along with the occasional birthday card that never showed up on the right date, and gift baskets from Swiss Colony for Christmas, even for her kids.

"Why does Grandpa think we like sausage so much?" Tess had asked one year, brandishing a two-pound beef log like a sword.

"Because he's firmly entrenched in the patriarchy and lacks insight and imagination," Mia had replied. She'd been twelve at the time.

Erin eyed Carli for another moment of speculation, then finally said, "Well, you know I support whatever you decide, but I hope you're not avoiding this job opportunity just because you're too scared to try. I think you'd be fabulous as a morning cohost. In fact, I don't know anyone else who is as chipper as you are at that time of day. It's annoying as hell, but you could put that cheerful attitude to some good use if you wanted to."

Erin's words were like a rubber band snapping against her skin. Not painful, but not pleasant, either. Because maybe Carli *was* too scared to try. So much in her life had changed since Steve moved out, and taking on a brand-new challenge could either be the best decision she'd ever made or end up being a massive error in judgment. Like letting the kids talk her into a dog or agreeing to be in charge of the parent/teacher appreciation committee at their school. Or not negotiating a better divorce settlement. The problem was, people didn't typically know a mistake was a mistake until it was too late.

"I'll think about it," Carli said. "But if I worked every morning, we wouldn't be able to have coffee as often, and I'd miss your ostentatious, two-thousand-dollar coffeepot. I save at least five bucks a day by getting my lattes from you. It makes up for having *just a job*."

Chapter 2

Not since college had Ben Chase woken up in a strange bedroom and not instantly recognized his surroundings, but this morning it took him a full five seconds to remember exactly where he was. *Oh, that's right.* He was in *his own* bedroom. In his *new* house. Today was the first day of the rest of his life and all that crap.

He stretched and yawned and tried not to think about the fact that right now, across town in his *old* house, his wife was tangled up in bed with some other guy. Not just any other guy, though. Sophia was in bed with Doug, his business partner. Because his soon-to-be ex-wife was sleeping with his soon-to-be ex–business partner. Four months ago, they'd confronted Ben with the old *the heart wants what the heart wants* speech and admitted to having had a yearlong affair. They said it was the *real thing*, and they wanted to be together forever. Quite frankly, Ben couldn't think of a more just punishment for the two of them. They deserved each other.

Ben stretched in the other direction, noticing a few aches and sore muscles compliments of his recent encounter with moving boxes. Not that he'd brought much stuff from the other house, but what he had brought had been heavy. A mattress and bed frame, lots of books, his weight bench, and every last not-nailed-down item from the bar he'd just finished building in their basement. He'd have torn up and moved the granite countertops if he could have. Not because he was that petty, but because he and Sophia had spent hours wandering around the granite showroom to pick out just the right piece. He was pretty damn proud of that bar, and of all the other projects he'd completed at that house, but when he learned his wife had adulterated all over it, he decided to move out and leave it all behind.

He'd spent the last several weeks at his sister's, brooding and trying to make plans, and now, here he was in a much smaller place, basically starting his life over while staring at the rattan ceiling fan circa 1980 wobbling precariously above his head with an annoying click. He felt like that fan. Spinning and spinning and getting nowhere, covered in dust from the past and making sounds that no one wanted to hear. He was tired of himself and all the shouting going on inside his head.

It was time to move forward, because his life, like the fan and the rest of this house, just needed some focused, intensive labor and maybe a little bit of TLC. He could've afforded a bigger, better place in a more prestigious location, but the distraction of working on an old, outdated house appealed to him, and it would certainly be easier to clean up this mess than the mess that was the rest of his life.

He eased into an upright position, his feet hitting the scratchy, stained Berber carpet. It crackled beneath the weight of him as he stood, and he was not optimistic about the state of the padding underneath.

He took a faster-than-ever shower because there was no curtain and he didn't want to get water all over the bathroom, then dried off with a T-shirt because his towels were somewhere in a box in his living room. He should've done some unpacking last night, but his brothers and son had been more interested in shooting hoops, and quite frankly, so had he. It had been good to blow off some steam after spending a few hours packing under the squinting, watchful eye of Sophia, as if she thought he'd take anything she hadn't agreed to. As if he even wanted to. Somehow, using a unique blend of ass-backward logic that wasn't logical at all, she'd decided to blame him for *her* infidelity. She reasoned away her betrayal by telling Ben he hadn't *been there for her*, which was absurd, because he was with her all the time. Except for all those times she was apparently with Doug.

All the muscles in his body clenched when he thought of *that guy*. The guy who'd been his friend since college. The guy who'd worked diligently by his side for the last ten years as they created and grew a very successful solar panel business. The guy who'd been the best man at his wedding. Ironic, really. Turns out Sophia thought he was the *best man* for her, too. But that was then, and this was now. The past was the past. Time to move on. Like it or not.

"How'd you sleep last night?" Ben asked as seventeen-year-old Ethan shuffled into the virtually empty kitchen an hour later, wearing nothing but a pair of navy basketball shorts and looking like he'd slept in a wind tunnel. His dark hair was shaggy and wild and desperately in need of a trim, but Ben had learned to pick his battles with this kid. The last few months had been rough on all of them, and since parenting seemed to be a no-win endeavor in the best of times, Ben decided not to pick at him about the less essential stuff.

"Okay, I guess," Ethan answered, his sleepy brown eyes scanning the countertops. "Where's the coffee maker?"

Ben bit back a snarky comment about how their coffeepot was still sitting on the counter at that *other* house, because according to his sister—a family therapist—it was up to Ben to set the tone for how this situation progressed. The kids would take their cues from him, and saying negative things about Sophia or the divorce or the fact that her actions had triggered this whole debacle would put Ethan and Addie in the middle. He didn't want to pile his stress on top of their own, and so he always tried to put a positive spin on things. He failed sometimes, but he was trying—just as he was in virtually every area of his life right now. That was the best he could offer. He was trying.

"I don't have one yet, but I've ordered a bunch of stuff that should be delivered in the next day or so. If you think of anything you or Addie might need when you're over here, just let me know and I'll get that ordered, too. In the meantime, we're sort of winging it."

Ben had never set up a new household, especially from scratch, and he was heavy on the clueless side about what his son and fourteen-year-old daughter might need. Since Addie was currently away at summer riding camp, her immediate needs were less of an issue, but he'd tried to cover all the basics. Pots, pans, dishes, bedding, towels. A toaster, a coffeepot, toilet paper. Worst-case scenario, he could get by with just those last three items for a couple of days, but he also needed groceries. A toaster didn't do him much good if there was no bread and no butter.

"Is there anything to eat?" Ethan asked, opening the avocado-green refrigerator. The door squeaked as it swung wide and bumped against the counter, where a permanent divot had been notched into the butcher-block surface.

Ben shook his head. "Sorry, dude, but if you throw on a shirt, we can go grab some breakfast."

Ethan ran a hand through that mass of hair and only made it look worse. "Can we go to IHOP?"

Ben chuckled. That would never be his first choice, but it was a small accommodation. The kid needed to eat, and clearly, they were both in need of caffeine. "Sure. I'm ready whenever you are."

His son turned to leave but paused for a moment at the doorway, glancing back at Ben. "Um, Dad," he asked, "are you, you know, thinking about making any changes to this place, or do you plan to leave it the same?"

Ben thought about toying with him, but it was too early in the day for that, and they were both too hungry for joking. "I intend to gut the whole place and start over from scratch. You okay with that?"

Ethan's smile was full of relief. "I'm very okay with that. My room smells like fried chicken."

"You love fried chicken."

"Let me clarify. It smells like fried chicken left in a dumpster that the rats thought was too gross to eat."

"Mmm, delicious," Ben answered, rubbing a hand over his belly. Ethan rolled his eyes and walked away.

∽

At nearly six foot three, his son could definitely pack away the food, and Ben observed in some fascination as Ethan scarfed down a double stack of pancakes along with half a dozen pieces of bacon and some hash browns before even slowing down. No wonder the kid was two inches taller than he was. Even so, everyone said they looked alike, both with dark hair and the same smile. Ethan had Sophia's eyes, though. A dark chocolate brown, whereas Ben's eyes were what his ninety-three-year-old grandmother always referred to as *the Chase family blue*. No one else ever called it that. Just her. But she said it often enough to make up for the fact that no one else ever mentioned it.

Throughout breakfast, Ben shared with Ethan the plans he had for the house. Tearing out a center wall and opening up the kitchen to the rest of the house. All new appliances and flooring and fixtures and paint. Ethan nodded while he chewed, not really voicing an opinion other than to say, "That sounds cool." He did like Ben's ideas for putting in a bigger backyard patio and adding a firepit.

"Maybe we can even build one of those backyard pizza ovens or something like that," Ben said. "Maybe a hot tub?"

"Can you add an outdoor TV screen so we can sit in the hot tub while eating pizza and watching football?" Now Ethan was finally getting engaged, but all Ben could think of was pizza clogging up the jets and drains of the hot tub. He might have to rethink this plan.

"Probably."

"Cool. But, hey, Dad, before we head back to Casa de Caca, can I talk to you about something?" Ethan wiped his hands on a wadded-up napkin and tossed it on his now-empty plate. Something in his tone told Ben this wasn't some run-of-the-mill topic. He leaned forward, resting his forearms on the table.

"Sure. What's up?"

Ethan stared at that napkin for a second before his dark eyes met Ben's blue ones. He took a shallow breath before saying, "I know you have to do a bunch of stuff to the house, and that's going to take a lot of time and all your attention and stuff, but I was wondering if . . . I want to live with you full-time. I don't want to switch between houses."

Ben tried hard to school his reaction, not wanting to immediately shout out a big *hell yes*, because this was a major development, and even though he'd rather not discuss anything about anything with Sophia ever again, they still had to coparent. They hadn't worked out any custody arrangements yet because Ben had been living with his sister. In fact, they hadn't even officially filed for divorce yet, because they'd agreed to wait until Ben had closed on his new house, and now that he had, they were about to begin the sure-to-be-unpleasant division of marital assets, not to mention the dissolution of Ben's partnership with Doug. Things could get very messy very quickly once they started talking about money, and if custody was also on the table, messier still.

"I understand, Ethan," Ben said calmly, "and I wish I could give you an answer right now, but that's a decision your mother and I still have to discuss. Can you tell me why you'd rather live with me full-time?"

Ethan's lips quirked into a half smile, reminding Ben of how his son had looked as a little kid. Impish and sassy and a bit too smart for his own good. "You've been talking to Aunt Kenzie again, haven't you?" Ethan said. "I can always tell when she's done the woo-woo therapy number on you." He waggled his fingers over his plate as if something mystical were happening.

Ben found himself smiling back, because his son was spot-on. Kenzie was his go-to these days for all things divorce and parenting related. Thank God for her. She was available 24-7, she was extremely respected in her field, and best of all, she worked for vodka. These past few months while he'd crashed at her house, they'd gone through at least three bottles of Tito's.

"I may have had some conversations with Aunt Kenzie, but I'd like to think I could have come up with that response on my own. So what's your reasoning?"

"Because I can't stand her." Ethan's smile faded, and all the light-heartedness in his tone escaped like steam. Ben felt a hot knife twist in his gut. For all the hurt Sophia had caused *him*, he was still surprised by the intensity of the anger bringing a flush to Ethan's skin.

"She's not the same, Dad. Ever since you left, she's just . . . different. She dresses different. She goes out all the time. I heard her on the phone being all gross and flirty with that asshat she's sleeping with." His tone was full of distaste, with undertones of hurt.

Another twist in the gut for Ben, followed by a virtual kick in the groin.

"What makes you think she's sleeping with someone?"

Ethan paused, staring at his dad with the *OMG, yer so dumb* expression that Ben chose to chalk up to standard teen attitude and not as a personal insult.

"Come on, Dad. I'm not a little kid, and Mom hasn't been all that discreet. Even Addie figured it out, and I didn't tell her. Isn't that why you're getting divorced? Because she's having an affair?"

Ben wished he had Kenzie on speed dial right now, because he had no idea how honest to be. Ethan was nearly eighteen, technically an adult, but this was his mother they were talking about. Her betrayal to Ben aside, could he—should he—admit to their son she was indeed cheating? Especially with good old *Uncle* Doug, whom Ben had been in business with for the past ten years? If there was a handbook for this sort of thing, he hadn't found it.

"It's not usually one single thing that breaks up a marriage, Ethan. It can be an accumulation of things, but . . ." *Oh, what the hell. The kid already guessed.* "Yes, she is involved with someone."

"Doug?" Ethan said as if on a dare, and Ben wasn't clever enough to hide his reaction that time.

"I thought so," Ethan said, falling back against his seat only to bounce forward again, his expression full of resentment. "He's around all the time 'helping.'" He made air quotes around the word. "He's a total douche, and Mom is a nutcase, and that's why I don't want to live there. I'm sure Aunt Kenzie would tell you it's an unhealthy environment. And anyway, once I turn eighteen, I should get to decide for myself where I live."

Ben stared at his son, feeling a dozen different emotions. Anger at Sophia for putting them all in this situation. Sadness that their family and their lives were being dismantled piece by piece. And respect for Ethan for being bold enough to put it all out there. Ben would never have had this kind of conversation with his own father. In fact, he still couldn't imagine it, and his father was seventy-one years old. Then again, no one challenged William Geoffrey Chase. It just wasn't done.

Ben pondered this situation, moving the facts around like pieces to a puzzle that had no image to work toward. Maybe in some cases total honesty wasn't the best policy, but it seemed like Ethan had earned it from him. He wouldn't embellish, but he'd tell the truth. Consequences be damned.

"Okay, kid. Here's the deal. I'd love to have you live with me full-time, and Addie, too, if she wants that, but your mom and I are just at the beginning of all the mediation crap, and that's going to take some time. If I go at her saying I want full custody, she'll flip her shit and then nobody gets what they want. Can you be patient and trust me to handle this?"

Ethan's eyes lit up like Christmas morning. "You mean I can come live with you full-time?"

"I mean I'll do my best to try to make that happen, but in the meantime, you and Addie will have to try and go with the flow. I know that doesn't seem fair, because you guys didn't ask for any of this, but I also know that your mom loves you and she's going to want to see you as much as possible. Plus, school starts soon, and then hopefully we'll all get into a new routine."

Ah, yes. A new routine. *A new normal,* as his sister had called it in therapistspeak. He wasn't really sure what that even meant, but she seemed to suggest it was a deliberate attempt to cast aside all the old shit that wasn't working in your life and focus on creating systems that did work. Again, he was kind of at a loss. What was going to work for him and his kids? How was he supposed to move on when all he really wanted to do was set everything on fire? Kenzie had said something to him about being patient, too, but patience was in short supply.

"I promise I'll see what I can do. Now let's get home, because you are on unpacking duty."

"Or . . ." Ethan dragged out the word. "We could go golfing."

Ben glanced out the window of the IHOP. It was sunny and warm and a great day to be outside. His son didn't ask him to do things very often, usually preferring the company of friends, and next year he'd be off to college. Days like this would be numbered. Maybe the boxes could wait.

"Golf it is, but I'm going to kick your ass, just so you know."

"Challenge accepted, old man."

Chapter 3

Getting the oil changed in her car had turned into an unexpectedly expensive endeavor and included a new air filter, new windshield wipers, and four new tires. Carli wasn't certain if she should be proud of herself for being proactive about her car's maintenance or feel foolish because a service mechanic had just sold her a bunch of stuff she didn't really need. He'd *said* she needed it, but weren't mechanics prone to selling you things that weren't essential? She had no idea. Steve had always handled the car stuff, just as he'd handled all the repair stuff around the house. It was frustrating to not know how to do certain things that needed doing, or to not be physically strong enough or tall enough to handle the more standard tasks, like trimming the damn shrubs. The forsythia bushes on the side of her house were about nine feet tall right now, and even though she had trimmers and a ladder, there was no way she could reach where she needed to reach. Hiring someone would cost a stupid amount of money, and although she knew she could summon one of the neighborhood husbands, she hated asking for favors. Especially nonemergency favors.

Gus shimmied in the passenger seat next to her. In addition to the car repairs, she'd also just paid a bundle to the dog groomer to give him a thorough (and essential) bath, thanks to his doggie misadventures yesterday. He'd run away into the woods behind her house and somehow managed to find the one and only marshy spot within a hundred-yard radius. Although she was grateful he'd come back when she called, he'd had more than enough time on the lam to roll around in the muck and returned covered in mud from the tip of his shiny black nose to the opposite tip of his gummy, goop-covered tail. She'd hosed him off as best as she could, dousing herself in the process, and he'd spent the entire evening in his crate making all sorts of sad puppy faces at her. She'd even made him spend the night in there, but now he was clean and fresh again and seemingly eager to be home. Then again, he was a dog. He was always eager about *something*. She lowered the window, and he stuck his nose out to show off his fancy shampooed head and spent the rest of the drive home barking at other cars.

It was late afternoon as Carli pulled into her driveway, and she sighed at the sight of meddlesome Lynette standing outside. At just five feet two inches tall, her neighbor had expensively maintained breasts that nearly doubled her body weight and white-blonde hair cut in an *I'd like to speak to the manager* style that, unfortunately, suited her perfectly. Carli didn't have the time or energy for her right now. She also didn't have the time or energy for the messiness of her own landscaping. Everything was overgrown, and if she didn't deal with it soon, she'd get a strongly worded letter from the homeowners' association. Maybe trimming the forsythia *was* an emergency. They had standards here in Monroe Circle, after all. Grass taller than six inches for more than three days would get her a warning, and wildly misshapen hedges would result in a personal letter from the board. Half the reason Carli maintained even a lukewarm friendship with her neighbor from across the street was because Lynette sat on the board and wielded her power with an overzealous enthusiasm. Pissing her off could mean a nasty note about those dandelions near the mailbox, and since Lynette was, at this exact moment, staring at Carli's house, it couldn't be good news.

"Hey, Carli!" Lynette called from the end of her driveway and trotted over before Carli could close the garage door. Sensitive about her vertical challenges, Lynette always wore high heels. They slowed her down, but not enough so that Carli could escape. She was wearing a white tennis skirt and a white tank top with a V-neck that amplified the length of her cleavage. That wasn't by accident. *Clackity-clack-clack.* Lynette's shoes on the pavement were like Morse code for *I'm coming to get you.*

"Hey, Lynette," she said blandly, wrapping Gus's leash tightly around her wrist. He had a habit of bounding from the car as soon as the door opened, and as much as she might enjoy letting him plow forward and knock Lynette over on her well-cushioned ass, she thought better of it. She eased her way out instead, and he jumped at the first chance, pulling her along until they'd reached the grass, where he stopped to pee. Lynette flinched at the sight of him, then said without preamble, "I've met the new neighbor, and I'm not impressed."

"Not impressed? Why?" Carli glanced over at his house. The garage door was open, and she could see the area was full of boxes and old carpet. The moving van was gone, and a shiny black sedan remained. She had no idea what kind of car that was, but it looked expensive. And it probably didn't smell like cold french fries and sour soccer cleats, like her car did.

"I found him very rude," Lynette said. "I took the time to make him an apple cobbler, and I delivered it while it was still warm—still warm, mind you! But when I offered to tell him more about the neighborhood, he told me he was too busy. And then, when I gave him the flyer for the End of Summer Barbecue, he hardly even glanced at it before practically kicking me out of his house. So rude! He is handsome, though. I'll give him that. Have you met him yet?"

"I haven't. It's only been two days. I'm sure he appreciated the cobbler, but he's probably pretty busy with moving and everything. Looks like he's tearing up the carpet." She nodded at the garage full of scraps.

Lynette arched a heavily microbladed brow. "Well, you're nice to defend him, but you weren't there. He was abrasive. He practically shut the door in my face."

Little did Lynette realize that everyone wanted to shut the door in her face.

"I'm sorry," Carli said, tugging on Gus's leash so he'd sit down.

"You don't need to be sorry. You weren't the one who was rude." Lynette glared over at the neighbor's house as if *it* had been rude.

Carli felt compelled to say *I'm sorry* again, but she didn't, because Lynette's intense gaze moved from the neighbor's house to Gus, and she knew the woman hadn't really forgiven him for chasing her precious maltipoo into a cluster of thorny rosebushes almost two months ago, even though that ratty little dog was a terror in her own right. Lynette's dog, Mitzee, was eight pounds of *yappity-yap-yap*, and the only reason Gus had chased her was because she'd egged him on from the edge of her own yard until he couldn't take it anymore. At least that's what Carli had decided. She'd give her own dog the benefit of the doubt. And now that she thought about it, maybe it was good that she hadn't gotten her daughters one of those little tiny dogs that went *yappity-yap-yap* all the time. Mitzee and Lynette had a lot in common.

"How is his training going?" Lynette asked, tilting her head in Gus's direction while looking skeptical. "That Mrs. Stern is a miracle worker. She's trained my little Mitzee to pee in the same spot in the yard every single time and to sit politely when people come to the door. Of course, that's Mitzee's personality, too. Mrs. Stern can only do so much."

Lynette did the pseudosympathetic *tsk, tsk, tsk*, but all Carli heard was *clackity-clack-clack* and *yappity-yap-yap-yap*. "His training is going fine. He just needs to mature a little bit. He still has all that impulsive puppy energy to outgrow." *Dear Lord baby Jesus, please let that be true.*

"Hm," Lynette said dismissively, her eyes scanning the perimeter of the yard as if she was *literally* looking for something to complain about. And, of course, she found it. "You are going to do something about your bushes soon, aren't you? Do you want me to have Mike come over and trim them? If those things get any taller, you won't be able to see your roof. We have bylaws to adhere to, you know."

Carli tamped down a sigh. She was well aware of the bylaws, and she did kind of want Mike Barker to come over and trim them for her, because he was the antithesis of his wife—cheerful and generous and he never complained about anything—but then Carli would owe Lynette a favor, and the thought of it rankled her.

"Um, maybe. I'll let you know. Thanks for the offer, though."

"Of course. I can't imagine how hard it must be to have your husband just up and leave you without so much as a hint of warning. If Mike ever did that to me—not that he would, mind you—but if he did, I'd make sure my substantial alimony covered the cost of a landscaper. A sexy, young landscaper." She laughed as if her clever quip were such a *very clever* quip, but it wasn't, of course, and Carli was left to wonder if her comments were supposed to be helpful. Supportive? Tone-deaf? Passive-aggressive?

She cleared her throat and shrugged them off, because educating Lynette was a waste of time, and she'd learned over the past months to not take these kinds of comments too personally. If she did, she'd spend all day, every day analyzing and agonizing over clueless people's thoughtless observations. The uninitiated had no idea the amount of legal and emotional untethering the end of a marriage required, or how delicate the balance of power became when you were talking about things like alimony and custody. Or how draining the whole experience was. By any standards, Carli knew her divorce from Steve had been about as passionless as their marriage, but even so, it was the worst thing she'd ever gone through. Having a sexy landscaper wasn't going to change that.

"Oh, and speaking of sexy, did you see Erin's new Mercedes?" Lynette asked, moving on to the next shiny topic, oblivious to any of Carli's discomfort or disinterest. "It's a red convertible. Utterly pretentious, of course. I mean, who needs a convertible in Michigan? How often will she even be able to take the top down? It's like having a sailboat in Nevada."

Lynette laughed again, and the one-sided conversation went on for another fifteen minutes before circling around to the new neighbor again, and then another fifteen after that before Carli finally managed to make a break for it and get inside her own house. She glanced at the clock in her kitchen, noting she'd have just enough time to change her clothes and bring the dog back outside to work on his training before her kids started clamoring for dinner. Such was her glamorous life in suburbia—full of nosy neighbors, hungry children, and lots of dog poo. Same shit, different day. Work, laundry, kids, gossip. Lather. Rinse. Repeat.

Yep, so glamorous.

Chapter 4

Ben's day thus far had been tediously long and thoroughly unpleasant. He'd spent the morning unpacking and trying to organize the meager belongings in his house and the afternoon tearing up rank old carpet, because the previous owners had obviously possessed a leaky dog with significant bowel issues. The humid weather outside amplified the stink and left him coated in sweat and itchy granules of disintegrated carpet padding. He'd known before buying the place he'd want to redo all the flooring, but this was more than he'd bargained for. Damn, that dog must have had one heinous anus.

He'd taken a short break when a too-chatty neighbor with jigundus breasts stopped by with some kind of apple crisp. She'd all but insisted on coming inside, practically shoving those jigundus breasts against his arm to force her way past, even though he'd told her he was in the middle of a phone call. In hindsight, he should have let her in and given up on the call, because it had been with Sophia, and intense, and had ended with a heated argument about her car insurance because his soon-to-be ex-wife thought he should pay for hers, and he thought, since she'd slept with another guy and asked for a divorce, maybe she could pay her own damn car insurance.

"Is that going to be your response to everything from now on? You're going to shirk your responsibilities just because you're angry with me for honoring my authentic self and speaking my truth?" Sophia had said.

"I'm not really sure how that has anything to do with expecting you to pay the insurance on the car you're driving, Sophia, and let's not talk about which of us is shirking duties. Not to mention the fact that the bill is at your house and I didn't even realize the payment was due. This may come as a shock, but I've got some stuff on my mind, and your car is pretty low on the list."

They'd gone three rounds until one of them finally hung up, and Ben followed up that call with one from his soon-to-be ex–business partner, who accused him of spreading malicious rumors to bring down the value of their company.

"I haven't said anything that isn't true, Doug, and trust me, I'm not thrilled about this story getting out any more than you are. All I'm telling clients who ask is that the company is restructuring the management team and we'll keep them posted."

Three brutal rounds with that guy, too. Now it was dinnertime, and Ben was spent and irritated. After a long, hot shower—with a curtain this time, because he'd finally bought one—he just wanted a big, fat steak, a tall, cold beer, and to settle in to watch some mind-numbing television. He still hadn't stocked the fridge or pantry very well, but he had stopped by the store yesterday and knew he had one T-bone in the house. Since Ethan was hanging out with friends, it was just him, and he didn't mind the solitude, grateful for some peace and quiet after a particularly fucktacular day.

He seasoned the steak with salt and pepper because that's all he had, and once outside on the patio, he tinkered with the nozzle of the propane tank on the grill, adjusting it before pushing the start button, but nothing happened. The rusty, beat-up piece of crap had come with the house and he planned to replace it very soon, but he needed the damn thing to fire up just one more time. He rattled the tank for a second and at last heard sounds of gas moving through the tube. Victory. Thank

God. He laid the steak on the grill, glad to hear the sizzle indicating the thing would hold up for at least one more meal.

Back inside the kitchen, he decided beer wasn't going to cut it. This kind of night called for something stronger, and although there was no bread, or vegetables, or condiments, he did have a nice bottle of blue-label Johnnie Walker. He put some ice in a glass that may or may not have been clean and poured a liberal portion of whisky on top. He listened to the ice crackle as he swirled it around in the amber liquid. He breathed in the scent before taking a sip and planned to enjoy this drink, dirty glass or not.

It was amazing the things you took for granted when you were married and living in a fully stocked house. Spices. Shower curtains. Towels. Coffee makers. A decent whisky glass.

Companionship.

He and Sophia had shared a good life. Or at least he'd thought they had. Money wasn't a problem, even after he'd left Chase Industries to branch out on his own. They'd dialed back their spending for a couple of years, which Sophia hadn't loved, but it hadn't seemed to be a real hardship. They still enjoyed each other's company. There were nice vacations. Their kids were happy and healthy and bright. They'd never wanted for more, and he'd sincerely thought Sophia was happy. He would've sworn she was happy—until he found out that she wasn't.

There'd been no talk of therapy or reconciliation. She hadn't been interested in that. When she was done with him, she was done, and in all honesty, Ben wasn't sure he could forgive her anyway. Being disillusioned with the state of their marriage was one thing. He could've worked with her on that if she'd been willing. But cheating on him with his best friend? That was more than he could process. He mused for another moment over his whisky, finding the clink of the ice against the glass oddly comforting, but then he heard a desperate shout and an earsplitting crash.

"Gus! Darn it, Gus. Come here!"

It was a woman's voice calling out, followed by the clang and the smash of something heavy and solid slamming against something else that was heavy and solid. He dashed from the kitchen down the staircase to the lower level of the house and yanked open the screen door before bursting out onto the back patio. And there, lying on its side, broken apart into multiple pieces, was his piece-of-shit grill. Ten feet away from that, in the space between his house and the one next door, was a woman, flushed cheeks, dark hair twisted up in what his daughter had informed him was called a *messy bun*. The woman was tense and standing as if about to pounce, and when he followed her gaze, he saw why. There was a dog, a big-ass dog . . . with Ben's dinner in his mouth!

"Hey!" he exclaimed. "That's my steak." He turned toward the pile of junk formerly known as his grill. "And my grill. Seriously?"

The brunette cast a glance his way, her face a study in apologetic exasperation. "I know. I'm so sorry. He's just a puppy."

"Just a puppy? Then maybe he should be on a leash and not rampaging through my backyard." Ben was a dog person, but he was hangry and on his last nerve and preferred the kind of dog that didn't steal his food.

"I know. I'm trying to train him on the electric fence, but he smelled the meat cooking and just took off, and now I'm trying to catch him. I can usually lure him with . . . treats . . ." Her voice trailed off as Ben found himself stating the obvious.

"Lady, no treat is going to make him let go of a T-bone steak."

"A T-bone? That's dangerous for him, isn't it? What if he chokes on it?"

"Well, he'll only make that mistake once."

He hadn't meant to say it out loud but realized at her indignant gasp that he had. It was a rotten joke, and he didn't mean it, but he also didn't want the damn dog devouring his dinner. And he didn't want his piece-of-shit grill broken into useless chunks of rubble on his patio. And he didn't want to spend another day tearing out old, disgusting carpet or fighting with Sophia about car insurance or defending himself to Doug about rumors he had no control over. But most of all, he didn't want his fucking wife fucking his fucking business partner, either.

This day just kept getting better and better. He clenched his fist and realized the drink was in his hand, so he tossed it back in one gulp, glad for the distraction of the burn as it sped down his throat and splashed in his gut with warm relief. He looked at the now-empty glass. His drink was gone. His steak was clearly gone as well. There was no way he'd be able to wrestle anything of substance from the dog, who was now trotting off to the farthest corner of his yard with tail waving high. He glanced over at the woman, and she was staring at him as if *he* should be doing something. But what on earth was he supposed to do? It wasn't his dog.

This night was a bust. In fact, the whole damn day had been miserable, but maybe after a couple more glasses of whisky, he might actually be able to find this funny. At the very least, he'd be able to sleep. For a while. He turned to go back into the house.

"Where are you going?" the woman asked.

"Um . . . inside my house."

"Aren't you going to help me?"

He looked back at her, taking note of her big, dark brown eyes and semipleading expression. She was attractive and looked good in those shorts. Too good for his own good, in fact, making something in his mind whisper *Warning! Complicated!* He'd heard from his real estate agent that his new next-door neighbor was a single mom and recently divorced. But Ben already had his hands full with enough of his own divorce drama. Hands that were currently covered in tiny puncture wounds from pulling up carpet-tack strips because of some *other* dog's bad behavior. Man's best friend, his ass. His fingertips were sore and raw, like his heart. It was all just a little too much. He should probably help her. It would be the neighborly thing to do. The gentlemanly, chivalrous, polite thing to do, but at the moment, he couldn't. All he wanted was to have another shot of whisky (or five) and fall into a dreamless sleep. He was done with people today. And their dogs.

"Sorry, ma'am. You're on your own." He reached down to make sure the propane tank was closed, because, even though the hose was no longer attached to anything, with his current run of shitty luck, the thing would catch a spark and set his house on fire. He heard her quiet yet judgmental scoff at his departure but didn't look at her again. He just locked the patio door with a loud click and went to find his good friend Johnnie Walker.

ᕲ

"So I just met the new neighbor," Carli said as she strode into the kitchen, where her daughters were sitting at the island and watching *Queer Eye* on an iPad. She'd caught Gus without much fanfare when he settled down in the grass to enjoy his meal of contraband beef. He'd given it up reluctantly, but she was relieved to see that the bone seemed to be intact. Nothing in his throat to choke on. Nonetheless, he'd probably be hurling something up before the evening was over.

Dark-haired Mia straightened from her perpetual slouch. "The new neighbor? What's he like?"

Carli scoffed and walked over to the sink to wash her hands. "Kind of rude. Probably hungry. Possibly drunk."

Tess laughed, her smile wide. "Wow, Mom. Why so salty? Was he at least hot? I mean, for an old guy? Lauren said her mom said he's hot." She took a bite of the red licorice in her hand and reached over to pet Gus with the other.

"I didn't notice if he was *hot* or not because I was too busy worrying about the guy's T-bone in Gus's mouth." Actually, she *had* noticed, and he *was* hot, which was why it was such a disappointment when he'd left her alone in the yard without even bothering to ask her name.

Mia turned to her sister. "She's talking about a steak, right? T-bone's not a euphemism for something, is it?"

At eighteen, Mia was two years older than Tess, but she sometimes missed the finer nuances of a conversation. She was what people called *book smart*, but when it came to common sense, not so much. She wasn't tuned in to the latest trends or the hot topics of the day, preferring to keep her nose in a book and her feet planted firmly in the clouds. An old soul. This week she was vegan, and she'd once been voted Most Likely to Save the World by her classmates at Glenville High School. She was about to start her senior year, a fact which Carli found both amazing and terrifying.

Tess rolled her eyes at Mia but glanced at her mother just to be sure. "It's a kind of steak, right? Please tell me it's a kind of steak." Her highlighted blonde hair glinted in the final rays of the day's sunshine. She'd recently turned sixteen and had just gotten her driver's license. Another fact which Carli found both amazing and terrifying.

"Yes, it's a kind of steak, and the damn dog tore through the electric fence, grabbed it, and knocked the grill over in the process. The thing shattered. It's in pieces, and now I'm going to have buy that guy a new one."

Of all the things she didn't want to spend money on, a new grill for the jerk next door was at the very bottom of the list. Especially considering how very *not helpful* he'd been. And even if he hadn't wanted to help, the way he'd just *dismissed* her and sauntered back inside as if the scene between her and Gus were nothing more than a commercial that he could fast-forward through was humiliating. For once, she agreed with Lynette. That guy was rude.

"Did you at least get a name?" Tess asked.

She had gotten a name. Not from Mr. Personality himself, but from Lynette an hour ago, in between her comments about how Gus was going to ruin the grass with his copious amounts of urine and how Carli really needed to paint her soffits.

"His name is Ben Chase," Carli answered. "He's got two kids at Glenville High. Addie and . . . Nathan, maybe? No, that's not right. But he's got a son who'll be a senior this year."

"Not Ethan Chase?" Tess asked, her shoulders lifting as her blue eyes grew wide and her lightly freckled cheeks pinkened in an instant.

Carli snapped her fingers. "Yes, that's it. Ethan. Why? Do you know him?"

"Oh my God, Mom. Ethan Chase is gorgeous. Like so gorge, I can't even. He's super tall and he has the best hair." She clutched fistfuls of her own as if to demonstrate.

Mia's face held none of the rapture being displayed by her sister. She looked positively sour. "Ethan Chase may be gorgeous, but he's also a douchetastic fuckboy. And he sucks at calculus."

"Please don't say *fuckboy* in front of me," Carli said automatically, more from habit than because of an actual rule. She knew most of the bad language her kids used, they'd picked up from her, although *fuckboy* was a new term. Definitely not one of hers.

"He's not a fuckboy," Tess answered, ignoring Carli's reprimand. "Maybe those guys he hangs out with are, but he's not. And being bad at calculus hardly makes him a bad person."

"No, it doesn't," Mia responded, the flush in her cheeks now matching her sister's. "Being bad at calculus makes you *dumb*, but hanging out with douchetastic fuckboys *does* make you a bad person. All those guys just think they're the shit, and personally, I can't wait to see them all ten years from now, when they come to the tragic realization that they peaked in high school." Her aspersions were paired with a practiced eye roll, and Carli chuckled in spite of herself, because she'd known her share of those kinds of boys. Handsome. Desirable. Immune to the awkward trappings of lesser-blessed youth. Actually . . . Steve had been one of those kinds of boys, cruising through life propelled by charm and buoyed by good looks. Collecting people like possessions. It had taken her years to realize she was just a checked box to him. Not special or unique. Not his soul mate. Just a willing woman in the right place at the right time. Like one of those little plastic pegs in the game Life, he'd chosen her because he thought it was *time* to get married, and she was convenient. Doting wife? Check. Two beautiful children? Check and check.

Midlife crisis? Check.

"Who's hungry?" Carli asked loudly, deciding that everyone's mood would improve with some pasta and marinara. And also deciding that she did not feel like cooking. "I'm starving. Let's go out to dinner."

Gus barked as if to say that he was up for anything.

"Sorry for you, pal," Carli said, leading him over to his monster-size crate. "You already ate."

"Can we get manicures after dinner?" Tess asked, hopping off her chair. "My hands are like claws, and school starts next week."

Carli tamped down a sigh. She'd just paid a ridiculous amount of money for new car tires and for Gus to get groomed, and now it looked as if she owed a new grill to the neighbor. Manicures times three meant more money out of her bank account, and although Steve did pay a modest amount in child support, that money went toward clothes and essentials. Did a manicure count as an essential? Some might say yes, and heaven knew Carli's ego could use a little pampering after her encounter with Oscar the Grouch from next door, but she really needed to start budgeting more strategically. She was one busted water heater away from disaster.

"Maybe." Her answer was deliberately noncommittal. "I'm not sure we'll have time, but we can try. Let's figure out where we're going to dinner, first. Mia, are you still vegan?" It was a fair question, since the cause du jour was often hard to keep up with. It cycled from vegetarian to vegan to pescatarian to whatever else Mia could come up with to render the meal Carli had cooked as being unacceptable. Basically, Mia was a contrarian.

"Of course I'm still vegan. Do you think animals deserve to suffer just so we can eat?"

"That's a nice leather belt you're wearing, Mia," Tess said sarcastically. She was pretty much a contrarian, too. Teenage girls were such a joy. But this was Carli's circus, and for better or worse, they were her monkeys.

Chapter 5

The Eighth Annual Monroe Circle End of Summer BBQ hosted by Renee Belmont was in full swing as Carli, Mia, and Tess made their way down the street toward the cul-de-sac. Red, white, and blue balloons and sparkly streamers decorated every mailbox. An inflatable bounce castle filled an entire front yard, and next to that was a tent full of eight-foot tables covered with cheerful red-and-white-checked table-cloths along with every kind of summer picnic potluck dish ever posted on Pinterest, including a watermelon carved to look like a pirate ship surrounded by little pirates made from marshmallows and Rice Krispie Treats dipped in candy coating. Renee never did anything halfway, and while Carli applauded her achievements, she also wondered if perhaps Renee might have a bit too much time on her hands.

She had just one child, a college boy about to start his second year of premed at the University of Michigan, and a firefighting husband who was at work far more often than he was at home. Renee rarely complained about his absences, and Carli sometimes suspected that was the secret to their happy marriage. Maybe if Steve had been home less, they'd have had a chance to miss each other and not take everything for granted.

"Wow," Tess murmured, staring at the elaborate buffet. "Mrs. Belmont strikes again. This is seriously extra."

"Did you put bacon in that?" Mia asked as Carli tried to wedge her humble bowl of broccoli salad in between a decorative platter of tomato-mozzarella-basil kabobs and an assortment of mini mason jars full of Tex-Mex dip adorned with one perfectly positioned triangle of corn chip.

"Nope, no bacon," Carli answered, wondering if she should have put more effort into her dish. On more than one occasion, she'd tried to pass off store-bought items as homemade, and Renee busted her every damn time. Today's contribution was sincerely homemade, but it looked sparse and bland next to the mini sandwiches cut into letter shapes that spelled **MONROE CIRCLE** and the cookies frosted to look like soccer balls and footballs.

"I miss bacon," Mia said wistfully.

"Maybe you could try that soy bacon. You know, that stuff Dad always calls fakon?" Tess added. "Definitely no animals were involved in the production of that stuff."

"Nothing organic was involved in the production of that stuff. It's like chemically treated cardboard," Mia answered dismissively, and Tess rolled her eyes.

It was the last Saturday of the summer, and Mia and Tess were here under duress, having both gotten invited to something better. Carli knew they'd rather be just about anyplace else, since they were too young to hang out with the adults and too old to play with the little kids. But she wanted them here. It was the annual summer barbecue. It was *tradition*, but her daughters were displaying all the enthusiasm of two teens about to get a flu shot.

Was she selfish for wanting them here when they could be with their friends? It was a constant tightrope walk in her heart these days, wanting to give them the freedom to be teens and all that entailed while also wanting them to be with her. Now that they spent part of their time at Steve's, she was particularly greedy about their attention. She knew that inevitably a cluster of teens from the neighborhood would end up taking over the play structure in Renee's backyard and socialize by texting each other about how lame this party was, but she was okay with that. She just wanted them *near*.

"It looks like there's lots of good stuff to eat," Carli said, hoping to stir some interest. Maybe she could at least appeal to their stomachs.

Tess leaned over and adjusted a couple of the Tex-Mex mason jars to make more room for the basic broccoli salad. Her blonde hair was in pigtails, making her look twelve instead of sixteen, and a spear of nostalgia pierced Carli right in the chest.

"Lots of good stuff," Tess agreed. "And your salad is really pretty, Mom."

Carli looked at her, wondering if her emotions were so obvious, but her daughter's attention was already drawn elsewhere—toward the nearest boy—and soon she and Mia were ensconced within a squad of like-minded kids all eager to talk about how much they dreaded school starting on Monday. And off they went.

"So have you met him yet?" Her neighbor DeeDee appeared at Carli's elbow just as Mia and Tess disappeared into the nearest backyard.

"Who?" She knew who. She was just playing coy. She'd gotten a dozen text messages from various factions in the neighborhood wanting to know if the new guy next door was as good-looking as *everyone* said, and if he was as rude as Lynette thought. Short answer: yes to both.

"The new neighbor," DeeDee said. "I saw a couple pictures of him on Facebook and this momma likey." She smoothed her hands over her torso and hips. DeeDee was twice divorced, constantly on the lookout for her next ex-husband, and spent so much time at the gym that most people thought she worked there. Her hair was cut pixie short and was a deep red hue found nowhere in nature.

Carli shook her head at DeeDee. "Well, he's all yours, because this momma no likey. He's kind of a jerk."

DeeDee sighed. "Ahh, wouldn't you know it? Jerks are my kryptonite. Let's get you a drink and you can tell me all about him."

Two glasses of pinot grigio later, DeeDee, Erin, and Lynette had heard every detail about the dog and the steak and the broken grill. They were now sitting in folding lawn chairs as far from the bouncy house as possible while Renee stopped by every few minutes to refill their glasses before flitting away to attend to something else.

"Oh my gosh," Erin said, laughing after Carli recounted the dog story one more time. "You had a meat cute. Get it? Like M-E-A-T? A meat cute."

"Hilarious," Carli said, *not* laughing. "And then he just walked back into his house. And he called me *ma'am*." The wine was hitting her hard, and every time she retold her story, she got more annoyed, because no woman in the world wants to be called *ma'am*, especially by someone their own age. Maybe it was understandable coming from a bagger at the grocery store or a kid selling candy bars door to door, but a grown man calling a woman *ma'am* was practically like saying *I find you sexless and overly mature.*

"See?" Lynette said. "I told you. Rude. I don't care if he is a Chase." Her concurrent scoff was well practiced and accompanied by a flick of a wrist.

"A Chase? Meaning what?" Carli glanced at her glass and noticed it was time for a refill. Where the heck was Renee?

Lynette gazed at her as if she were clueless. "You know. He's a Chase meaning he's, like, you know, *a Chase*. Like Chase Industries. The Chase Foundation. The Wallace-Chase Arena. Didn't I mention that the other day?"

Lynette hadn't. Carli would've remembered that. "He is? He's that kind of Chase? What the heck is a guy with that kind of money doing living in our humble little neighborhood?" Their neighborhood was actually a few steps above humble, but it was hardly Chaseworthy. That family was Midas rich and well-known, with their names on buildings all around Glenville. There was the Lila Chase Pediatric Cancer Ward, the Saundra Chase Equestrian Center, and the Chase Art Gallery, which Carli had gone to once and discovered was full of really peculiar sculptures by an artist who simply called himself Alex.

"Word is he paid cash for the house, but I've also heard his divorce is going to be . . . very . . . expensive," Lynette added, leaning forward. She said the words *very* and *expensive* with equal gusto.

"I'd imagine it will be, if he comes from that kind of money," DeeDee said, tapping her french-manicured fingers against her wineglass. "Still, I'm sure there'll be enough left over for him to support me in the lifestyle to which I'd like to become accustomed."

Erin chuckled. "Well, rude or not, I'm sure once word gets around about a Chase being on the market again, women will be lining up for miles."

Carli shook her head, feeling a little sloppy from her wine. "Well, I sure as hell won't be in that line. He may be rich, but I think that guy's an asshole."

∽

Something loud and carnival-like was happening at the end of Ben's street. He had a vague memory of his busybody neighbor lady handing him a flyer along with the apple thing, but he'd tossed the paper into a stack of mail without paying much attention. Maybe he should read it and find out why family after family seemed to be walking past his house with coolers and wagons full of kids. He sifted through the pile, tossing out the obvious junk pieces until he came to the sunny yellow sheet of paper with the words *Eighth Annual Monroe Circle End of Summer BBQ* splashed across the top in some very elaborate font. From the looks of it, he was supposed to bring a dish to pass, his own beverages, and a lawn chair.

Or he could just skip it, which seemed like the best option. The kids were at Sophia's, and Ben had work to do while they were gone. He'd torn down the wall between the kitchen and living room, and drywall dust was everywhere. His refrigerator was practically in the middle of the kitchen. Plus, all the stuff he'd ordered last week had finally arrived and needed to be unpacked. There were boxes over by the fireplace containing plates and bowls and glasses, pots and pans, sheets and towels. Best of all, he now had a coffee maker that was currently sitting on the counter in his master bathroom to protect it during his kitchen reconstruction. All things considered, he should probably keep at it . . . but he could hear the music from down the street and people shouting and laughing.

Ben appreciated his solitude, but he hadn't talked to anyone outside of his family, his lawyer, and a handful of clients in days, and since he had no idea how long he'd be living in this house, maybe it would be worthwhile to go meet some of his neighbors. Undoubtedly, they'd ask questions. Uncomfortable questions, like basically anything pertaining to the catastrophic status of his marriage, his business, and his treacherous business partner, or his new yet mostly empty house . . . but he could handle it. What the hell? How bad could it be?

He opened his fridge and pulled out a bag of grapes. Not exactly a dish to pass, but this should count. He looked around for a moment before realizing he had no cooler. He'd add that to the growing list of stuff he still needed to buy, but for right now, he just grabbed a beer and figured he'd walk back when that one was empty, which would also give him a handy exit strategy if the situation called for it.

It felt a little odd walking down his new street with an open beer in one hand and a plastic baggie of freshly washed grapes in the other, but as he got closer to the melee of people, he was greeted with smiles and waves. A dozen different neighbors introduced themselves, and he tried to commit as many names as possible to his memory but was pretty sure he was going to forget them all. He was typically good with names, but this was too many at once.

"Hello, there. I'm Renee. You must be Carli's new neighbor," said a woman with intricately braided hair piled high on her head and a smile so bright it made him automatically smile in return.

"Carli?" he asked before making the connection. "Oh, is that the woman with the dog?"

Renee's laugh was as infectious as her smile. "Yep, that would be Carli. And Gus. He's not so much a dog as he is a furry disaster, but she's working on that."

Ben shook his head. "She wasn't having much luck the last time I saw her."

"Well, he's a work in progress, and speaking of progress, how goes your unpacking? Are you getting settled into your new place?"

"That is also a work in progress. I should be unpacking right now, but I heard there was food down here."

"That there is. You can put your . . ." She glanced at the bag in his hand. "Um, grapes right over there on that table and help yourself to whatever you want to eat. The guys are just firing up the grill to cook some hot dogs and hamburgers, so let me know if you need anything." She pointed in the direction of a white tent full of tables, and Ben blinked in surprise. There was a ton of food here, and suddenly his grapes felt very insignificant. Was that a pirate ship?

He made his way toward the tent, passing behind a cluster of women sitting in lawn chairs, and his footsteps faltered as he heard one distinctly say, "Well, rude or not, I'm sure once word gets around about a Chase being on the market again, women will be lining up for miles." Then the woman next to her said, "Well, I sure as hell won't be in that line. He may be rich, but I think that guy's an asshole."

Great. That's just great. He took a step backward, nearly bumping into someone behind him, and as the women in the chairs turned, Ben saw the only familiar face at this entire party. His next-door neighbor with the messy bun and the very bad dog.

She had the decency to blush when she spotted him and quickly turned back around. Her companions did more of a long stare, and he felt very much as if he were being appraised, but for what, he couldn't guess. It certainly wasn't the first time he'd been called an asshole, but it was the first time he'd been called that by a virtual stranger. Usually one had to earn that kind of comment, but all he'd done to this woman was leave her alone to deal with her own damn dog.

He watched Messy Bun's head drop for a second before she stood up from the chair. She walked around it and up to him, extending a hand and offering up the most lackluster smile he'd ever seen.

"Hi, I'm Carli from next door. We sort of met the other night. Um . . . Welcome to the neighborhood?"

He lifted his hands to establish that he had a beer in one and grapes in the other, and he was pretty sure his expression said he wasn't all that interested in shaking her hand. That's the look he was going for, anyway.

"Here, let me get those for you," said one of the other women, popping up from her chair and joining them, pulling the bag of grapes from his grasp. "I'm DeeDee. That house right there is mine, and if you need anything, and I mean *anything*, you just let me know." She pointed to the beige two-story house mostly obscured by an enormous bounce castle that must've had thirty kids in, on, and around it. "Welcome to the Monroe Circle Barbecue."

He let himself be guided away from the scene of the crime, only because he didn't want to walk in and kick up a fuss in front of a bunch of people who didn't know him. The short-haired woman leaned against him as they walked, and if he didn't know better, he might think she'd just grazed her boob across his arm on purpose. "Don't pay attention to Carli," she said. "She was just joking, and that dog is a real sore spot for her. Everyone wants her to get rid of him, but she's determined to train him."

His judgmental neighbor having a steak-snatching, grill-busting mutt hardly entitled her to call him an asshole, especially to a group of women who didn't know anything about him. He'd seen enough episodes of *Real Housewives*, thanks to Sophia, to know how this would play out. They'd all form opinions about him and he'd endure the next however many years trying to make up for one moment of unfriendly behavior. But trying to defend himself would only dig the hole deeper. All he could do now was be the friendliest SOB at this party and show everyone he was not an asshole. He definitely should have brought more than one beer.

Fortunately, people seemed to be in a sharing mood, and he spent the rest of the afternoon feeling as if everyone *else* seemed to like him just fine. All the guys offered him beer and asked which sports teams he liked, and all the women offered him food and asked how the unpacking was going. He was chatty and inquisitive and replied with friendly yet vague answers. He made a show of smiling at everyone's little kids and sharing how Addie loved to babysit. This barbecue, with the standard, superficial chitchat, wasn't all that different from galas and fundraisers that he'd been to while working for his father. It wasn't different from the parties he and Sophia had gone to. No one asked anything too invasive, although the redhead who'd taken away his grapes kept staring at him in a way that felt overly familiar.

Meanwhile, Carli With the Bad Dog kept her distance. They caught each other's eyes once or twice, and she gave him a feeble half smile each time, and he'd responded with an equally tepid and anemic half smile in return, like they were politicians forced to share an elevator with a crowd of reporters. Eventually, thanks to the copious amounts of beer he'd been given, he decided to be the bigger person and worked his way to her side. Her cheeks were flushed, and her messy bun seemed even messier than before. It was late in the evening now, and the drinking had been going on all day. She might be a little drunk. He knew he was. Not sloppy or anything, but talking to all those people had made him thirsty.

"Hi," he said.

"Hi," she said back.

They stared cautiously at each other for a moment, like cats who wanted you to know they were there just so they could ignore you, until she finally said, "Are you having a good time?"

"Uh-huh. You?"

"Yep." She took a sip from a plastic wineglass. Another pause filled the empty space until she added, "I'm sorry I called—"

"I'm sorry I didn't—" he said at the same time, then they both chuckled, popping the tension like a soap bubble.

"Okay, you go first," he said.

She sighed, big and deep, and he couldn't help but enjoy the view of her breasts rising and falling under her pink T-shirt. She wasn't particularly busty but had enough curves in all the right places, and he appreciated that. She had the whole girl-next-door vibe going on that the other women in this neighborhood did not. Nothing against the other women, of course, but the redhead was a little too obvious for his taste. He'd passed by her at one point earlier in the evening and could've sworn he heard her smacking her lips.

"I'm sorry you heard me call you an asshole," Carli finally said.

He let that work its way through his beer-laden brain fog. "Are you sorry you *said* it, or just sorry I *heard* you say it?"

Her smile was the subtlest of quirks. "I'm definitely sorry you heard and . . . yeah, I'm sorry I said it, too." In the scheme of apologies, that was about a two on a scale of one to ten. But he'd take it.

"I'm sorry I didn't help you with your dog. Is he okay? He didn't choke or anything, did he?" His apology was an eight.

She shook her head, and the messy bun went *flip, flop, flip.* "No, he's fine. I'm really working with him on the electric fence. I promise I'll get him trained."

"I'm sure you will. It's fine." And in that moment, he meant it.

She took another sip. Gave up another little sigh. "I'll replace your grill if you just tell me how much that will be."

He shook his head and laughed. "That grill was worth less than the steak, so don't worry about it. We're good." He meant that, too.

Her relief was palpable, and she smiled up at him so suddenly it caused a tiny hitch in his breath. For what reason he could not identify. Blame it on the alcohol.

"Are you sure? My dog did break it," she said.

"I'm sure. Just . . . try to keep him in your own yard from now on."

"I will. I promise." After an awkward pause and another sip of wine, she added, "I think your son was in calculus with my daughter last year."

"Oh, really? What's her name?"

"Mia Lancaster. She's pretty quiet, though. He might not have noticed her."

"Does she look like you?"

"Yes."

"Then I'm sure he noticed her." Ethan noticed every pretty girl. And pretty much every less-than-pretty girl, too. The raging teenage hormones gave him radarlike focus, but at Carli's sideways glance, Ben realized how flirtatious that had sounded. And he had no business flirting with his new neighbor. Because in spite of what those women thought, he wasn't on the market. Not yet, and now she was going to think he was an asshole again. Or even worse, she'd think he was deliberately flirting, and he did not need that kind of complication in his life.

It was time to leave. His brain was tired and his words were getting clumsy, and since he'd achieved his goal of being nice and overtly friendly to every single person here, including this woman who'd insulted him, it was time to call it a night before he gave in to the urge to flirt with her for real. Because she was cute, and he was worse for wear thanks to all the beers pressed into his hands.

"I think it's time for me to head home," he said. "See you around."

"G'night," he heard her say quietly as he stepped away, and for the first time in a long time, he wondered if there just might be life after divorce.

Chapter 6

Just as she had every year on the first day of school, Carli made her kids smiley-face pancakes with whipped cream hair and chocolate chip eyes and a red maraschino cherry nose. Of course, they were far too old for that kind of thing now, but it was tradition, and since it was a tradition they could do without Steve, she wanted to stick with it. The fall and winter holidays would be awkward this year, their first ones celebrating as a family divided, but the start of the school year was something she could keep just the same. The continuity was comforting, and yet she found herself blinking back nostalgic tears. Mia would be off at college next year, and everything would be different. Soon, Tess would be gone, too, but she couldn't think about that just now. It was too overwhelming.

So today she'd have chocolate chip pancakes with her two best girls, and they'd make predictions about the upcoming school year. Then they'd make a fuss while she insisted on taking their pictures before they left the house. Just as they did every year.

"Oh, Mom," Tess said as she peeled around the corner at a full run, "I'm so sorry. I don't have time to eat. Becca is picking me up in like two seconds."

Carli's heart fell to the floor. "Becca? You're not riding with Mia?"

Tess shook her head, sending golden-blonde waves over her shoulders. She was wearing jean shorts and a Glenville High School T-shirt with pink high-top tennis shoes. If not for the curves and the mascara, she could've passed for an eighth grader. "Nope, I thought I told you. Becca got a new car for her birthday, and she offered to drive me. Those pancakes are so funny, though. You are too cute, Mom." She rushed over and kissed Carli's cheek before giving an equally loving kiss to Gus, who was prancing next to the door in the hopes that, wherever Tess was going, he could go, too. And then she was gone.

Carli stood motionless in the kitchen, staring at the space her daughter had just vacated. Did she not remember the tradition?

Mia came down just a moment later, dressed in head-to-toe black. Cropped black leggings, a black T-shirt, black flip-flops, even a black scrunchie holding her dark hair up into a high ponytail. She was heading either to school or to a bank heist. She was staring at her phone as she entered the kitchen.

"Good morning, honey," Carli said brightly. Too brightly.

Mia looked up and glanced at her before her eyes traveled to the pancakes. "Thanks for breakfast, Mom, but I can't eat that. Full of eggs and dairy and probably sugar and carbs. I'll just grab a vegan protein bar at school."

Tears sprang to Carli's eyes, and she turned away to hide them, embarrassed at her own heightened emotions. They were just pancakes. Nothing to cry about. Except it wasn't the pancakes. It was the tradition. It was the moment of connection with her daughters before they parted ways. And this was a big day! The first day of Mia's senior year, but she was acting as if it were just any old morning on any old day. Carli blinked back the stupid tears. All this time she'd thought she was doing it for them, to give them a sense of comfort and security before facing the hard, cold world, but in that moment, she realized she was really doing it for herself. She was the one who needed the connection. Especially now, when so many aspects of their lives were changing, but her daughters were perfectly ready to leave the nest. It hurt far more than it should.

"Can I pack you a lunch?" she asked, trying to keep her voice steady, but Mia was already back to staring at her phone.

"What? Oh, um, no, thanks. Some of the parents bring in lunch for the seniors on the first day and make a whole big deal about it. It's kind of stupid."

"Parents? What parents?" How had she not known about this? This was right up her alley. And it wasn't stupid. It was kind and thoughtful and generous. Those were very nice parents!

Mia shrugged and tucked her phone into the pocket of her (naturally) black backpack. "I don't know. Just some group of parents. They do stuff every month for the seniors. You can ask Mrs. Tully about it. She always seems to be around."

Elizabeth Tully was a PTO mom on steroids, running every fundraiser, every special event, baking cookies and taking names. She'd scolded Carli once for bringing in store-bought brownies for Mia's birthday during the second grade, and ever since then, any time Carli volunteered to help at a school party, Elizabeth put her in charge of paper products. Everyone knew that if you got assigned to paper products it was because you couldn't cut it as a properly vetted homemaker.

"Okay, well . . . can I take your picture? Tess ran out of here before I got a chance to get one of the both of you."

Mia posed, but her strained smile was so insincere it was practically a mug shot. Carli made her pose for another. A slight improvement. It looked like a passport photo, but it was clear that was the best she was going to get. She gave her a hug, and although Mia hugged her back, Carli could already feel her pulling away.

"I gotta run, Mom. Thanks for breakfast. Sorry I can't eat it."

"That's okay. I love you. Have a wonderful first day of senior year."

Mia smiled back. "Thanks, Mom. I love you, too."

And with that, her other daughter was gone, and Carli was all alone. Except for Gus, who was now prancing at the door in earnest. He needed his walk, and she needed to shake away the sudden melancholy taking over her morning. But first, more coffee.

She poured herself a second cup and sat down on the floral sofa on her sunporch, her favorite room of the house, where she could look out over the trees of her backyard. She'd let herself mope for as long as the coffee lasted, and then she had to be done. That was a trick she'd learned over the years, especially right after Steve had moved out. Sometimes she'd even set a timer and let herself sink into her sadness, but when the timer went off, she had to stop wallowing. Otherwise she'd waste the whole day, and there was simply no time for that.

Gus joined her on the couch, realizing his walk would have to wait. He slowly eased his way up, one clumsy paw at a time, so she wouldn't notice his mammoth presence. She scratched him behind his big, floppy ears, and he let out a soft woof as he heard neighborhood kids walking past the house. Then she heard the brief honk-honk of the school bus as it left the stop, and she sighed. That was the sound of time marching on, and Carli realized in that moment, if she didn't make some changes, she was going to spend the rest of her life with nothing interesting to do. Her kids were growing up, and Erin was right. Carli needed a better job. A bigger job. Something challenging and rewarding. Something new and exciting. Something to keep her mind occupied on stuff other than the tick-tock of the proverbial clock and wondering who would win the latest season of *Survivor*. The position for cohost of the new morning show at Channel 7 was still up for grabs, so maybe, just maybe, she should give that a try. She glanced at her watch.

All the other neighborhood moms would be gathering at Renee's house for mimosas—or as Renee called them, mom-osas—to celebrate the kids being back in school, but Carli wasn't up for it today. She had errands to run and plans to make, and Mrs. Stern was coming later. If Gus was going to get any kind of exercise, she'd have to take him now. She downed the last of her coffee and pushed him to the side so she could stand up. It was time to move.

"How about a nice long walk, Gus?"

He perked up at the question, and she knew some fresh air would do them both good. Exercise always made her happier. Maybe not while she was doing it, but she certainly felt good when it was over! She glanced down at the old Wonder Woman T-shirt she was wearing. It had outlasted her marriage and showed about as much wear and tear as she did, but everyone would be at Renee's and she'd be back home before any of them were done sipping their morning cocktails. No one would even see her.

Chapter 7

Ben was sitting amid the rubble of his kitchen, his laptop open on the table while he prepped for a phone meeting scheduled later that morning, when he spotted Carli From Next Door walking her hellhound past his house. The dog was pulling, but she seemed to be holding her own, and that said something, because if Gus decided to drag her all the way to Florida, he probably could. Ben observed through the window as they went down the street toward the cul-de-sac, reluctantly acknowledging she looked cute again in shorts and a faded red shirt. She had on a baseball hat with her ponytail swinging out the back, looking more like a teenager herself rather than the mom of two.

A memory of their brief conversation Saturday night brought a smile to his face, and he decided not to question his reaction. There was nothing wrong with smiling at a recollection. No harm in it. Besides, their talk had been humorous. She'd seemed so reluctant to apologize for calling him an asshole, which maybe should bother him, but it didn't. He'd been called all sorts of names over the years. He had three brothers and a sister, after all, not to mention the fact that he owned a company with two hundred employees and had a board of directors to answer to. He'd had names thrown at him by all sorts of people, because not everyone liked his decisions. You couldn't please everyone all the time and still expect to be a successful businessman. No, none of that bothered him.

What had bothered him in the wee hours of the morning, however, was the fact that sleep had been so elusive last night. And the night before, thanks to a vision of Carli and her pink top that kept tapping at his brain. Yep, that was annoying as hell at 2:00 a.m., but now it was daytime, and Ben wasn't stupid. He wasn't naive. He'd worked with women all his life. He knew that the attraction he felt for her was primal, but that didn't mean he'd act on it. It was biology, not destiny. And exploring it would certainly lead to a dead-end road. One ending at the edge of a steep, rocky cliff. Sure, she was single, and he was virtually single—except for the formalities, anyway—but everything about the situation pointed to this attraction being nothing but an inconvenience and an inconceivably bad idea. She was his *neighbor*, and the proximity wasn't a bonus—it was a deal breaker. And besides, even if he did try to pursue something with her, she'd probably shut him down. She clearly had no issue with calling him names.

Thirty minutes later, after he'd successfully pushed thoughts of Carli from his mind, he saw her again, only this time she marched right past his front window and then dropped from view. Dropped, as if she'd sunk down to the ground. He got up from the kitchen table to get a closer look, and there she was . . . on her hands and knees nosing around in his hydrangeas.

Why the hell was Carli From Next Door rooting around in his shrubbery? Was she . . . weeding? He didn't see her pulling anything up. After he watched for another full minute, curiosity got the better of him. He opened his front door and stepped out onto the brick-lined porch and leaned forward around the post just far enough to see her more clearly. And yes, there she was on her hands and knees, running her hands over the ground in his landscaped beds.

He stepped into full view, and when she failed to acknowledge him, he cleared his throat. "Um . . . What are you doing?"

Carli sat back on her heels with an excessively demonstrative sigh and frowned up at him, shading her eyes from the sun. "I'm looking for my house key."

He leaned against the porch post. "You think you lost your keys in my flower beds?"

"Not lost. Hid. When the Mortons lived here, I kept a spare house key inside one of those decoy rocks in case I ever locked myself out, and now I can't find it."

"Why wouldn't you just keep that decoy rock on your own property?"

She shrugged, tossing up her hands impatiently. "I don't know. I just didn't because the Mortons and I swapped rocks a long time ago, and when they moved, I forgot to say anything about it. I have a key to your place, by the way. I'll give that back to you."

"Thanks. I'd appreciate that." He didn't think she'd take advantage of having his house key, but then again, she wasn't currently coming across as the most stable of neighbors. Best for him to keep track of his own keys.

"Have you seen any decoy rocks around your front door? I don't think the Mortons would've thought to move it when they sold you the house."

Ben had a phone conference about to start, and yet it seemed that once again, Carli From Next Door had a personal dilemma that somehow required his participation. No wonder the Mortons had moved away. She was a nuisance—even if she was cute.

"What did the rock look like?" he asked. The question seemed legit, but her frown increased and her tone grew more exasperated.

"It looked like a rock. With a key inside."

Really? She was going to get indignant with him when she was the one crawling around in his bushes? This was an important call he had scheduled with one of his clients, and yet he knew if he went inside without helping her look, she'd be back to thinking he was a jerk.

"Well, I haven't seen anything like that, but then again, I haven't looked. It never occurred to me that someone else would be hiding stuff on my property." He thought his tone was pretty neutral, but her frown increased, and she squinted at him for a split second before letting out another long sigh.

"Awesome," she said.

Clearly not awesome.

"Don't you have a spare?"

"That was my spare. Actually, it was the spare to my spare, because I keep one in the garage, and I keep one in the glove compartment of my car, but I can't get inside the garage because that door is broken, which is why I'm locked out in the first place. I normally use the service door, but since I can't get into my garage, I can't get to the door that's unlocked. I can only get to the front door of my house. Which is locked."

Confusion swirled as Ben lost the trail of her story right around the time she said *spare to my spare*. And while this sounded very much like a Carli problem and not a Ben problem, he wasn't about to walk back inside his house like he had last time.

"Did you leave any windows open?"

"Only the one to my bedroom, which is way up there." She pointed off toward her house, but he already knew which window was her bedroom window, because she'd walked around in a nightgown last evening and apparently thought the flimsy little curtains she had were sufficient. That corner of her house was shielded from the street and all the other neighbors, but if he was in his room, and she was in her room, well, he was no peeper. He didn't *stare*, but he could *see* her. And maybe once he'd realized she was in her nightgown, he may have looked back once or twice. He was only human. That had kept him awake, too.

"And you checked all the lower windows to make sure they were locked?" Ben was still hoping to fix this quickly and efficiently.

She rolled her eyes at his persistent questioning. "I know I locked them all last night before I went to bed. Like I said, the only open window is the one to my bedroom. I guess I'll have to call a locksmith . . ."

He waited and watched as her expression changed from decisive to one of dawning realization. He could guess what was coming next. "Can I borrow your phone, please? Mine is sitting on my kitchen counter. Inside my tightly locked house."

That was just no way to start the day, and he found himself chuckling. Not at her, of course, but rather because he'd had those kinds of days. In fact, he'd had about four months straight of those kinds of days. "Do you have an extension ladder?" he asked.

"Maybe? But it would be in my garage along with my car and my extra key."

"Maybe? How do you not know if you have an extension ladder or not?" That wasn't really the point, but still, he was curious. It wasn't like an ink pen or a paper clip. If you had something as big as an extension ladder, it seemed like you'd know it.

"My ex-husband has a habit of coming over here and borrowing stuff without asking. I'm sure there used to be one here, but who knows if it's here now? Do you have one?"

He did have one. At the moment, he kind of wished he didn't, because then he could've called her a locksmith and been done with it, but she looked so very *woe is me* sitting there on her knees in his grass with her Wonder Woman T-shirt and baseball hat. His sigh matched hers. He had a metric ton of work to be doing right now, but he couldn't *not* help her.

"Yep, I'll get it."

He texted his client to say the conference call would have to be postponed and then went into his garage. It was no small task getting the ladder down from the wall, because there were still boxes of stuff and rolls of old carpet in there, but he managed. Gus barked as Ben carried it over to Carli's yard. She'd hooked his leash to a tree, which the dog seemed none too happy about.

"Maybe the dog ate your rock," he said, causing her to blush.

"Sorry again about that. Are you sure I can't pay you to replace the grill?"

"I'm positive. How about you buy me a steak and we'll call it good." Her frustration seemed to dissipate in an instant, and her sudden, bright smile made his chest tighten in a way that wasn't at all helpful to him.

"I can't tell you how much I appreciate that," she said. "Thanks for being such a good sport."

He paused for an enjoyable moment, just to tease. "You must be confusing me with someone else. I'm an asshole, remember?"

The pale blush turned crimson. "I apologized for that."

"Yes, you did, and I accept your apology, so let's take this ladder and break into your house, okay?"

"Sounds good. How long can you make that thing?" she asked innocently, and he passed on the perfectly good opportunity to make a big-dick joke, because he figured he was still on probation with the neighborhood women. Instead, he extended the ladder to its full length, glad that the task occupied him so she wouldn't notice how all her adorable blushing was making him fidgety. She seemed wholly unaware as she helped to position it against the house, right beneath her bedroom window.

With the slope of the yard, that window was three stories high, but before he could put a foot on the bottom rung, she said, "How do I get the window open once I'm up there? I mean, the glass window is open, but how do I get the screen out so I can climb inside?"

"I can do it for you," he said, but she shook her head immediately.

"No, it's my problem. I can solve it. If you can tell me how to open the screen. Or am I just supposed to cut it with something?"

He swallowed down a chuckle. She was determined, yes, but perhaps lacked a little finesse. "You can use a screwdriver. Just push the top of the screen up and then slide the screwdriver in under the bottom. It should pop right out."

She took a deep breath, still staring upward. "Okay. Got it." Then her face fell. "Do you happen to have a screwdriver?"

He smiled. "I do. I'll be right back." He had one on his kitchen table, because he'd been using it incessantly over the past few days. When he returned with it, he could see the warring indecision on her face. She did want him to do it, but she wouldn't ask, and his impression of her adjusted slightly. Maybe because Sophia had been so deliberately helpless when it came to things like this. For as long as he'd known her, she'd never hung a picture, changed a battery, or replaced a light bulb. She'd also never killed a spider, once waking him up from a sound sleep because she'd seen one in the bathroom. Never in a million years would she have climbed this ladder.

"Are you sure you wouldn't like me to go up there?" he said after she'd taken another deep breath.

"No, thanks. I can do it. Of course I can do it."

But she couldn't.

To her credit, she did go all the way to the top of the ladder, but once she got to the window, she couldn't seem to maneuver the screen out. After a full five minutes of working it over, he heard her mutter, "Fuck this." Then more loudly, she said, "I'm coming down for some scissors so I can just cut the damn screen."

He watched her slow descent, trying not to take advantage of the view she was currently presenting. Those shorts were taunting him. Carli From Next Door had long, strong legs, and he could hardly help but notice. She had a round butt, too. He was a real fan of the round butt and the long, strong legs. Especially when they were right at eye level. He finally looked away and cleared his throat. That inconvenient sense of attraction scratched and stung like kitten claws in his gut. Not terribly dangerous, but definitely there. He reminded himself that it was just the circumstances and not anything real. Not anything to worry about, anyway. His emotions had been so worked over during the past few months, he could've just as easily found himself attracted to a pockmarked, toothless carnival worker if she smiled at him long enough. That's all this was. Just nature's way of letting him know there was a pretty girl in close proximity. Very close proximity.

Carli's feet hit the ground, and she hung on to the ladder rung for a moment, her face pale and her breath shallow, and he realized—ah, crap—she'd been scared up there. And no wonder. That three-story climb was nothing to take lightly, and only a true chickenshit asshole would send her back up there.

"How about if you give me that screwdriver and let me try," he said.

She took a short little breath. "No, that's okay. I'm sure I can do it with scissors. I just have to get some."

"It might be nice to not have to mend the screen," he said. "Do you mind if I at least try?"

She wanted him to. That much was clear. What wasn't clear was why she was so determined to do this on her own. He was able and mostly willing. Maybe it had something to do with his refusal to help with the dog, and he felt a fresh flush of remorse about that. "I really think I can get it," he added.

Reluctantly, she handed him the screwdriver. "I'm sorry to ask you to do this for me. I can usually manage stuff on my own."

"I'm sure you can. Maybe this will make up for me not helping with your dog the other night."

"You weren't obligated to help me with my dog. He was in your yard, and he had just stolen your dinner."

"True. So how about I get your window open so I can let you in your house and then you can go to the store and buy me a steak. Sound good?"

She nodded, wiping a few tiny dots of perspiration from her forehead.

He climbed the ladder, going a little faster than he was actually comfortable with, because he was a dude and didn't want her thinking a three-story climb was enough to rattle him. Thankfully, once at the top, he managed to open the screen without much effort. It popped out within seconds.

"Are you kidding me?" she shouted from the ground. "How was I not able to do that?"

"It's all in the wrist," he called back down, now realizing he had to crawl in through the window to let her into her own house. "I'm going in."

"My house is a mess. Please don't judge me."

He laughed at her concern, because unless she had crime-scene photos taped to her bedroom wall, or an actual dead body on the floor, he was sure he'd seen worse. Sophia was a slob, and even though they'd had a weekly housekeeper, the amount of clutter and crap she could accumulate between cleanings was indescribable. He'd started using the guest bathroom a few years ago just so he could have some counter space. There was also Ethan and Addie adding to the general mess, so whatever Carli and her daughters doled out, he could handle.

He turned the screen at an angle and maneuvered it inside, dropping it to the floor of her bedroom, then hoisted himself in behind it. That was no easy task, and he knocked nearly everything from the surface of her nightstand in the process. Once inside, he quickly put the screen back in place and then tried to rearrange her stuff back on the table. First the lamp, then an iPhone charging dock. There was an empty water bottle, a stack of books, and, finally, a frame. He took a second to look at the photo inside it. There was Carli in the center with a teenage girl on each side of her, obviously her daughters. One had thick, dark hair and long-lashed brown eyes like Carli, and the other was a blue-eyed blonde with dimples. He'd caught glimpses of them at the barbecue. Both dangerously pretty girls. He'd have to keep Ethan on his side of the property line. Ben took an extra second to admire Carli in the photo, too, noticing the curve of her mouth and the way her smile created the tiniest crinkles in the corners of her eyes. Then he set the frame down a little too hard on the surface of the nightstand, because he had no business staring at Carli. That would only lead to trouble. Where was that pockmarked carnival worker when he needed her?

~♋~

"Thank you so much," Carli said as Ben greeted her at her own front door. She very nearly hugged him but, all things considered, decided against it. "I owe you big-time. I'm going to find you the thickest, juiciest, most tender steak on the planet. I swear."

He chuckled and stepped outside. "And I'm going to let you, because climbing through that window was not easy."

"I believe you." It hadn't looked easy. Even climbing up the ladder had been enough to give Carli a case of vertigo. If she'd managed to get the screen out, she wasn't sure if she'd have had the courage to try to climb through, and a rush of gratitude flooded her senses. Perhaps she'd been a little hasty with her judgment of Ben Chase, because all signs were indicating that maybe he wasn't such a jerk after all. In fact, he'd seemed like kind of a nice guy the other night at the barbecue. Friendly and forgiving and even a little flirty. Sure, she'd had about five glasses of wine and their conversation wasn't crystal clear in her mind, but at the very least, he'd been much nicer than he'd been the night her dog stole his dinner. And today he'd literally gone above and beyond to help her out. Like, above the ground and beyond the window frame.

Gus barked, and she turned to watch him roll over onto the grass, his legs up in the air as he gave his back a good scratching. The sun was bright in the sky and it was warm, and she suddenly realized how thirsty he must be after their walk.

"Oh goodness. I need to get him some water. Can I get you anything? A glass of water or some iced tea or something? A beer?"

Ben's smile was quick, and she mentally acknowledged that the rumors were true. He was very nice-looking, with dark hair just a hint on the long side and eyes so blue they were almost sapphire. He was tall, and although his shoulders were broad, he was a little on the slender side. Not skinny, but not bulky and physically imposing the way Steve was. Just nicely muscled. She'd noticed that when he was carrying that big, heavy ladder. And right before she made a truly unfortunate comment about the size of it that really sounded like she was asking Ben about his penis.

"It's nine in the morning, so I think I'll pass on the beer," he said. "Another time, though. For now, unless you need something else, I think I'll collect my ladder and head home. I actually have a conference call waiting."

"Oh yes, of course. I'm sorry to keep you," Carli said. "How's the unpacking going, by the way? Is there anything I can help with? Seems like I owe you a favor."

He walked over to where Gus lay and bent down to scratch the dog's belly, apparently forgiving his earlier transgressions. Lynette should take a page from Ben's book. "If I get locked out, I'll let you know. Word around town is that there's a key around here someplace, hidden inside a rock."

His easy teasing sent a tingle through her veins. One she hadn't felt in far too long. Clearly she needed to get out more. "I'll get that back to you as soon as I can find it. I think it's behind one of my lilac bushes on the side of the house."

"No worries." He stood up. "I hope the rest of your day is . . . uneventful."

"Me too. And just so you know, I am working with a dog trainer. Mrs. Stern is supposed to work miracles." Although the woman was going to bump Carli and Gus up to three sessions a week once she heard about the broken-grill incident.

Ben shook his head, a warm chuckle spilling forth. "Honestly, it's not that big of a deal. I was just having a really bad day that day and feeling . . . unsociable. Now that I think about it, it was actually kind of funny."

"Was it?" *Really? Was it?*

"Sort of. Kind of like how all this is sort of funny." He gestured to the side of the house where the ladder remained—just as a breeze kicked up, blowing the front door shut.

"No!" Carli gasped, jumping toward the porch to try to catch it before it closed. She wasn't fast enough, though, and her heart plummeted right to the soles of her cross trainers. She grabbed ahold of the doorknob and gave a twist, but it resisted. Her chin fell to her chest like dread descending.

"You're not going to tell me that door is still locked, are you?" he asked, his tone suggesting he already knew the answer.

She met his eyes. His really nice, dark blue eyes. "If you don't turn the little tab thingy, the door stays locked from the outside. It's okay, though. I can go up and through this time."

He sighed and cast a glance toward the sky as if hoping divine intervention might rescue him. Then he looked back at her. "No, I got it," he said, walking dejectedly toward the ladder. "But forget what I said about this being kind of funny."

Chapter 8

Channel 7 producer Marlow Rees greeted Carli at the front door of the station with a bright, friendly smile. Her bold red lip color perfectly matched her cherry-red dress, and thick eyeliner and shiny black patent-leather Mary Janes completed her retro fashion look. She had bleached-blonde hair that bounced off her shoulders like she was perpetually in a shampoo commercial, and although her style was breezy and almost cartoonish, Marlow knew her job and did it with panache. She'd been with the station for five years, heading up their new program development department, and everyone liked her. Even Jessica Jackson, the news director. And Jessica didn't seem to like anybody.

"I'm so excited you're giving this a try," Marlow said, giving Carli a friendly hug. "I'm super proud of you in a totally nonpatronizing way."

"Thanks," Carli said, her voice barely above a whisper, "but I'm nervous as hell, and I don't want anyone else to know I'm doing this."

Marlow's expression dimmed a bit. "That kitty cat may have already sauntered from the bag," she said. "It's Sunday, and I had to ask a couple people to let us use the studio for your test tape. Floyd wants to get some still shots of you, but don't worry. Honest, everyone is rooting for you to do a good job."

Everyone? Everyone knew she was making an audition tape?

After a bit more prodding from Erin and a long conversation with her daughters about what the change in her schedule might mean to their family unit, Carli had decided to at least *apply* for the on-air position. She probably wouldn't get it, because there were certainly more qualified and experienced candidates in the running, but it was worth a shot. Right? At least that's what she'd told herself in the mirror this morning, but now she was having second, and third, and fourth thoughts about the whole thing.

"When you say everyone, do you mean, you know, like, everyone?" Carli asked, all but stepping backward out the door. Marlow grabbed her arm and pulled her forward and into the lobby.

"You'll be fine. I promise. Let's scurry into the dressing room, though, and do a little tweaking. The camera will wash you out, especially when you're sitting next to Troy. He fell asleep in his tanning bed again, and his face is on fire today."

"Troy? I'm doing my test tape with Troy?"

Marlow nodded, leading Carli down a narrow hallway as if she'd never been there before.

"Yep, that was Jessica's idea. She wants to see how you two play off each other, since he's already got the job as the other cohost. Don't forget, he's only got two settings: on-air friendly and off-air inappropriate. But since this is only a practice tape, he'll probably be full-on offensive. Just roll with it. You know he's gross but harmless."

Troy Buckman was Channel 7's perpetually gregarious on-air personality, a hometown hero clinging to his past glory days as a Detroit Red Wings hockey player. It was a *blink and you missed it* career, ended by a knee injury, but he was known locally these days for his work at the station. And for his multiple ex-wives. One of whom was a strip . . . um, an exotic dancer named Tallulah DeFleur.

Marlow nudged Carli into the makeup chair in the tiny dressing room and began to scrutinize her face in much the same way a myopic dermatologist might study a curious growth on someone's eyelid. It was not a good feeling.

"You're making me even more nervous. Do I look that bad?"

"No, you look great. You just look . . ."

"Tired?" Carli offered. At least tired was something she could fix.

"Mature."

"Mature? That's another word for *old*, right?" Erin had said she looked thirty-five. Was she just being polite?

Marlow chuckled and dabbed some powder on Carli's temple. Probably to cover up an age spot. "You don't look old, but high def is no one's friend, and when you have tiny wrinkles around your eyes, we have to make sure that makeup doesn't settle in there and get cakey. It's fine, though. There are tricks."

"You're not really bolstering my confidence right now, Marlow." Carli's chest felt like it was filling with cement. This was a mistake. Like worse than a buying-a-huge-dog kind of mistake. She was a receptionist, not an on-air kind of person. "We don't have to do this. I really don't want to waste anyone's time."

Marlow squeezed her shoulder. "Relax and trust me."

"Trust you? You just said I looked old."

Marlow giggled. "I did not call you old, and anyway, Troy is fifty-seven, although he'll tell you he's fifty-one. You'll look like a prom queen next to him, and honestly, all that really matters is your chemistry with him. And that should come naturally, because you already know each other."

"I wouldn't exactly say we know each other," Carli corrected. "He walks by my desk every afternoon when he leaves the station, and I swear every single time he calls me either Sheila or Gretchen. He has no idea who I am."

"Yeah, he's not so great with the names. He usually calls me Margo, but at least that's closer than Gretchen. Anyway, just be your regular charming self and laugh at his awful jokes and it'll be great."

Fifteen minutes later Marlow led a slightly dazed Carli to the recently reconstructed studio, a brightly lit area with a shiny white desk and a backdrop of royal-blue panels interspersed with brushed nickel and chrome. The ultramodern look was softened by window-size photographs of local landmarks. The Monroe covered bridge. The Glenville historical museum. The new Wallace-Chase Arena. Next to the studio, just on the other side of a movable folding wall, was the main studio, where the news and weather were done. Carli could see the weekend anchor chatting it up with meteorologist Allie Winters through a slightly opened door.

"After we do the taping, Floyd will do some test shots, and we'll send everything over to Jessica so she can decide if she wants to talk to you or not."

"That sounds awesome," Carli said, and by *awesome* she meant whatever was the exact opposite of awesome. Awful? Miserable? Nauseating? She was twenty thousand leagues out of her depth right now. She should not be this nervous. It was just an audition tape for a job that she probably didn't want to get anyway. Yes, the extra money would be nice and would allow her to make all those home repairs her place needed, and it might be just the thing to nudge her from the security of her mostly dull life, but who wanted to get up at five o'clock in the morning every day? And have to banter with Troy Buckman on a regular basis?

"What exactly is it I'm doing here right now on a Sunday?" Troy asked as he strode into the studio, wearing a plaid sport coat of navy blue and kelly green. His white dress shirt was open at the neck, exposing overly tanned skin. He was generically handsome in a soap opera star way, with perfectly styled hair and teeth a little too white to be natural. Everything about him was just a little bit extra.

"You're doing a test tape with one of our potential cohosts for *Glenville in the Morning*," Marlow answered patiently. "And it's going to be wonderful."

Carli turned toward him and smiled, extending her hand for a handshake. She may as well at least try to act professional, especially since this was technically the first time she'd been introduced to Troy.

He gave her an exaggerated perusal, as if she were an Armani suit he was thinking might look good on him. Mild recognition glazed over his expression. "You look familiar. Have we slept together?"

A chuff of nervous laughter escaped Carli's throat. Clearly the entire #MeToo movement had gone entirely over Troy's expertly coiffed head.

"No, we have not slept together."

"Would you like to?" he asked, grinning broadly.

"Troy!" Marlow barked. "You are going to get us sued one of these days, and then Jessica will fricassee your carcass and serve you to her cats. Behave yourself."

"My apologies," he said, the picture of amused insincerity. "But you do look familiar. What station have you worked at before? Nine? Eleven? Are you that sassy girl from Channel 4 who does the traffic reports?"

Should she tell him she was Carli/Sheila/Gretchen from the front lobby?

"Troy, this is Carli Lancaster, and we're a little behind schedule," Marlow interrupted before Carli could respond. "Let's get your mic packs on so we can get started."

Lester, the floor director, came out from the control room and handed a slender cord to Carli, instructing her to run it down inside the back of her dress, then he handed her something that looked like a wide headband.

"That's your girly garter," Marlow explained at Carli's obvious confusion. "You pull it up high on your thigh, and then the mic goes in there. You won't need that if you're wearing a jacket or strictly sitting at the desk, but most times we'd have you moving around. We want the feel of the show to be fluid and energetic. Almost like you're with a couple of friends at a cocktail party sharing stories about all the fun things going on in Glenville."

Marlow kept offering advice, Troy kept making inane remarks, Lester was giving technical instructions, and Carli thought maybe she might like to go lie down for a bit. This was a lot to soak up and remember. The lights were bright and hot, her Spanx were too snug (weren't they always?), and the two camera towers were flippin' enormous. How had she never noticed that before? They were like robots moving around the room, tethered by a single thick cable that linked them to Lester's board in the control room. Between them were the teleprompter and a digital countdown clock to keep the talent on pace. She'd been in the studio before, and in theory, she knew all this stuff, but this was the first time those big-ass cameras would be pointed at her and the first time she'd be expected to articulately read the digital script.

"Let's start with them both sitting behind the desk," Lester suggested. "I want to make sure the chairs are adjusted to the correct height so Troy doesn't look shorter than Carli."

"I'm comfortable with my compact stature," Troy said, adjusting his lapel.

"It's all the same when you're lying down, right?" Carli said without thinking.

Troy crooked an eyebrow in her direction, then his smile grew wide. "I like you, kid. I like the way you think. We're going to get along just fine."

Chapter 9

It had been almost a month since Ben had moved into his modest house on Monroe Circle, and he'd already made a lot of improvements to the place, although you couldn't really tell by looking at its current state of demolition. He'd finished removing the wall between the kitchen and the family room, torn up every last bit of the old flooring—including the peeling linoleum from all the bathrooms—and had his brothers scheduled to come by tomorrow to help him remove all the old kitchen cabinets so he could replace them with new ones. The rancid chicken-in-the-dumpster smell was gone, and the drywall dust was cleaned up, so even though there was still a lot to do, Ben was feeling moderately accomplished.

Today he was taking advantage of the cooler weather to do some work outside, and the first order of business was setting up his new gas grill, on which he'd spent far too much money. The thing was a beast, with more bells and whistles and smokers and burners and rotisserie arms than any man needed. But he hadn't bought this particular grill because he *needed* all the extras. He'd bought this top-of-the-line, envy-of-the-neighborhood grill because he'd *wanted* it. He wasn't the type to splurge, but he felt like he'd earned this, and that wasn't something he took for granted. In spite of growing up surrounded by the Chase family wealth, he and his siblings had been taught to appreciate the value of a dollar. As a kid, when Ben wanted a Sega Genesis gaming system, his father hired him to do work around the house until he'd earned enough money. That's when Ben had learned about taxes, too, which his father took from his salary. Nothing was given easily. That had annoyed the hell out of him as a teenager, but now he was grateful.

Well, mostly grateful. Either way, he intended to enjoy this fine piece of equipment, which would go nicely with the pizza oven/hot tub/outdoor television setup that Ethan was hoping for. Jury was still out on most of that stuff, but the patio certainly needed an overhaul. Currently it was nothing more than a ten-by-ten cement slab with a few fieldstones around the perimeter. So not so much a backyard oasis as it was an eyesore. But for now, he just needed it to support this mammoth grill.

He'd just attached the final knob when, through an open window, Ben heard his front doorbell ring. Rather than going through the inside of his house, he walked up the sloping hill of his yard and around the corner to find his sister standing on his front step.

"Hey," he said, causing her to jump and turn at the same time.

"What the hell? You startled me," Kenzie said, laughter filling her voice.

He smiled, suddenly realizing he'd missed her. Kenzie could always make him smile and was one of the few people whose advice he trusted. Not just because she was a therapist, but because he knew she'd always give it to him straight. She was always honest. Sometimes brutally so, but without her support over the past few months, he'd be a blob of a man with no idea how to move on with his life after Sophia had gutted him.

Kenzie took a step toward him, extending her arms, which held at least half a dozen gift bags.

"Happy housewarming," she said. "I meant to bring this stuff last week, but work has been crazy."

Ben chuckled. "Interesting choice of words for someone who works with actual crazy people."

She laughed again. "I don't work with too many actual crazy people. My people are mostly stressed and depressed and sometimes confused."

"I guess that explains why you've been able to help me. Come on inside."

He led her in the front door and gave her a quick tour of the house, showing her his room, which still had nothing but a bed and a floor lamp and laundry baskets full of the clothes he hadn't hung in his closet; Ethan's room, which had a bed and floor lamp *and* a beat-up old dresser that had been Ben's when he was a kid; and Addie's room, which was completely empty.

"I like this industrial flooring you've got going here," she teased as they returned to the family room, pointing to the exposed subfloor where he'd torn up the carpet. "Very cutting-edge design."

"Thanks. I'm not sure the look will catch on, but at least I don't have to worry about spilling anything."

"Convenient," she said with a nod. "What do the kids think of the house?"

"Addie hasn't seen it yet. I'm hoping she'll come this weekend, though, and Ethan seems to like it just fine. In fact . . ." He paused for effect. "He wants to live with me full-time."

Kenzie's eyebrows rose slowly. "He does? So what do *you* think about *that*?"

It was an issue he'd thought about almost incessantly, but he had yet to bring up the matter of custody with Sophia. He was waiting until she was in a good mood but was starting to realize that might never happen. For a woman who was getting basically everything she was asking for, she sure as hell was grumpy about it.

"I'd love for either of the kids to live with me full-time, but I'm not sure it's the best thing for them to do. Ethan's really mad at Sophia, and if he's here all the time, I'm afraid they'll never get past that. Then again, maybe a little space will give him time to cool off and work through some stuff on his own. What do you think?"

She looked around the room before returning her gaze to him. "Honestly, I'm not sure. I do think it's important that they keep spending time together, but from what you've mentioned before, it sounds like Doug is over there quite a bit. That's really hard on kids, seeing one parent being romantically involved with someone new, especially if it happens before they've had a chance to grieve what they've lost. You're all grieving the loss of your family as you knew it, so now you and your kids will have to create your own unit, and Sophia will need to do the same with them. But if Doug is already in the picture, it changes the whole dynamic."

Ben felt his mood shifting, the thrill of the new grill taking second place to the current drama with his wife. "Yeah, that's the circle I keep going in. I've tried to say as much to Sophia, but she thinks it's just my jealousy talking. And I can't deny that I don't like Addie being there with him around. I mean, she's always known him as Uncle Doug, so I know she's comfortable with him as a person, but both kids understand what's going on behind closed doors. Ethan says Sophia hasn't been very discreet."

Kenzie slowly rolled her eyes before saying, "What a bitch."

Ironically, Ben found himself smiling. "Is that your professional opinion?" he asked.

"Yes." She nodded. "Yes, it is."

He chuckled as he grabbed them beers from the fridge, which was still sitting in the middle of the kitchen, and they continued talking about the kids and the divorce and Sophia and the fact that she was a grumpy bitch. The line between family therapist and supportive sister was definitely blurred, but Ben appreciated that Kenzie could commiserate with him about the misery of his failed marriage while still offering good advice and making him laugh at the same time.

"Want to come outside and see my new grill?" he asked a while later, realizing yet not caring that he sounded like a little kid with a new toy. They went out to the patio, grabbing a second beer on their way.

"Now, what we have here," he said, doing his best game-show prize-hostess impression, "is a state-of-the-art Genesis Napoleon Prestige PRO 825 gas grill with infrared rotisserie and side burner. I could cook an entire Thanksgiving dinner on this thing and still have room to throw on a couple of extra hamburgers."

Kenzie nodded, her face devoid of either the awe or the respect his kick-ass grill deserved. "Sure, because who doesn't want to be standing outside in November in Michigan waiting for a turkey to cook? Good plan. Totally worth the money."

"I'm not saying I *would* cook Thanksgiving dinner on it. I'm just saying I could. It's the principle of it."

Kenzie smiled and took a sip of her beer, looking around the rest of his yard. "This is pretty nice back here. It's got potential."

"Ethan thinks I should add a hot tub/pizza oven/big-screen TV combo. That would be pretty sweet, right?"

"No wonder he wants to live here."

❧

"Hello?" Carli heard voices in Ben's backyard. One masculine, one feminine, and she hoped she wasn't interrupting some kind of romantic encounter. That would be awkward on a variety of levels. Then again, it was four o'clock in the afternoon, so whatever tryst he might be having would probably be pretty PG-13.

"Back here," she heard Ben answer as she made her way down the gentle slope into his backyard. He was on his patio next to a massively large and shiny grill and someone who looked very much like him, with dark hair and sapphire-blue eyes. If not his sister, then certainly a relative.

"Hi," Carli said, suddenly feeling a bit breathless, although she wasn't sure why. It wasn't from walking down the hill, and it wasn't from lugging the big basket she had in her arms. But she felt . . . anxious?

Jittery? Eager? She'd been looking forward to delivering this belated *welcome to the neighborhood, here's your compensatory steak* basket, but suddenly she felt awkward. Maybe because Ben wasn't alone. Or maybe it was because he was the first man she'd felt the stirrings of attraction for since the day she'd met Steve, and those sensations were a mixed blessing. It was good to know her long-dormant libido wasn't completely squashed, but getting revved up by watching her neighbor do yard work wasn't exactly satisfying, and anything beyond *watching* was out of the question.

"Hi," he said as she reached the patio's edge. "What have you got there?"

She held up the basket. "Just a small token of appreciation for your willingness to break into my bedroom. Twice."

The woman next to him tilted her head, her mouth widening with an instant smile. Carli flushed, realizing how that sounded. "I got locked out."

Ben chuckled and took the basket, perusing the contents while tilting his head toward the woman. "Wow, this is impressive. Thanks, Carli. This is my sister, by the way. Kenzie, this is Carli. She lives next door, and she has a very big dog."

"Hi, Carli. Nice to meet you." His sister's smile was warm, her gaze a little speculative, but no wonder after that bedroom comment. *Great first impression, Carli.*

"Nice to meet you, too," Carli answered. "Do you live around here?"

"Not too far. I live over in Elmwood Springs."

Elmwood Springs was the most affluent section of the mostly affluent East Glenville Township. Probably where all the other Chase family members lived, instead of over here in regular middle-class suburban Glenville. Someday, when she knew Ben better, she'd ask him why he was living over here instead of with his people. Especially since he'd obviously lived in this school district even before his divorce.

"What is all this stuff?" Ben asked, setting the basket down on a nearby lawn chair and shuffling around the items. "You put a lot in here."

"Oh, nothing much," Carli answered. "Just some craft beers and cheese to go with your steak. That's in there, too, by the way. It's wrapped up in plastic inside that white paper bag, so you'll want to put that in the fridge. I see you've replaced the grill." She still felt a little breathless and disconcerted as she looked past him to the huge, shiny, stainless-steel minikitchen now sitting on his patio. If Gus knocked that thing over, Carli would have to sell her car to replace it. The thing must've cost a fortune. It was the biggest, fanciest grill she'd ever seen and looked ridiculously out of place on his tiny patio.

"I *have* replaced my grill. Would you like to see it?" He sounded oddly hopeful, so she nodded, following him over to it so he could lift the lid and show her the spotless, cavernous insides. Yep. It was a grill. Other than being brand-new and the biggest she'd ever seen, it honestly looked like most other grills. She didn't have the heart to say so, though, because he was so clearly proud of it.

"That's really nice," she said. "I'll do my best to keep Gus away from it."

"I doubt he could knock this one over, but I'm going to move it against the side of the house anyway, just in case."

"Who is Gus?" his sister asked.

"My dog," Carli said with a sigh. "He broke the last one. My obedience trainer is coming over tonight to help me train him on the electric fence. She hates me, but fortunately she loves my dog, and everyone says she's got a magic touch."

"Why do you think she hates you?" Kenzie's question was direct, and Carli felt her cheeks getting hot, because she hadn't really meant that. It was a joke. Kind of. Although, come to think of it, it was entirely possible that Mrs. Stern did hate her . . .

She shifted from one foot to the other. "Um, I think she kind of hates people in general."

"Ah, I see." Kenzie took a drink.

"Um, so anyway, enjoy the steak and the beer, Ben. I didn't know what kind you liked to drink, so I got an assortment."

He looked at the basket again. "Thanks. This was totally unnecessary, but I do appreciate it."

"You're welcome. Oh, and here's your key. I found it in my lilac bush, right where I thought it would be." She reached into her shorts pocket and produced the key. She'd kept the decoy rock. He could get his own.

His fingers brushed against hers as he took the key from her hand, an entirely innocent bit of contact that triggered an irrational ripple through the rest of her.

"Thanks," he said. "If I ever find yours, I'll let you know."

"Do you have kids?" Kenzie asked, almost interrupting.

Carli nodded. "I do. Mia is eighteen, and Tess turned sixteen a few weeks ago."

"Oh, that's interesting. Ben has a son who's almost eighteen. They must know each other."

Carli nodded. "They've had a few classes together." She didn't mention that Mia considered him a douchey jerk, or that Tess had recently taken to loitering in the front yard just hoping to catch a glimpse of him. At first, Carli had thought her daughter was finally interested in helping with the dog, but she'd caught on to Tess's motives pretty quickly.

"Oh good. It'll be nice for Ethan to see some familiar faces in the neighborhood. Do they live with you full-time?" The question seemed a bit presumptuous. Kenzie either assumed Carli was divorced, or Ben had told her. It wasn't like it was a secret, but maybe that was a little personal? A little abrupt? Or maybe Ethan's aunt was just looking out for him and hoping he'd have friends nearby.

"Not exactly full-time. They stayed with their dad on and off during the summer, but now that school has started, we're going to see how things go. We're still making adjustments to the schedule."

Kenzie nodded. "It's good to be flexible as long as the kids know what to expect."

"My sister is a family therapist," Ben added. "She loves doling out unsolicited advice, so ignore her if you want to."

Oh, okay. Now the questions made a bit more sense, even if the delivery was somewhat awkward, and Carli smiled. "I'm always open to advice. Dole away."

Kenzie laughed and said, "Well, then maybe you should stay and drink one of those beers with us."

Carli stole a glance at Ben. It wasn't really up to his sister to do the inviting, and she didn't want to overstay her welcome. She wasn't *Lynette*, after all. But Ben smiled and pulled one from the basket.

"Looks like I have plenty," he said. "Interested?"

"Mrs. Stern is coming later. If she smells alcohol on my breath, she might add that to her list of my inadequacies, but honestly, a drink before dog training might be just what I need."

"Mrs. Stern?" Kenzie said with a chuckle. "That's an unfortunate name."

"It suits her," Carli answered, taking the beer from Ben's outstretched hand.

Chapter 10

"I'd like to say there's a job for you, Ben, but you chose to leave the company. You can't just waltz back in after ten years away and expect a vice presidency."

William Chase Sr. sat behind an imposing mahogany desk in a high-backed leather chair. He wore a pin-striped suit and a sedate burgundy tie in spite of it being a Sunday afternoon and them being in his home office. The room was as expansively large as it was expensively decorated, with floor-to-ceiling windows providing a stunning view of rose gardens that Ben's mother had meticulously designed herself. A double-wide bookshelf of gleaming teak held numerous awards from various business and charity organizations around the city. William liked to think of himself as a philanthropist, but at his core, he was a capitalist. He expected a return on his investments—and the one investment that had yet to pay off was Ben.

"I'm not asking for a vice presidency, Dad. I'm asking for a job. You know my situation and my qualifications. I don't want any special favors. I just want to know if there are any current positions within the organization that I'd be suitable for."

William steepled his index fingers as his elbows rested on the desk. It was a posture Ben had seen dozens of times over the years. It was his father's *I'd like to make you uncomfortable* pose, and it was pretty damned effective. It was also exactly what Ben had expected. Since leaving Chase Industries ten years earlier to start his own company with Doug, Ben had been considered the Chase family black sheep, at least as far as his father was concerned. He was the foolish, ungrateful son. Even Sophia had thought his decision was ill conceived and shortsighted. She'd liked the security of him working for his father, and the wealth and prestige that came with that, but Ben had wanted to be his own boss for a change. To branch out on his own and see what he could make of himself. He was also tired of being his father's employee.

"Do you have a résumé?" his father asked.

Ben felt his jaw clench. "Seriously? I have an MBA from Harvard Business School, Dad, and I've run my own company for ten years. We started turning a profit almost immediately and have continued to increase our revenue every year since, so let that be my résumé."

"I thought you said you didn't want special treatment. Any other candidate would certainly need a résumé."

Now his father was just being a dick. Ben shouldn't have bothered with even asking, but he was here now, and he may as well play along.

"Fine, Dad. I can get you a résumé if that's what you want. Or I could just call up Dave Price and see if Talbott Industrial Designs has something for me. Maybe that's a better fit anyway."

William frowned. "Well, now, Ben, you don't have to get huffy. I'm just trying to negotiate and see how serious you are. Frankly, I don't want to get you settled into some position here only to have you abandon us a second time when you get another wild scheme about starting your own company. What's going to happen to your partnership with Doug?"

The question was inevitable. "Pretty much the same thing that's happening to my partnership with Sophia. I'm insisting they both buy me out. He can give me half of what the company is worth, and she can give me half of all our marital assets."

"She doesn't deserve half, you know," William said, leaning back in his chair. "Your mother thinks she's rapacious."

Ben nodded slowly, and although he'd never in his life discussed something so nebulous and mundane as *feelings* with his father, he may as well tell him the truth.

"I'm inclined to agree with you about that, but I'm not in the mood to fight her. I'm not up for a fight with Doug, either. We're letting our company lawyers hash it out, and since he and I had agreed on how we'd divide things in the event that one of us ever wanted to leave the company, it's pretty fair and equitable to us both. On paper, anyway. Except for the part about him getting my wife. We didn't really include anything about that in our articles of incorporation."

Ben knew the family was entirely up-to-date on all the happenings within his marriage—the one downside of having your personal therapist also be your sister. Kenzie didn't necessarily honor that whole confidentiality thing when it came to her brothers, and if you missed a Sunday dinner, which Ben often did, then you were likely to be the topic of discussion.

"So right now, Dad," Ben continued, "I just want a job that's stable and predictable, that keeps my mind occupied and pays the bills."

William offered up a mild scowl. "That's a terrible thing to say to a prospective employer. You're basically telling me you have no ambition."

Ben's chuckle came out as more of a sigh. "I do have ambition, Dad. You know I do, but right now I'm juggling a dozen chain saws in the air and trying not to drop any of them on my head. Or on my kids' heads. Sophia pulled the rug out from under us all, and right now my cash is essentially frozen until our mediation is over. Same for my business assets. I'm not broke, but I'm also not solvent. I need some cash flow so I can remodel my new house. Plus anything I earn from a job at Chase Industries from this point forward is mine, free and clear. Any earnings from my company will be tangled up in my division of assets. It's just simpler to make a clean break, even though I don't love the idea of giving up my own company."

William gazed at him for a moment, and Ben could tell his father was ruminating about something. He braced for the next response. "What if we bought it?"

"Bought it?" Ben hadn't seen that one coming and was surprised that his father could still surprise him.

"What if Chase Industries bought your company? Then you could still run it. It would be your company but under the Chase umbrella." His father seemed to be in earnest, his posture relaxing, and Ben's capacity for being surprised increased again. "Let's bring Terrance in on this," William added. "He'd have to look at the numbers and make sure it was a sound investment. I assume you won't mind sharing your financials with him?"

"No, of course not."

Terrance was Ben's younger brother and CFO of Chase Industries, while his older brother, Bill Jr., was vice president in charge of real estate development. Then there was Alex, the oops baby who was eleven years younger than Ben, who'd completely broken the Chase family mold by becoming a sculptor. No one in the family was really certain how he was perceived within the art community, because all his pieces were on display at the Chase Art Gallery and buildings with ties to the family. Ben also wasn't certain how his brother had escaped the emotional wrath of not working for their father. Maybe because Alex had never shown any aptitude for business. Kenzie, on the other hand, had escaped because she was a woman, and their father was a chauvinist who didn't think females belonged in the corporate world.

William glanced at his Rolex diving watch, a gift from Ben's mother even though his father had never, to the best of Ben's knowledge, gone diving. "That's settled, then. Let's go have lunch. Your mother's waiting."

Ben bristled slightly. It wasn't settled. It was a generous offer his father had made, but there were still a lot of variables to consider. He wasn't even sure he wanted to keep the company. There were a lot of memories tied up in that place, and some of them were better left behind. He wasn't sure he wanted to hand a forklift full of cash over to Doug, either, but his father had already stood up and started walking toward the door. William Chase had a habit of doing that—making a unilateral decision and just assuming everyone would go along with it while simultaneously making you feel as if he were doing you a favor, even though he'd certainly benefit.

Then again, his father was offering him a real lifeline. A chance to keep his company if he wanted to. Either way, he'd end up working for his dad again. That was not his favorite option, but maybe there was more ego than common sense in what he was feeling. He'd once asked Kenzie if she thought he had a chip on his shoulder when it came to their father.

"Of course you do," she'd answered. "We all do, but that's because Dad put it there."

∽

"I'm not sure why we're even looking at Fairfield College, Mia," Steve said as he turned the leather-bound steering wheel of his brand-new Ford Expedition with just one thick finger as he careened in and around traffic. "Your grades are certainly good enough to get you into the University of Michigan, and everyone knows that's a far superior school."

Carli was sitting in the cushy passenger seat of her ex-husband's new-car-smelling vehicle while simultaneously having flashbacks to all the times she'd wished he'd drive with more caution. Steve was a cruise-controlling, tailgating lead foot who never used his turn signals and only rarely used his brakes. If she had a dime for every time someone honked at him, or flipped him off, or swerved to get out of his path, she'd have enough dimes to fix every broken thing inside her house.

They were, at this moment, on their way to tour a college campus located in the northernmost reaches of Michigan's Upper Peninsula. A spot so far north it took six hours to get there, meaning they'd arrive tonight, tour tomorrow morning, and then drive back home. A full twenty-four hours together, and just forty-five minutes into their trip Carli was certain that any of the brief, random moments she'd entertained over the past eight months about maybe, just maybe, missing being married to Steve had been swept away right along with the paper food wrapper he'd just thrown out the open window.

She should've made Mia sit up here in the front. At least in the back seat she could've drowned out the unresolvable, circular argument they were having about Mia's decision-making process. Her hyperanalytical daughter wanted to gather all the data from every possible location before thoughtfully weighing the pros and cons of each university, and this was the very last campus tour they were scheduled to take from the list Mia had crafted after hours of online research. A dozen other visits had occurred before Steve had moved out, so this was the only one they were taking postdivorce, and while Carli didn't disagree with what Steve was saying, as usual, his heavy-handed *father knows best* manner made their daughter want to argue. Of course, everything made Mia want to argue, but Steve could push her buttons faster than anything or anyone else.

"Superior is relative, Dad. I hope I do get into U of M, but I should at least consider some of the other, smaller schools. Fairfield might have things to offer that the other schools don't."

"That's ridiculous. A smaller school will have fewer options, not more, so you're actively limiting your opportunities."

"I didn't say Fairfield would have *more*, Dad. I said it might have something *different*. You're missing my point."

"No, you're missing my point. A larger institution is going to have more choices. More clubs, a wider variety of majors, better sports teams, so if you're looking for something different, you'll have a much easier time finding it at a bigger school. I should think that would be obvious."

This had been going on for the last fifteen miles, and Carli knew there was no point in engaging in this conversation. Nothing she added would have any impact, because Steve thought any opinion that didn't match his own was somehow inferior, and yet she didn't want to leave Mia to fend for herself, either. Her daughter had, thus far, been holding her own, but Carli could sense her frustration building. Fighting with Steve was like having pebbles thrown at you. Individually, it didn't hurt that much, but cumulatively, it left a bruise.

"It's not just about the size of the school, Steve," Carli finally said. "It's also about the atmosphere and the environment. Mia needs to choose someplace she'll feel comfortable. You know every campus has a vibe to it, and finding the right fit is just as important as size."

Personally, Carli thought Mia would thrive at a smaller school and that the University of Michigan might just swallow her up. Her oldest daughter was more on the shy side, and a lecture-style classroom with two hundred other kids in it could leave her feeling anonymous and overwhelmed. Then again, Mia was stubborn enough to succeed at anything she put her mind to, so no matter where she went to college, she'd be okay.

Steve frowned behind his aviator sunglasses. He was a big guy, very broad in the chest with close-cropped hair that was now more silver than blond. "You can't choose a school based on something as intangible as a *vibe*, Carli. That's ridiculous. The main thing to consider is academics. People go to college to get the best education their money can buy, and I'm not going to fork over an arm and a leg for her tuition so she can go to a lower-quality school just because it makes her feel all warm and fuzzy. She needs to go to the one that'll provide her with the best training for her future."

This might be a good time to remind Steve of all the partying he did in college, and all the fraternity pranks, and all the late nights he crammed for an exam because he hadn't studied in advance. He hadn't been thinking about his education or his future back then. He'd been thinking about fun. He'd been enjoying the vibe, but there was no point in bringing that up. Somehow, he'd twist it around, changing the argument until she felt as if she were the one being obstinate. It was a real skill of his. Her neighbor Renee had once joked that Steve was the type of guy who'd want to give his own eulogy, just so he could have the last word. Carli hadn't had the last word since the day she'd met him.

"I haven't even decided for sure what I want to study yet, Dad, so how am I supposed to figure out which school will prepare me with the best training?" Mia said, scowling at the back of his head.

"That's all the more reason to choose a larger university. If not U of M, at least go to Michigan State, where you'll have lots of majors to choose from. And besides, I thought you wanted to be a lawyer. When did that change?"

"It hasn't exactly changed, but I think I should keep my options open."

His sigh was big and heavy and full of judgment. "I knew by the time I was fifteen years old that I wanted to study business and finance. You millennials or Gen Zs or whatever you're calling yourselves these days, you seem to think you have all the time in the world to make up your minds, but life just doesn't work that way. While you're busy trying to figure out what to be when you grow up, other people are going to snap up all the good opportunities. Ya snooze, ya lose, kid."

Something inside Carli snapped. She'd grown numb to him criticizing her, but she wasn't going to let him do it to her daughter. "She's not snoozing, Steve. She's being thoughtful and reflective and trying to figure out what her interests are. This decision is important, and she's taking the time to get as much information as she can so she can make the best choice for herself. How about you lighten up a little, huh? Maybe not suck all the joy out of her college decision process?"

From the corner of her eye, she saw Mia giving her a thumbs-up, and Carli felt victorious, even as the muscles in Steve's jaw visibly clenched.

"Yes, Carli. This decision *is* important. That's why I don't want her focusing on intangibles. She needs to be focusing on the facts, like what academic programs they have and the employment rate of their alumni."

"That's on my list, Dad," Mia said. "Basically, all the stuff you've mentioned is on my list of things to consider. Could we maybe talk about something else for a while? You know, save some of this fighting for the ride home tomorrow?"

"We're not fighting, Mia. We're discussing. There's a difference," he said, because only Steve could quarrel about whether or not something was a quarrel.

"Is there a difference? Really? Because it always sounds like you're trying to start an argument, Dad."

He paused for a few seconds before muttering, "And you're starting to sound a lot like your mother."

Carli smirked and decided to take that as a compliment.

The conversation was sufficiently snuffed after that, and they drove on in silence for the next half an hour or so. Carli watched the scenery roll by as she stared out the window, her mind filled with other things. Gus and his latest training session with Mrs. Stern, Ben and how excited he seemed to be about his new grill, and her career prospects. Or apparent lack thereof. As she took a sip of coffee from the thermal Channel 7 travel mug that Marlow had given her in honor of her bravery for making the audition tape, it seemed as if applying for the job had gotten her exactly nowhere. The tape had been turned over a week ago and still, not a peep from the news director. Carli had worked Monday through Thursday last week, just as she always had, and there'd been no note, memo, email—nothing to indicate that Jessica was remotely interested in talking to her about the job. And Troy had walked past her every afternoon, just like always, with a wave and a smile and a "See ya later, Sheila." As if the experience had never even happened. As if she'd imagined it. Carli had stepped out of her comfort zone just as Erin and Marlow, and even her kids, had encouraged her to do and ended up with nothing but a new coffee mug. Had *she* snoozed too long and missed her opportunity?

"God, he's so frustrating!" Mia said five hours later, after chucking her backpack onto the hotel room bed and flouncing her body down next to it. "Why does he have to nitpick every single thing I say?"

Carli had no good answer for that, other than the obvious one—which was that Steve was a self-absorbed pain in the ass. Tomorrow was going to be hellish.

"For what it's worth, he thinks he's helping."

"How can he possibly think he's helping when he undermines all my opinions? I'm the one who has to live at the college I choose. I'm the one who'll be dealing with the professors and the homework and the students and the—" And with that, stoic Mia burst into tears.

Yep. Tomorrow would be absolutely hellish unless Carli took some action. She sank down onto the bed and pulled Mia half onto her lap to stroke her hair, just like she'd done when her daughter was little.

"Tomorrow will be just fine, Mia. Don't let Dad get under your skin, okay? I am one hundred percent confident that no matter where you go to school, you're going to love it, and you're going to figure everything out just like you always do. And you're going to make some amazing new friends."

"Maybe I should just keep living at your house and go to community college until I know what I actually want to study." Mia snuffled against Carli's leg, and as much as the lonely-mom part of her wanted to say that was a great idea, the more forward-thinking mom in her said, "You need to live on campus someplace, honey. I don't care where, but I think getting the full experience includes dorm life. Some of the best friends I've ever had were the ones I met my freshman year in college."

Another snuffle. "I have literally never heard you talk about college friends."

"You haven't? I'm sure I told you some of the stories. I had a great time in college." She *had* had a great time in college, but those memories were dusty and tucked away, like old photos lost and forgotten in a shoebox in someone's attic. "You've heard me talk to Mary Ann on the phone, right? Or Kristi or Jill?"

Mia shook her head, and Carli tried to recall the last time she'd actually *spoken* to any of them. Those women were once so large a part of her life, but she'd let those relationships drift away as Steve and then Mia and Tess became the center of her universe, and now she only knew what they were up to through Facebook posts about vacations and their kids' accomplishments. She resolved, in that moment, to rekindle some old friendships. Maybe a conversation with old college friends would help Carli remember who she used to be, so she could figure out who she *wanted* to become.

In the meantime, she'd settle for regaling Mia with stories about her own college days, and by the time they were ready for bed, Mia was full of giggles and optimism about tomorrow's tour. And after her daughter was tucked into bed like a toddler, Carli told her she was running down to the lobby to get some ibuprofen. She went to Steve's room instead. The surprise on his face as he opened the door was priceless.

"Is this what I think it is?"

"Oh, for God's sake, if you're referring to a booty call, that's a huge, emphatic no. I'm here to tell you to back off on your constant criticism of Mia about this college stuff. She's a smart girl with a good, sensible head on her shoulders, and you've got her so stressed out about making the wrong decision that she can't think straight."

His expression of bemused surprise morphed into a scowl. "Don't come knocking on my door at eleven o'clock at night just to tell me what to do. And I'm not criticizing her. She's a seventeen-year-old girl who needs adult guidance."

"She's eighteen, you moron, and she's got plenty of adult guidance. She has listened to what you have to say and she's not dismissing it, but now you have to be quiet and let her sift through the facts on her own. So tomorrow, I want you to smile and nod and let Mia take the fucking tour without your constant commentary. Got it?"

He rubbed a paw across the top of his buzz-cut hair, and Carli wondered how she'd ever found him attractive. "Couldn't you have just texted me that?"

His lack of emotion nearly made her smile. She'd been prepared for a much more vigorous debate. "You never respond to my text messages, and I wanted to make sure that you heard me this time. Are you hearing me?"

"Loud and clear."

"Good. I'll see you in the lobby tomorrow morning at 8:00 a.m."

"Yes, sir!" He saluted her with his middle finger, but at least he didn't argue.

Carli all but skipped down the hall back to her room after he'd shut his door.

"Did you get the ibuprofen?" Mia mumbled as Carli got back to her room.

"What? Oh, I forgot I already had some in my purse. Do you need some?"

Mia offered up a sleepy smile. "No, but we're probably both going to have a headache after spending the day with Dad."

"Maybe he'll surprise us," Carli answered. She picked up her phone from the nightstand where it had been charging and noticed a missed call from Marlow. Why would Marlow call her so late in the evening? Unless . . . it must be something about the job. She stared at the screen, wanting to listen to the message, poised on that fragile bubble of optimism while hoping that maybe it was good news. Still on a high from having told Steve to shove it. But if Marlow was calling to notify her that the position was filled, the bubble would burst.

Carli brushed her teeth and washed her face and put on her pajamas and set the alarm on her phone and adjusted the thermostat and checked the locks on the door and got into bed, and when there was absolutely nothing she needed to do other than go to sleep, she finally listened to the message.

"Hey, Carli! I know you're in Northern Timfucktoo or wherever, but I thought you might like to know that the news director wants to see you. She didn't specifically tell me any details. She just asked me to arrange a time. Can you come in early the day after tomorrow? Text me back as soon as you can. I'm heading to bed, but you can call me tomorrow if that's easier. Good luck, babe! We're all rooting for you."

She listened to the message three more times and finally fell asleep with a smile on her face.

Chapter 11

"Good morning, Carli. Thanks so much for coming in early today." Jessica Jackson greeted Carli with a mild but sincere smile and gestured to the chrome-and-black-leather armchair on the other side of her immaculately tidy desk. "Please, sit down." The news director was soft-spoken and direct, with her jet-black hair pulled into a no-nonsense bun at the nape of her neck. It might have looked severe on someone else, but on Jessica it looked sleek and elegant. Her cream-colored suit and pale pink scarf complemented the rich hue of her skin, leaving Carli to wish she'd worn something with a little more pizzazz. She had on a navy-blue pantsuit with a plain white blouse. She'd wanted to look professional but now felt a bit drab. She needed to update her scarf collection.

She perched nervously on the edge of the seat, keeping her spine straight and holding on to her purse tightly enough to stem the quiver of her hands. She shouldn't be this nervous. Jessica knew her. Not well, but well enough. And she'd seen the audition tape, so that was either good news or bad.

Thankfully, the news director got right to the point. "Carli, I think we both know that your lack of credentials and minimal on-air experience make you a real risk for this job."

Carli felt all the air leave the room, and her vision wavered for a moment as Jessica continued, "But your test tape with Troy had a lot of sparkle to it. Troy's personality is big, and not everyone can share the screen with him. I think you handled him deftly, and your delivery was natural and engaging. I think our audience would respond to you, but I wonder if you're up to the challenge. Do you think you are?"

Jessica was asking *her*? Good Lord. No one ever asked for her opinion. Should she tell the truth and say, "Um, probably not"? Or should she blast out of her comfort zone and lie like a teenager getting caught after curfew? She chose option B.

"I am absolutely up for the challenge," she said brazenly. "I've got a degree in broadcast journalism, and although I haven't been on air since my college internships, I've been with this station for four years. I know the ins and outs. I know the people, and I know Glenville. I think I can do this job, Jessica. In fact, I'm certain of it."

Ohmygosh, ohmygosh, ohmygosh! Erin would be so damn proud of her right now. She'd just sold it.

The news director arched a dark brow and nodded. "I like your confidence. That's the kind of bold energy you'll need to keep up with Troy. So I'd like to make you an offer. As you know, this is a brand-new show. I'm certain there will be some bumps in the road as we fine-tune things, weeding out what doesn't work and building on what does, but I expect everyone involved to deliver their best work, every time."

"Absolutely," Carli said, not certain if she was supposed to agree or just listen.

Jessica continued. "We've decided to include Allie Winters as an additional cohost on occasion. That will give us some flexibility with regard to on-location segments."

Allie Winters was Channel 7's newest meteorologist, and she had a great personality. Carli liked her a lot because, unlike Troy, Allie knew everyone's names and had a habit of bringing in cupcakes for the staff. She'd be fun to work with, and maybe doubling the estrogen on set would help dilute Troy's overpowering, heavily cologned testosterone. That was a relief.

"We already have a great lineup of local guests to interview," Jessica added. "And the marketing team will be developing our ad spots over the next few weeks. If you decide to take this job, we'll have you, Troy, and Allie do a few promo bits soon, just to show to our test group, but we want to get ads going as soon as possible. We need to build up the buzz a bit. Next week we'll start rehearsals and do some full run-throughs, although we won't be going live with the show for a few weeks yet."

That was also a relief. Carli needed the practice. So much practice.

Jessica pulled a few sheets of paper from a folder and slid them across the desk for Carli to see. They were photographs, one of a stylish, attractive woman of around thirty wearing a fitted black cocktail dress and strappy high heels while holding an adorable baby in one arm and a gym bag draped over the other. The second photo was a man golfing in a suit and tie. And the third was the image of a solidly average woman in jeans and a pale blue sweater. Her hair was shoulder length and brown, her ethnicity ambiguous. She was holding a Starbucks cup in one hand and was staring at a cell phone in the other.

"These are our target demographics for the show," Jessica said, spreading the photos out in front of Carli. "Allie hits our younger viewers. The young career women, the new moms, the ones who've grown up being told they can have it all and are now working to balance life and careers. Troy is for our male viewers. In all honesty, they're a secondary market, but we want to see how he does. And for some reason, he appeals to our over-sixty-five crowd of both genders. And then there's you." Jessica smiled again, but Carli was not really liking the photo that she was supposed represent. "Your aim is to appeal to our forty- to sixty-year-old female market. The women facing various life transitions. Menopause, empty nests, aging parents. Women who are starting a new career or transitioning into retirement. This audience is middle-class with a college education. Basically, you."

The words individually were not an insult, because yes, Carli did indeed fit that bill, but suddenly her joy at being chosen for this cohost position dimmed. A sick sort of swelling took over in her stomach, but she tried to tamp it down. She was being too sensitive. There was nothing wrong with being a forty-something woman. She *was* facing an empty nest. She *was* starting a new career. So why did that photo bother her so much? Maybe it was the mom jeans or the bland hairstyle. Or the notion that she'd only gotten this job because she fit a cookie-cutter mold of what they needed. The one that said she hadn't gotten it because she was special or talented or in any way unique. In fact, she'd been hired for exactly the opposite reason. She'd been hired because *she* was solidly average. A relatable everywoman. Just the way Steve had asked her to be his wife because she'd been in the right place at the right time, Jessica Jackson had given her this job because she was common and unprovocative.

The news director said more about the format of the show and the advertisers and audience they hoped to attract. She talked about scheduling and training and a multitude of other details, and Carli tried to absorb it all while ignoring the negative voice inside her head. The high-maintenance, critical voice that sounded a lot like Steve, but twenty years of him telling her she was *less than* were hard to shake off. She'd wanted to be hired on the strength of her audition tape and her style. Not because of her age or commonality.

But then Jessica started talking about salary and bonuses and overtime, and Carli's mood swung from *why do they want me?* to *holy shit, that's a lot of money!* Working as full-time, on-air talent was definitely more lucrative than being a part-time receptionist. So she just needed to tuck away those feelings of unworthiness and focus on making sure everyone knew she *was* somebody special. Even if she didn't really believe it.

"So that's about it," Jessica finally said. "After seeing your tape, I do think you have what we're looking for. You'll have to work hard and hit the ground running, but if you want the job, it's yours. Now, what questions do you have for me?"

There were dozens of questions, but the only one she dared to ask was "When can I start?"

Chapter 12

"So now that you have that amazing new job—and congratulations and you're welcome, by the way—have you given any thought to redecorating?" Erin asked as she sat on the floor of Carli's bedroom, playing half-heartedly with Gus. He was trying to tug a rope toy from her hand while Carli was in the master bathroom, putting on mascara before they headed off to brunch with DeeDee and Renee.

"Redecorating?" Carli said absently, only half listening. She was busy thinking about her new and improved job and wondering if she should use her first new and improved paycheck to buy a new and improved vacuum, since hers didn't seem to be doing the trick anymore. There was probably too much dog hair sucked up into it.

"Yes, redecorating," Erin repeated. "I don't mean to be rude or anything"—that was a first—"but everything in this house still has Steve's man stink all over it, even your bedroom. Don't you think it's time to freshen things up? Show some of your own style around here?"

Carli paused, a mascara wand halfway to her eye, and looked over at Erin. "What makes you think this house isn't my style?"

"Um, that?" Erin pointed to a golf trophy on the dresser. "Steve won that thing six years ago. Why is it still here? And how about that?" She pointed again, and Carli peered around the corner at a framed picture of her ex and his buddies all wearing tuxedoes and smoking cigars.

"That's a wedding photo," Carli said.

"Okay, but you're not married anymore, and you're not even in that picture."

Carli frowned and looked into the mirror once more. "I get what you're saying, and I don't disagree, but I didn't want to make a bunch of changes the minute Steve left. I felt like it was better for the kids to keep things similar so they wouldn't think I was trying to erase him."

Erin gave an unladylike snort and dropped the rope toy to scratch the dog's belly so vigorously he wiggled with joy. "It's not about erasing him, although it would be okay if you did. It's about claiming your own territory. I don't even know how you can sleep in here with his picture still on the wall. He's been out of here for what . . . nine, ten months? It's time to let go."

Carli glanced over at the family portrait hanging above the bed, a shot taken several years ago of her and Steve with Tess and Mia in between, the four of them smiling from a Bell Harbor sand dune. The gold-framed picture had hung in that spot for so long she never even noticed it anymore. Or maybe she did but still cherished the memory of that day. It was yet another area of divorce that was hard to navigate—how to remember the good times without getting caught up in wanting to recapture them. There *had* been some good times. Magical times, even, but if she sat with those memories for too long, it just made her sad and remorseful. Not because she thought she and Steve should still be together, but because she wished they could have made those magical times last longer. Then she remembered the fresh hell that was her recent college tour with him and realized Erin was right. Those memories needed to be put in a box and stuffed into the attic.

"I suppose I could do a little rearranging," Carli said.

"Screw rearranging," Erin said, getting up from the floor. "You need to Marie Kondo the shit out of this place. Have a massive garage sale or just donate a bunch of stuff to charity and start over. Paint the walls.

Get a new bedspread. Buy some throw pillows. All those knickknacks in your family room? They are all about Steve. It's time for a purge."

Carli frowned at her, starting to feel defensive. Sometimes Erin was a little pushy under the guise of *just being honest*. "And how exactly am I supposed to pay for all new stuff? My new job hasn't even started yet, and I'm a little more worried about fixing the broken air conditioner than painting the walls."

Erin blushed. "You know if you need money, you just have to ask."

Carli blushed as well. "I don't need money. I appreciate the offer, but that's not the issue. I can pay my bills, but I don't have a lot left over for frivolous stuff like décor. I'd rather spend that money on my kids."

"But . . . ," Erin said slowly, "maybe teaching your kids that putting your own needs first once in a while is an okay thing for a woman to do. You deserve to have a pretty house and a pretty bedroom. I'm not saying break the bank by buying a ton of new stuff, but a can of paint is, like, forty dollars. Tell you what, after brunch, let's go to the home-goods store. I haven't gotten you a birthday present yet, so how about I buy you a new comforter and some new sheets? Please?"

Carli felt a stab of longing and forgave her friend's pushiness, because a new bedspread might be nice. The one she had right now was tan microfiber with Sherpa fleece on the other side. It was at least ten years old and the only one that she and Steve could agree on, because he'd refused to have any *girly, floral shit* in his master bedroom. "My birthday isn't until December."

"Okay, then let's call it a *congratulations on your new job* present. And if you're worried about paying for any new décor, you know you can sell the old stuff online. I made a tidy bundle with my stuff by doing that."

Carli chuckled as she swiped on a bit of lipstick, all agitation now gone. "I imagine your hand-me-down items were a little less worn, torn, dented, and chipped than mine would be, but it's something to think about."

And think about it, she did. In fact, during lunch, it was practically all the four of them talked about. After the inevitable and much appreciated well wishes about her job upgrade, they spent the next two hours planning her home improvements.

"Even the things you don't get rid of, you can repurpose," Renee said. "Recover the dining room chairs, paint the armoire, add trim to the lampshades."

Carli chuckled. "I can pretty much promise I'm not going to add trim to my lampshades. That's just not me," she said as they sat in the booth at the Chrysanthemum Café, a trendy little bistro in downtown Glenville.

"Don't knock it until you've tried it," Renee replied. "I have mad skills with a glue gun, and I'm happy to embellish anything you'll let me at. In fact, I think we should make a girls' day of it. I'll help you sort through what you've got and sell the stuff you want to get rid of. I don't have a project right now, so please let me help. You'd actually be doing me a favor, because Rob's been picking up extra shifts and RJ never answers my text messages. I'm bored out of my mind. Let me help you purge and redecorate."

"You're that bored?" DeeDee asked. "Jeez, as soon as you're done with her house, will you come do mine? The only thing I seem to be good at getting rid of is husbands. I have way too much stuff in my house, and I'd love to unload some of it."

Renee's eyes lit up. "Really? You'd let me do that?"

DeeDee laughed. "Let you? Hell yes, I'll let you."

After lunch, Carli went home and strategically strolled through her house with a (mostly objective) critical eye and realized Erin was right. She was so right! The artwork on the walls, the knickknacks on the shelves, even the furniture and the color schemes all said *Steve*. He liked earth tones like rust and beige and chocolate brown.

Staring into her family room as if for the very first time, Carli had a realization. Or perhaps it was a full-blown and final acknowledgment of something she'd known, deep down, for a very long time. She frickin' hated earth tones. She might not have minded them at first, and she'd wanted to be a good sport and a supportive wife, so she'd let Steve have his way with most of the choices—it was just easier that way—but this was her house now. Just hers, and it was time to make some changes.

By the time her daughters got home from school, Carli had loaded dozens of things onto the dining room table to have Renee sort through to sell or donate, including a set of tarnished brass candlesticks that Steve's grandmother had given them as a wedding present. Carli had always thought they looked like weapons from the game Clue, but Steve insisted on displaying them because they looked expensive. She'd stacked up all the biographies about dead presidents he'd purchased but never read. Those books hadn't fooled anyone. Everyone knew he never read anything except *Golf Digest*. There was the buffalo figurine he'd bought during a business trip to South Dakota, the metal B-17 bomber replica he'd built when he was twelve, and a set of bookends shaped like peacocks his mother had given them for Christmas the first year they were married that Carli had hated from the first second she'd seen them.

She scooped up all the rust and beige accent pillows and the brown plaid throw blanket that always hung over the back of the sofa and took down most of the artwork. Pictures of the kids she left in place, with plans to update them, but the prints of flying geese were history. Carli was on a roll, and she wasn't stopping now. She could hardly wait to get up to her bedroom and take down that picture over her bed. This place was no longer Steve's castle. It was Carli's castle.

"Wow, Mom," Tess said that afternoon, walking into the family room and spinning around slowly to take in the absence of what had once been there. "What'cha doing?"

"Just a little redecorating."

Mia wandered in behind Tess, her eyes surveying the now nearly barren room. "Cool, but I think you might be taking the minimalist look a bit far, Mom."

"I plan to get replacements and paint the walls," she said. "Maybe get some new pillows and area rugs. You guys don't mind, do you?" She suddenly wondered if she should've asked them first. It was her house, of course, but it was also theirs. Maybe they were emotionally attached to that cheap-ass print of the goose flying over a stone bridge that used to hang by the front door.

"Mind?" Tess said with a chuckle. "I'm thrilled. This place always looked like Grandma and Grampa's house." Then she blushed. "I mean, I'm sorry. That sounded really rude."

But Carli laughed right along with her, because Tess was right. It looked like Steve's parents' house, right down to the heavy, ostentatious curtains and the fake Persian rug under the cherrywood dining room table. This place wasn't her style at all. How had that happened? How had her own personality been so thoroughly subdued in her own house? And why had she let it happen?

"Sometimes relationships are like two balloons inside a shoebox," one of the marriage counselors had told Carli during a private one-on-one session shortly before Steve had moved out. "There's only so much room inside the box, and as one balloon gets bigger, the other balloon has to shrink or one of them will pop. From what I've seen between you and Steve, he's one of those larger-than-life kind of people who doesn't like to yield much space, either physically or emotionally. You've chosen to get smaller to accommodate him."

Carli had bristled at the time, saying, "I don't think I've exactly *chosen* it."

But the therapist had gone on to explain, "It probably doesn't seem that way because you didn't deliberately choose it, but you've allowed it, and I don't mean that to sound judgmental. You allow it because it's how you've learned to function within the framework of your relationship. If a day comes when you decide you deserve to thrive rather than just survive, Steve will have to adapt. If he can."

Her words had stung at the time, and they'd left Carli with a sense of dread rather than hope, so she hadn't gone back to that counselor again. Now she realized the woman had been right on the money. Any time Carli tried to assert herself, to make herself bigger or even equal, Steve had squashed her. Once, when the kids were little, Carli had wanted a new bike. A cute bike in a pastel color with a wicker basket. Steve kept insisting she get a ten-speed. Something with gears that she could shift to make pedaling easier, but Carli had been twenty-eight years old at the time, and if she wanted the turquoise-blue bike with the tan wicker basket, then damn it, that's the one she was going to buy. They'd had a huge argument in the bike store with all the salesclerks surreptitiously observing until Steve finally blurted out, "Fine. You know what? Get the blue bike. I've decided I'm going to let you make this mistake just so you see how wrong you are."

She'd been so stunned and humiliated at the insult she'd walked out of the store without another word. And without either bike.

For her birthday a few months later, Steve presented her with the ten-speed along with an assurance that it was the right bike for her. She should have driven over it with her car and given the mangled metal back to him for *his* birthday, but he'd given it to her with such elaborate ceremony and with the kids watching, and so she accepted it graciously. Because she thought that was the mature thing to do. But every time she rode that damn bike, and every time she shifted the gears, she thought of how she'd felt that day in the bike store. Stupid. Small. Voiceless.

But she wasn't voiceless, and Steve wasn't here anymore, and now she could grow as big as she damn well pleased. And if she wanted to get a floral bedspread and paint her bedroom pink or orange or lime green, it was her choice. She crossed her arms and surveyed the nearly empty living room and decided she liked this house better already.

"So, girls," she said as they walked into the kitchen. "This weekend, we're going to the paint store. And the home-goods store. And maybe the furniture store, too."

"I like what this new job is doing to you, Mom," Tess said. "Can I paint my room, too?"

"Absolutely," Carli answered without even hesitating. "Mia, how about you? Would you like to paint your bedroom?"

Mia shrugged as she took a container of soy yogurt from the fridge. "Sure, I guess. Except I'll be moving to college next fall. Is it worth it?"

Carli refused to let that reminder sink her good mood. She'd cross that bridge later. "Yes, of course it's still worth it. That's almost a year away, and I think we could all use some fresh, new colors around here."

"I want my color scheme to match my Nolan Hart poster," Tess said with a giggle. "And then I want to hang the poster on my ceiling."

Carli smiled. "Who is Nolan Hart?"

"Don't you remember? He was on the Disney Channel, and then last year he put out an album. You know that one song, the 'Love You for Forever' song?" She hummed a few bars, but Carli shook her head.

"Sorry, still not ringing any bells."

"Alexa," Mia said loudly, standing in the kitchen and eating her yogurt. "Play 'Love You for Forever.'" Seconds later the room filled with music.

"Oh, that song," Carli said. "Yeah, I like that song. Not sure about you putting a poster on your ceiling, though."

Tess pulled out her phone and tapped on the screen. "Let me find a picture of him. You might change your mind. He's so hot he makes Ethan Chase look like Shrek."

Carli laughed, and as the music played, and her daughters began to sing along, she felt a new sort of peace. She felt like she was standing on the bubble of optimism again, where all was right with the world. It might not last, but she was going to enjoy it for as long as it did. Then Tess showed her a photo of the infamous Nolan Hart, and damn, that was one good-looking kid. If it wouldn't be so unseemly for a woman of her *demographic*, she'd put a picture of him over her bed, too.

Chapter 13

"And this is your room," Ben said to Addie as they walked to the end of the hall. "You can pick out whatever color scheme you want. The carpet will be installed next week, and we'll get you a desk and obviously a bed. I would've gotten one for you before, but I thought you might want to pick it out yourself. I know the house is still kind of rough, but I'm working on it."

He was nervous. He wanted her to like it here, but so far, the visit wasn't going all that well. His daughter's wavy light brown hair hung halfway down her back. She'd grown over the summer, and in spite of her new height, or perhaps because of it, she was as reed slender as ever. And significantly less chatty than he was used to. Thus far, his fourteen-year-old had yet to express any kind of opinion on the house. Or about anything else, for that matter. He'd picked her up from Sophia's almost three hours ago, and so far all she'd said was that school was *okay*, her friends were *nice*, and she was *fine*. Even for a woman of only fourteen, he knew that *fine* was typically indicative of virtually anything other than fine. Logically, he also knew that seeing this house might be hard for her. Kenzie had warned him that she'd see it as proof that he and Sophia probably weren't going to get back together.

"Fathers and fourteen-year-old girls rarely speak the same language," Kenzie had told him. "So don't try to use dad logic with her. She won't buy it. Just listen and nod your head and keep asking her how she feels about stuff. She might have trouble articulating it, but she just needs to know that you're willing to listen. And don't be surprised if she treats you like the enemy."

"Me? I'm the enemy?" he'd said. That couldn't be right.

But Kenzie had explained it this way. "To her, you're the one who moved out. You're the one who let Sophia down. It's bullshit, I know, but Addie won't really be able to separate her emotions from her need to get things back to the way she wants them to be. And at her age—shit, at any age—it's hard for kids to understand all the layers. Just give her time. Be patient."

That's how all his conversations with his sister ended these days. With her reminding him to be patient. So that's what he was trying to do, but Addie sure wasn't making it easy. He'd been at this house for over a month now, and this was the first time he'd been able to convince her to even come see it.

"So," he prompted. "What do you think? You got the room with the best view of the backyard so you can see the trees. And if you want, I can hang some bird feeders out there, and maybe we can attract some hummingbirds."

Her expression suggested that she thought *she* was the one being patient with *him*.

"I'm kind of over the hummingbird thing, Dad. I haven't been interested in them in, like, a year."

He nodded. "Okay, what are you interested in?"

Her shrug was minute, a visual indicator of her total indifference. Patience, Kenzie had said. He needed patience.

"How about ice cream? Are you interested in ice cream?"

"I guess. Not sure what that has to do with my room."

"Nothing, but I've really missed you, so I feel like being together is something to celebrate." He could see the wheels turning in her head, and he had no idea if bribing her with treats was the way to go. She was fourteen, not four, but at least he got a nod out of her.

"Ice cream sounds okay."

"Awesome. There's a place not too far from here. There's a theater, too. Feel like watching a movie? Have you seen the latest Avengers yet? I heard it's pretty good."

"Um, yeah. I saw that a couple days ago with Mom and Doug."

His stomach clenched like he'd taken a hearty punch to the gut, and Addie immediately added, "Oh my gosh. I shouldn't have said that. I'm sorry, Dad."

"It's okay." *God damn, it's so not okay.*

"No, it isn't," Addie said, reaching out to touch his arm. "Mom shouldn't be hanging around with him all the time. I didn't want to go to the movies with them, but . . . I really wanted to see the Avengers." Guilt swirled over her expression as her face fell.

He covered her hand with his own, noticing how small and delicate it was. Addie was a strong girl, and yet she'd always be his baby. "You don't need to apologize, honey. And you don't need to hide anything from me, either. You're stuck in the middle of something that you didn't create and that you don't have much control over. Honestly, right now none of us have much control over this. We all just have to kind of ride it out and try to be patient." There was that word again, but Addie didn't seem to be a fan of it, either.

"I don't like Doug. I mean, I used to, but I don't get why he's over all the time. I mean," she said again, "I do *get why he's over*, and that's just gross. So gross."

Ben agreed. It was gross. And inappropriate and unfair, and it made him want to punch his fist into a wall while simultaneously scooping his daughter up into the tightest hug since the invention of hugs. He chose the latter, and having her in his arms felt bittersweet.

"I'm so sorry, sweetheart. I wish I could fix all this."

"You could come home," she said, snuffling the words against his shirt.

"I wish that would work, but coming home wouldn't fix anything."

Her sigh was one of decades of sorrow, even though she was just fourteen. "I know. Mom wrecked it. She wrecked everything. I still love her, but I don't know why she's being so stupid."

Maybe Ben should tell Addie that calling her mother stupid was disrespectful, but this might be one of those times when he was just supposed to listen. And besides, he couldn't argue with his daughter about something if he agreed with her. Sophia was being stupid. And she had wrecked everything. Maybe he hadn't been the perfect husband—in fact, he knew he hadn't been—but he also hadn't once looked at another woman from the day he'd met her. She'd been all he wanted. And now all he wanted was to put that beautiful, innocent smile back on Addie's face.

"Mom's doing her best, I guess," Ben said, stroking her soft hair as they stood close together. "I don't really understand it, either, but I do know that she loves you very much. Just like I do."

Addie snuffed again. "Can I get a bed that has a cushy headboard?"

He leaned back and looked down at her. "A cushy headboard?"

"Yeah, like one made of fabric, and maybe could we get a new light for the ceiling, because that one is seriously ugly." She pointed to the ceiling fan, which was the same awful 1980s rattan style as in his bedroom.

"Yes, you can absolutely get a cushy headboard, a new fan, some cool posters. Whatever you want. We can even go to the furniture store right now if you want to. Do you think you're up for some shopping?"

Her tiny smile felt like a major victory. "I guess."

❦

"Isn't that Ethan's dad?" Tess whispered to Carli as they stood at the counter of the Home Depot paint department.

Carli turned to look, and sure enough, there was Ben strolling down the paint aisle next to a striking young girl with thick light brown hair and blue eyes. She had the look of a Chase for sure.

"Ben?" Carli said, her voice full of more surprise than was warranted. Tess gasped beside her, embarrassed by her mother's loudness. Mia wasn't paying much attention, more focused on watching the paint shaker do its shaking.

Ben turned at the sound of his name, and his smile was slow but genuine.

"Carli. Hi. Are you here getting some extra keys made? Maybe some more decoy rocks?" he asked as he reached her side.

"No, but thanks for reminding me. I probably should. I'm actually here getting some paint." She pointed to the can of Periwinkle Paradise that Tess had chosen for her own room as the sales associate set it down on the counter with a thunk.

He glanced at it and nodded. "Ah, me too. Lots of paint, lots of fixtures, lots of everything." The girl at his side brushed against him, and he put his arm around her slender shoulders. "This is Addie, by the way. My daughter."

Addie's smile was shy and hesitant, her head dipping after brief eye contact.

"Hi, Addie. How are you?" Carli said.

"Fine, thank you," she murmured and blushed.

"Hi, Addie. I'm Tess, and this is Mia." Carli's daughter pointed over her shoulder toward her other daughter. "Do you go to Glenville High?"

"Sort of. I go to the middle school." Glenville High School and the middle school were part of the same campus, but they were housed in different buildings. They shared a media center, gymnasium, and lunchroom, but the classrooms were separate.

"Cool," Tess responded. "Do you have Mr. Evens for history? He's the best teacher because all he ever does is show movies and then you talk about them for, like, ten minutes."

Carli turned to Tess. "All he does is show movies?"

Mia moved forward, now facing in the direction of the conversation. "Oh yeah. I had him, too. Lots of movies."

Carli's cheeks flushed, not that she had any reason to feel embarrassed about this, but it seemed like something she should have known about. This made her look like a negligent parent. And she wasn't. For some inexplicable reason, she didn't want Ben to think that she might be. He already thought she was a lousy dog trainer and an unreliable keeper of her own keys.

"My son had him," Ben said, as if noticing her discomfort. "I didn't know about the movies, either, but that might explain how Ethan got an A."

Now Tess's cheeks turned pink. "Oh, that's right. Your son is Ethan." What a cool liar she was, as if she hadn't been staring out her window incessantly or standing in the yard with the dog for the past month trying to catch a glimpse of him. Still no sightings. He was like Bigfoot.

Ben nodded. "Yep, he's a senior this year. You are, too, right, Mia? Your mom said you guys had a class together last year. Calculus, maybe?"

His questions to her made them a trio of blushing Lancasters as Mia nodded and simply said, "Yeah."

"Do you have any classes with him this year?"

She nodded again. "A couple. Physics and Spanish."

"If he ever needs a ride to school, we can take him," Tess interrupted. "We'd be glad to."

Carli bit back a smile. If Ethan Chase had been a scrawny, pimply nerd, Tess would not have made the offer. That's why rich, handsome boys grew up thinking they were just a little bit better than everyone else. Stuff was just offered to them, and if this kid was the player they said he was, Carli wasn't sure she wanted him socializing with her daughters. Well, at least not Tess. Mia's force fields were firmly in place when it came to boys. She didn't dislike all of them, but she didn't find many of them very entertaining, either. Tess, on the other hand . . .

"Thanks very much," Ben responded to the offer. "I'll let him know that. He has his own car, but maybe you guys can work out some kind of carpool for when you're all around at the same time."

"Awesome." Tess smiled.

"So awesome," Mia muttered under her breath so only Carli could hear.

The sales associate plunked another gallon of paint down on the counter. A shade of the palest pink called Fresh Renewal. Based on the name, it seemed like a good choice for Carli's bedroom, because never, ever in a bajillion, gazillion years would Steve have let her paint their bedroom walls pink. She wasn't even sure pink should be her first choice, but it was an act of pure empowerment to decorate her bedroom in the girliest way possible. She'd even bought some fur pillows this morning at a different store. Fur pillows! And lampshades with little tiny crystal pendants hanging from the rim. Renee was going to love them.

"Do you want this one in eggshell or satin?" the associate asked, pointing to the last empty paint can. Their cart was already full of their other choices.

"Satin, please," Carli answered.

"Well, we have some other stuff to shop for," Ben said. "It was nice to meet you girls."

"Nice to meet you, too," Tess answered brightly, while Carli smiled and Mia just gave a mild wave of her hand, which she then used to thwack Tess against the back of her head as soon as Ben had rounded a corner and disappeared from sight.

"Ow, what was that for?" Tess demanded, thwacking her back.

"For inviting Ethan Chase to ride with us. Ohmygosh, what's wrong with you?"

"Nothing is wrong with me. I was just trying to be nice."

"Pffffft. Nice, my ass," Mia said.

"Girls!" Carli said. "Watch your language. And Mia, stop picking on her for being nice."

Carli knew Tess wasn't just being nice. If this Ethan kid looked anything like his father? Well, nice had nothing to do with it at all.

Chapter 14

After days of rehearsals, Carli was finally starting to get the hang of things in the studio. Troy, to his credit and much to her surprise, was a decent mentor and really did know his stuff when it came to broadcasting and camera angles and how to sit in your chair so you looked like you had perfect posture but not so ramrod straight that you seemed to be tipping forward. He'd coached her on how to pace her speech so she sounded natural and conversational, and he'd even managed to teach her some breathing exercises and not turn it into some kind of sexual innuendo. They were developing into a nice team. And he'd started calling her *Carls*, which for some silly reason made her feel like she was one of the cool kids. At least he'd stopped calling her Sheila or Gretchen.

Today she was learning something new, and working with Allie Winters was like a crash course in how to record a remote segment. Carli was in awe of her ease in front of the camera. The meteorologist-turned-cohost was friendly and approachable and made it all look so easy. She somehow managed to make the interviewee look good, too, and that was often the biggest challenge. They were currently at the Glenville Museum standing next to a new exhibit called The Science of Weather. Marlow was there as well, along with Hannah the videographer.

"Thanks so much for having us here today. What can you tell us about this new exhibit?" Allie asked smoothly before tilting her microphone toward a thick-browed woman wearing a short lab coat and a T-shirt that said **I Take Weather Cirrusly**.

"We here at the Glenville Museum are thrilled to share this new exhibit, and we're certain it'll be a big hit with our visitors." She gestured stiffly to a wall mural of various weather events. "We've got a combination of visual and interactive displays to engage all age groups," said the woman. She gestured just as stiffly in the opposite direction, obviously nervous to be in front of the camera. "Over here we have some historical artifacts, such as the first Doppler weather radar console, a few portable tornado-detection devices, and some items damaged by Michigan twisters. That's another name for tornados. But even more exciting than that, we also have on loan to us a tornado vortex generator, a wind tunnel, and a cloud chamber." Her voice rose an octave, and Carli got the impression that that stuff was supposed to be cool, although she really had no idea what it was.

"That's wonderful," Allie said, nodding as the woman continued.

"Over on the other side of the room, you'll find information about research aircraft and weather radar antennae, along with a green screen so kids can perform their own weather forecast in front of a camera. They love that."

"Carli and I are very familiar with the green screen, too, aren't we, Carli?" Allie said, turning toward her.

Carli actually wasn't all that familiar with the green screen. She knew what it was, of course, but she'd never worked in front of one. They hadn't gotten to that part of her training yet.

"Yes, very familiar," she said, hoping to sound experienced and convincing instead of newbie-ignorant and uncertain of herself.

"Maybe it's just the weather nerd in me, but I think kids are going to love this," Allie added. "What about over there?" She pointed to a double-wide door located under a big sign that said GLENVILLE MUSEUM PRESENTS.

"That's our IMAX-style theater, where we'll be showing a fifteen-minute movie on a continuous loop with footage of historical weather events," the woman said. "And we even have a few special events scheduled where actual storm chasers will come to speak. People love storm chasers."

"I definitely love storm chasers," Allie said, her smile deepening, and Carli found herself smiling as well. Everyone at the station knew how Allie had gone storm chasing just last spring and come home with a fiancé.

"It all looks so exciting on TV," Allie said later that day as they were all having a postinterview lunch at the museum café. "Moments of it are so intense that you can't believe you're really there, but a lot of it is just driving around trying to figure out the best spot to be and then hoping all the weather elements align to give you that perfect storm."

"It's definitely a week I'll never forget," Hannah added. "I was scared out of my mind half of the time, but the other half was pure entertainment watching you and Dylan fall in love."

"You actually fell in love in a week?" Carli hadn't meant to sound so shocked, but her current stance on romance made the very concept all but impossible to believe. She'd heard the rumors around the station, of course, but this was the first time hearing the story from Allie herself. She'd assumed the details had been exaggerated. No one could fall in love that fast. Honestly, how did anyone fall in love ever? She couldn't even remember the feeling anymore. Oh sure, she enjoyed the random zing she got every time Ben Chase popped up in her field of vision, but that wasn't about romance. It was just hormones.

"I know it sounds pretty accelerated, but we'd dated before that, and something about being in such extreme circumstances kind of crystallized for me what I wanted from my life," Allie said. "Once Dylan came back into my orbit, I realized I'd been chasing after happiness in all the wrong places. Now I can't imagine my life without him. He's my person." Her eyes got teary with emotion, and she blushed.

Carli gazed at her and felt a surge of envy and awe and sadness. Oh, to be so certain about happily ever after. To enjoy the falling and the optimism about the future. To have hope, and to believe that you had a person who was there just for you, all the time. She hoped Allie was right and that she'd picked the right person. Because during those long, heavy moments in the middle of the night, when Carli was being brutally truthful with herself, she knew, deep down, that Steve had never really been her person. Somehow, they'd been playing the roles of husband and wife without really owning it. They'd done all the things married people were supposed to do. They had sex and professed love and had game night with friends. They had babies and took vacations and bought a house. They argued about inconsequential things and then made up, but somehow, through it all, Carli had felt . . . alone. Like she was looking at her own marriage through frosted glass. She'd known for a very long time that something was out of focus, but the harder she'd struggled to make things right, the blurrier it all became. Like fog rolled in and surrounded her. She just couldn't see her way clear.

Sometimes while cooking dinner, she'd imagine a scenario where Steve came home with flowers for no reason at all, just because he'd been *thinking* of her, and then they'd share some engaging conversation over wine and cheese, followed by intuitive and mutually beneficial sexy time. But then in reality, he'd come home, burst in through the front door, drop all his shit in the foyer, and say, "God, Carli. I have a ton of hair in my ears. Why the hell didn't you tell me? I need you to trim it. I'm late for fantasy football."

Sigh . . .

So she'd trim the hair from his ears and then watch him gobble down that dinner she'd just made so he could rush out the door and give all his attention to his buddies instead of her. She'd give the kids their bath and read them stories and tuck them into bed before pouring herself a glass of wine and watching home-improvement shows until midnight. Sometimes she'd pour a second glass if she thought Steve would come home feeling amorous, but more often than not, she'd climb under the covers and pretend to be asleep when he arrived so he'd leave her alone. He'd once commented on how she was such a sound sleeper. He never realized she'd hardly slept at all.

⁓

"A python," DeeDee said later that night. "He promised to get our daughter a kitten, and he got her a frickin' python instead. What's my ten-year-old little girl supposed to do with a frickin' python?"

On the third Thursday of each month, the ladies of Monroe Circle gathered at someone's house for cocktails, gossip, and bunco. In reality, it wasn't all that different from lots of other evenings when they got together for drinks and conversation, but on the third Thursday it also included dice. And like most other evenings, DeeDee was regaling the women with yet another transgression committed by one of her two ex-husbands, the fathers of her four children.

"What did Maisy say?" Erin asked, picking up the dice and rolling them across the table. "Does she even like snakes?"

"No, she likes kittens, and that's what her father promised her, but now he's trying to say that he's allergic and if I want her to have a cat then I should get her one myself. But I'm not the one who said she could get a pet, because you know who'll be cleaning up hair balls from the floor? Me. I'm not doing it. I'm not falling for it this time. He makes me so mad, I swear I need a support group for it. You know, like Ass-a-holics Anonymous?"

Laughter circled Renee's impeccably decorated family room, where the twelve women sat around card tables draped with cream-colored linen cloths. No one else ever had tablecloths for bunco. The last time Carli had hosted, she wasn't even sure if she'd wiped the tables off before anyone arrived, but as usual, Renee's place looked like a Pinterest board. The kitchen island held a bevy of decorative bowls filled with various dips and spreads and chutneys. There were crackers of various sizes, shapes, and levels of crunch and saltiness. There were gluten-free options, too, of course. Renee would never be so negligent a hostess as to ignore the needs of her celiac-challenged guests. And for those with a sweet tooth, there were cookies decorated to look like dice.

"Maybe he's trying to get even because he figured out you hacked into his Netflix account and filled up his watch list with Nicholas Sparks movies," Lynette said.

DeeDee smirked. "I didn't hack anything. If he's too dumb to change his password, then why should I pay for my own account? He's just lucky I didn't use his toothbrush on the dog's teeth. Again."

More laughter. DeeDee's subtle methods of exacting emotional revenge on her previous husbands were mostly urban legend. Carli wasn't certain which things she'd actually done and which things she only thought about doing, but there was a very convincing story about her taking an old toilet, putting it in the middle of her ex's driveway, and filling it with fast-drying cement. He'd backed out of the garage without seeing it. Rumor had it there was significant bumper damage to his car but no way to prove it had been DeeDee who'd caused the accident. Her ironclad alibi placed her nowhere near the scene, but Carli suspected she'd had outside help.

DeeDee definitely had outside help with letting a box of crickets loose in ex number one's basement, filling his coffeepot water reservoir with vinegar, and leaving stinky cheese in his floor vents. Ex number two had been the target of her technology war when she signed him up for every digital newsletter that she could find online and changed his Alexa password so she could control it from her own phone. She'd randomly make it blast out "Eye of the Tiger" or "The Piña Colada

Song" whenever she was feeling irritated with him about something. Sometimes Carli wished she had the energy and imagination to torment Steve the way DeeDee tormented her ex-husbands, but Erin said it was self-destructive to hang on to such bitterness, and that clinging to the negative energy of resentment was like drinking poison and expecting the other person to suffer. That made sense. Still, every time Carli saw an online newsletter, it crossed her mind to enter Steve's address.

Chapter 15

Apparently, it was time to celebrate autumn. Ben now knew this, because someone had tucked a flyer into his mailbox declaring it was time for the Sixth Annual Celebrate Autumn Fest down at Renee's house. There would be cookies and popcorn and cider and . . . a leaf-blowing contest? That last part had left him really perplexed until Carli explained it meant each little kid would try to blow a single leaf down a driveway obstacle course and across a finish line using only their breath.

As much fun as that didn't sound like, Ben opted to pass. He had a meeting with his brother Terrance to go over the financial reports of his company to decide if Chase Industries would make an offer to buy it. Honestly, that didn't sound like much fun to him, either, but he needed to make a decision about this once and for all so that he and Sophia could move forward with their mediation. Yep, the fun was just coming at him from all sides.

"Everything here is pretty straightforward," Terrance said to him as they sat in his office in downtown Glenville. "I think it's a sound investment, and your solar panel company would fit in nicely with our portfolio, but I have to ask, are you sure you want to keep it? Maybe it would be better to just move on."

Ben crossed one leg over the other and pondered the question, although it was one that had bounced around in his mind like a Ping-Pong ball ever since the meeting with his father.

"I don't know. It was Dad's suggestion. On the one hand, it seems like a great solution. I get to keep my company, and Doug has to give it up. I've built some great professional relationships and have a loyal client base in a field I know a lot about. On the other hand, there's certainly something to be said for walking away, free and clear. I could take that money and go start something else or come work for Dad in some other area. It might be a nice change of pace to not be the big boss for a while."

Terrance toyed with a pen and then tapped it a couple of times on the surface of his desk before saying, "Do you want my opinion?"

"Sure."

"Okay, here's what I think. I think you wanted to prove you could start a successful company and build it from the ground up. You've done that. You achieved the goal you'd set, so I say let Doug buy you out. Then you invest that money and come work for Dad. He's seventy-one years old, Ben. He's talking about retiring, and then it would be you, me, and Bill running the show. How great would that be? Just like old times. We'll get the old band back together. The Chase brothers."

Ben chuckled. "Dad's never going to retire, and he's never going to die. He's going to be cryogenically frozen and kept in a cooler in his office until medical technology figures out a way to give him fifty more years."

The pen slipped from Terrance's hand, and he leaned over to pick it up. "Mom will make him retire eventually. She says she wants to get a villa in Tuscany and live out their golden years eating pasta."

"Now I know you're making shit up. Mother never eats pasta."

"Well, maybe she'll drink champagne and let him eat the pasta, but at any rate, Dad's time with Chase Industries is winding down, and both Bill and I would love it if you came back. We've got a consultant reconfiguring our management team as we speak, and there will be a job for you if you just say the word."

"Great, that'll make it look like some poor bastard lost his job because I wanted to come home. That's not cool. Plus, Dad was very clear that I couldn't just waltz back in here after ten years and expect a vice presidency. That's a direct quote from the man himself."

"He was just trying to give you shit. You know how he is. You could be VP of new product development, or VP of green technology. You name it and we'll figure it out."

"We don't have a green-technology division, do we?"

"Not at the moment. Seems like just the thing for you to create. Very cutting-edge. Very trendy. Very eco-aware."

"And a perfect place for a solar panel company."

Terrance shrugged. "Yeah, but I still think you should sell it. Just cut your losses and come back here for a fresh start. You know we can tweak the formula of your current panels, start producing them at Chase, and run Doug right out of business if you wanted to."

"Well, as tempting as that sounds, I'd rather not have all those employees lose their jobs."

"We'll hire them here. For our new green-technologies division that you'll be the vice president of. I don't know why you're fighting this so hard. I'm starting to take it personally." His easy smile suggested otherwise.

"Are you sure Dad is on board with this version of events? When I talked to him last, he wanted to see my résumé. I'm not sure he wants me back at Chase Industries at all."

A look passed across Terrance's face, and the pen tapping resumed. His brother was avoiding eye contact.

"Terrance? Is there something you're not telling me?"

"No," he said too quickly. "I mean, not exactly."

"Not exactly? What does *not exactly* mean?" he pressed.

Tap, tap, tap of the pen.

"Stop tapping that damn pen or I'm going to ram it up your nose. Now tell me what's going on."

Terrance looked around the office as if someone might be listening, but it was just the two of them in the room.

"Look, Dad really wants you to come back, but he'd never admit it. You know he's still pissed you went off on your own. He took that personally, but he's getting older now, and he's had a couple of health scares. Kenzie says Mom thinks Dad is worried that if you don't come back now, you never will."

"Health scares? What kind of health scares?"

"Nothing major. Just your basic aging stuff. He fell at the golf course a few months ago, and Mom was convinced it was the sign of terrible things to come. Personally, I think he's fine, but I also think he needs to step back from some of his work responsibilities. If you stepped in, he could bow out gracefully and not have to admit to anyone that he's only human."

Ben's brain was still focused on the health-scare part of this conversation, but he couldn't help asking, "If he wants me to come back so badly, why did he give me such a hard time a few weeks ago, when I asked him for a job?"

Terrance chuckled. "Because he's Dad. You know he's not just going to hand you something. My guess is he thought that once Doug bought you out, you'd take that money and go start something somewhere else. Buying your company was the one surefire way to make sure you came back for good."

"You really think it's that important to him?" It was mind-boggling to think that his father really cared one way or the other. It wasn't as if there was animosity between them. They still saw each other for holidays and Sunday dinner when Ben took the time to go. Was it possible that his father . . . missed him?

"It is important to him," Terrance said. "I don't know why. You're not that great." There was that smile again, and Ben suddenly realized that returning to Chase Industries wasn't indicative of failure. It wasn't a compromise or an inferior option. He could prove himself within the family business just as well as he could by starting something new. And maybe it would be nice to see his brothers more. And his father. Because Terrance was right. His dad wasn't getting any younger, and if this divorce was teaching him anything, it was that time is precious and nothing should ever be taken for granted.

"I am that great," Ben answered, returning the smile. "And you guys will be lucky to have me."

Terrance's eyes lit up as his brows rose. "Does that mean you'll come back and work here? Or does it mean you still want us to buy your company?"

Ben gave it fifteen more seconds of thought before tossing up his hands.

"Screw my company. Doug can have it. And I like your idea of taking that buyout money and investing it. Ethan's going to college next year, and he sure as hell isn't going on any academic scholarship. Looks like I'll be paying full tuition to wherever he goes, so I can use every penny."

Ben had walked in not knowing exactly what he wanted from this meeting, but the spontaneous decision felt entirely right. The past was the past, and Ben was looking toward the future. Relief flooded over him as a new sense of purpose took hold. Working with his brothers would be a good thing. He wasn't doing it for the perks or prestige or because it was convenient or safe. He was doing it because he had something to offer. "I like that VP of green technologies idea, too. Sign me up for that. Does it come with a parking spot?"

"Yes, but only for an electric car," Terrance answered with a grin. He stood up and held out his hand. "Shake on it and I'll get the ball moving."

Ben stood up, offered a quick handshake before his brother leaned in and gave him a hug.

"Welcome home," Terrance said. "It's about damn time."

Arriving back at his house an hour later, Ben spotted Ethan's car parked on the road. He pulled into the garage and got out of his own car just as his son rolled up into the driveway on his skateboard.

"Hey, buddy. I thought you were at your mom's tonight."

"I am. I mean, I was, but can I stay here tonight? Mom's not even home."

"Where's your sister?" Ben asked.

"She's with Mom. They went to some face lotion thing." He brushed the hair back from his face. Still no haircut.

"Face lotion thing?"

"Yeah, you know. One of those party things that moms have where you try out lotion and face wash and makeup and stuff and then you have to buy some. Girls are so weird."

Ben chuckled and didn't disagree. "It's fine with me as long as your mom knows you're here. Did you ask her?"

"No, but I'll text her and make sure it's okay."

"Sounds good. You hungry?"

"Starving." Naturally. When wasn't Ethan starving?

"I'm not sure what I have in the house. Hop in the car and we can go grab something."

"I was hoping you'd say that."

Five minutes later they were on the road with Ben thinking how good it felt to have his son by his side. Was that how his own father felt? Was that why it had bothered William so much when Ben left the family business? It had never made sense to him before. But it was starting to.

Chapter 16

Carli's heart was slamming so vigorously against her rib cage, she thought for certain her microphone would pick up the erratic *thump, tha-thump, tha-tha-thump*. It was the first day of the live show, and she was so full of butterflies that, had they been real, they could have lifted her up and carried her away. In fact, she wished they *were* real and that they *would* do that.

She gave a short exhale, breath not coming easily.

"You'll do fine, Carls. Just imagine it's another rehearsal. We got this. I like your new hairdo, by the way. Hope you don't mind me saying so." Troy reached over and patted her knee, but the gesture was one of support and encouragement rather than anything flirtatious. He'd dialed way back on all the innuendos and crass jokes, and for all his obvious flaws, Carli suspected he was a clueless guy trying to put on an entertaining morning show. She also suspected that Jessica had put him on a very short leash. In spite of his years of experience, Troy was as much on probation at this morning show as the rest of them. And he needed this job. He had multiple ex-wives to support.

"Cue Troy, in five, four, three . . ." The last two cues were silent, and Carli kept her eye on Lester, the floor director, as he pointed.

"Goooooooood morning, Glenville!" Troy's voice boomed, causing Carli to giggle and nearly lose it, but she pulled it together quickly and grinned at the camera as he continued. "Welcome to the maiden voyage of Channel 7's latest and, if I do say so myself, greatest addition to our fall programming lineup. *Glenville in the Morning* will come to you live every weekday morning, and we'll keep you informed about all the great haps in our area, from hayrides at the local cider mill to the opening of the new downtown Wallace-Chase Arena. You'll hear about it first from me and my lovely cohost, Carli Lancaster."

The camera-one light turned off as the camera-two light flashed on, and just like that, Carli was on live TV. She froze for what felt like an hour, but she could see the blinking countdown clock, and it was only a second before she exhaled and began her introduction.

"That's right, Troy. We here at *Glenville in the Morning* look forward to becoming a part of your morning routine, and we can't wait to get to know you better. Not only will we provide up-to-date information live and on air, but you can also check us out on our Facebook page, Twitter, Instagram, and Snapchat. Just go to Channel7.com, and you'll find all the links. You can send us questions, comments, photos. In fact, since today is our first day, it's kind of like a birthday, so we'd like you to send us your cutest baby pictures, and at the end of this week, we'll share some of the sweetest, chubbiest, most adorable photos. And speaking of photos, for those of you with high school students at home, it's time to start thinking about those senior portraits."

Carli segued into a segment with a local photographer while sweat trickled down her back. Thank goodness for face powder and commercial breaks, because she was certain her face was shining with perspiration. But she was doing it! She was on TV. Lester held up his hand, indicating they'd switched to the prerecorded element that Carli had taped earlier in the week at the photographer's portrait studio. A segment she'd taped all on her own, without the assistance of Allie Winters.

"And we are off to the races, hot stuff," Troy said.

"Did I talk too fast?" Carli asked. "I felt like I was talking really fast."

Troy smiled, his veneers glinting under the powerful lights. "You were perfect."

She smiled back and felt a rush of gratitude for this job and this moment. It was the first time in ages she'd felt proud of herself. Actually proud. She was doing something that had nothing to do with being a wife and nothing to do with being a mom. This was her—adulting. And doing just fine with it.

Once the taping was finished, her elation lasted exactly fifteen minutes.

"Congratulations on the first show, everyone. Now let's talk about all those rough edges," Jessica said abruptly as they all sat down in the conference room for the postshow meeting. "Definitely some clunky transitions. Troy, you can't veer off script that way, and Carli, if he does, it's up to you to get him back on track. Allie, your remote segment was fine. Now let's talk about tomorrow's show."

Carli's eyes prickled with instant tears, but she blinked them away as quickly as they'd threatened. Over the past few weeks, she'd learned that Jessica was stern with direction and frugal with her praise. The criticism could have been far worse, and while a learning curve was inevitable, being able to hear the criticism and grow from it rather than letting it undermine her self-confidence was essential. This was their first episode, and Jessica had warned there'd be kinks to work out. Carli just needed to listen and learn. And not cry. She should very definitely not cry.

Arriving at home later that day, though, she did cry, but fortunately for an entirely different reason. Someone had tied an enormous balloon bouquet to her mailbox, which held a plate of chocolate chip cookies, and on her front step was an arrangement of sunflowers tied with a green bow. The note tucked in between the stems read, "We're so proud of you! Can we have your autograph? Love, Erin, DeeDee & Renee."

Her eyes welled with tears. The good kind, because she had some amazing friends. And thank goodness for them and that bright spot in the afternoon, because the emotional whiplash continued as she stepped inside her house only to discover a disaster of mammoth proportions. Dirt from broken potted plants covered her floor and furniture. Sofa cushions lay in a heap with stuffing erupting from torn seams. A ceramic lamp lay shattered on its side near an end table, and big, dark doggie footprints were everywhere. The floor. The furniture. Even on the walls.

Gus scampered to her side, tail wagging, body shimmying with excitement to show her his artistic masterpiece, and in that moment, she realized what must've happened. In her haste to get to work this morning, distracted by nerves about her first day on the air, she'd forgotten to latch the door to his crate.

This was not the way she'd hoped to end her day. Today was supposed to be glamorous and fabulous and make her feel as if she'd finally *arrived*. But life had a way of doing that—handing you a gift with one hand while slapping you with the other. You had to take the awesome with the awful. The yin with the yang. She sank down on the part of the sofa that still had a cushion intact and wondered where to begin the cleanup. Gus pranced and licked her hand, and she scratched him behind the ears with a sigh. This wasn't his fault, but oh my, how she wanted to be angry.

The one upside to this entire mess? Now she had the resources and the motivation to hire some painters. She'd planned to do all the painting herself to save a few dollars, but maybe this was a sign from the universe telling her to go with some professionals.

And then she did the next best thing. She called Renee. This kind of mess was right up her alley.

Chapter 17

Ben was trimming back the sadly overgrown and misshapen bushes in the front of his house when Carli's white SUV pulled into the garage next door. Moments later she appeared outside with Gus on a leash, and after he did his doggie business, she slowly walked with him around the perimeter of her yard, where just a few of the electric-fencing flags remained. Ben had seen her doing this a couple of times a day, and the dog seemed to be catching on. From the looks of things, Ben's future dinners were safe.

"Good boy, Gus," Carli said, patting his head. Her hair was loose today, and she wore the same formfitting, sleeveless red dress she'd been wearing on TV that morning. He knew because he'd watched her show for the past week. He wasn't sure exactly *why* he'd watched her show, because he was more of a breaking-news, stock-market-report, daily-weather-update kind of viewer, but Addie had ridden home from school with Mia a few days ago and had heard all about it, so he'd decided to tune in just to satisfy his curiosity.

Watching *Glenville in the Morning*, he'd discovered a much different Carli Lancaster staring back at him through the TV screen. Gone was the typically flustered woman who lived next door. This Carli was polished and poised without being the least bit artificial. She seemed remarkably adept at making conversation with that asshat she shared the anchor desk with, and that guy was a complete tool. Ben knew him from the Glenville Estates Country Club, where everyone jokingly referred to him as Troy Fuckman because he always cheated at golf.

Carli seemed to have a nice, easygoing camaraderie with the blonde, too, but aside from being a savvy cohost, Carli was damn easy on the eyes. He'd determined that a couple of weeks ago, of course, but seeing her on camera made it even more obvious. Something was different about TV Carli. Something basic and biological that continued to trigger familiar cravings deep inside and tug at him in inconvenient ways.

He took a hearty chop at the branches of his shrub, a physical *nipping it in the bud* sort of gesture that made him laugh at himself. Yes, Carli was attractive, but he had the good sense to recognize that the stirring in his gut had less to do with her and more to do with the fact that he missed sex. Sophia, for all her complaints and avoidance, had at least been around enough to fill that void. Maybe he needed a night out with friends. Or a booty call. With someone other than his next-door neighbor. There'd been a handful of women who'd reached out to him after hearing of his impending divorce. How they knew about it, he couldn't imagine. But they'd homed in as if he'd sent out a bat signal. He could call one of them, right? Certainly, that's why they'd called. Right? Maybe a little no-strings sex was what he needed.

"Hi." Carli's voice cut through his thoughts, and his skin burned, as if she could tell he was standing there in his front yard trying to figure out how to get laid.

"Hi," he said, his voice cracking. He cleared his throat.

"Do you mind if I ask for a favor?" she said.

Sweet Jesus. If she asked him for a booty call right now, this was going to be the best day ever.

Gus was sitting patiently beside her, his tongue wagging as he panted in the afternoon sun, and Ben quickly realized her favor was going to be far less fun that what he hoped for.

"Um, sure." He dropped the gardening shears onto the grass and walked her way. "Please tell me you're not locked out."

Her smile was warm, and that tug in his gut gave another yank. "I'm not locked out. I'm trying to test Gus on the fence, but I need someone to hold his leash so he doesn't run through. He needs to learn that I can leave the yard, but he can't. Mrs. Stern says that every time I let him fail, it takes ten times as many successes, so would you mind just holding on to him for a minute?"

"Mrs. Stern?"

"The dog trainer. She scares me."

"Ah, yes. I remember you mentioning her before. Is that the woman in the tweed jacket?" He'd seen her in the yard with Carli and the dog. She was scary.

"Yes. And I'm paying her one hundred million dollars to help me turn Gus into a useful member of society."

"Rehabilitation from his meat-stealing days?"

"Exactly."

"In that case, I'd be glad to assist." This would not be as fun as a couple of hours of afternoon delight, but it was also far less fraught with potential complications. Ben crossed over to where she stood, and Gus began to shimmy with the joy of having someone to say hello to. He petted the dog with both hands, getting a smattering of doggie kisses in return.

"Thanks a bunch," Carli said. "I appreciate it. The kids are supposed to help me with training him, and yet they're always scarce when I need them."

"I can relate. I asked Ethan three days ago to unload the dishwasher. He's still warming up to the idea."

"Sounds very familiar. How's he handling everything? Does he like the new house?"

Ben straightened up from his stance over the dog and brushed dirt from his shirt. He was grimy from yard work and wished he wasn't. Not that Carli would care one way or the other, but Ben had been brought up by a man who wore suits every day, including Sunday.

"He likes the house all right. I mean, it's not quite what he's used to, but now that the refrigerator is fully stocked and the internet works, he's satisfied." Ben was tempted to add that Addie still hadn't slept over but thought it might seem odd, or too personal. Or that maybe it wasn't a great reflection on him. The furniture they'd ordered for her was scheduled to arrive tomorrow, and he hoped to get her bedroom set up by the weekend. The flooring was in the process of being installed, and the upstairs bedrooms were carpeted. There were couches and some chairs, and the new kitchen cabinets were also installed. Every day something happened to make the place a bit more livable. He'd even invited Kenzie and her husband and kids over for dinner on Friday night, thinking that might give his place more of a family feel. That was another thing he now realized he'd taken for granted—that sense of belonging to a family unit. It took some time becoming a party of three.

"How about Addie?" Carli asked, as if she really could read his thoughts. "Mia gave her a ride home the other day and said she's very sweet."

"Thanks. I think so, too, but it's always nice to hear someone else confirm. And please tell Mia she appreciated the ride. She hates taking the school bus, and I was in a meeting that day."

Carli nodded and stroked the dog's fur. "Of course. Anytime. And if you ever, you know, need to talk about the whole single-parenting thing, I'm available. It's a whole new world out here."

Ben paused, thinking it might be nice to confide in someone other than his sister. "You're telling me. I've had conversations with my kids over the past couple of months that I never thought I'd be having."

"Yep. Every day is an adventure. Anyway, thanks for giving me a hand with the dog."

"No problem. It's in my best interest to keep him on this side of the fence."

Carli handed Ben the leash, and they walked around for a minute before she stepped into his yard. Gus twitched and most definitely wanted to follow her, but his collar gave off a high-pitched tone every time he got too close to the edge of the yard. After a couple of minutes, he just sat down and waited. The three of them went through the motions a few more times, and each time, the dog seemed less agitated by the fact that she wasn't next to him.

"Hey, good job this morning, by the way," Ben said as she stepped back and forth from her yard to his.

"This morning?"

"Yeah, on TV. You did a good job."

Her brows rose in surprise. "You saw that?"

"Um, it was on TV. I think a lot of people probably saw it."

"Right. Of course. I mean, I hope a lot of people saw it, I just . . . Well, thanks. I'm a little green. It's my first on-air job. I've been pretty nervous."

"Really? You didn't seem nervous at all."

"I breathe into a paper bag during every commercial break."

"If that's true, you cover it well. I'm totally impressed. I had no idea I'd moved in next door to a celebrity."

Carli's laughter burst forth like confetti, and he found himself laughing with her, although he wasn't sure why. He wasn't sure why it was such an appealing sight, either. But it was, and he decided to quickly change the subject. "Hey, by the way, did I see painters here the other day? I need someone to paint all my interiors."

Carli's laughter dwindled away, but her smile remained. "I had someone here to paint my living room and kitchen. They have to come back to finish the rest. I'm doing a few rooms at a time but started there because this guy"—she thumped Gus on the head—"demolished a couple of houseplants one day and did the doggie equivalent of finger painting all over my floors and my walls."

"Bad dog."

"Uh-huh. And all over my couch and kitchen cabinets. Plus, he's been pooping out sofa-cushion stuffing for days."

"Very bad dog."

"But at least he's catching on to the electric fence, and he did give me an excuse to do the painting that I'd been wanting to do."

"In that case, I guess good dog?"

"Jury's still out, but if you'd like the number for the painters, I can give it to you."

"That would be great. Thanks."

"My phone's in the kitchen. Come inside and I'll find their contact information." Then she chuckled again as she turned away. "A celebrity," she muttered under her breath and shook her head.

⟲

"That is the biggest frickin' dog crate I have ever seen in my life," Ben said as he followed Carli into her house. He kicked off his shoes and nudged them onto the new rug she'd left by the front door. It was bright yellow with a big butterfly on it. Steve would've hated it, which made her like it that much more. She'd bought it the day after the houseplant incident, along with some new pillows and a few other things, since it seemed like the universe, by way of Gus, was telling her to get some new stuff.

Gus ambled into his pen without being asked and settled down on his bed with a satisfied sigh. A couple of jolts from an electric fence were bound to tire a boy out.

"I know," she said to Ben. "I should've checked the measurements more carefully before I bought it, but once I'd put it up, it was too much trouble to return. Let's just hope he doesn't grow into it."

Gus's crate took up one full corner of her front living room, and next to it sat a laundry basket full of gigantic chew toys and plush stuffies. "I'm trying to train him to put his toys away at the end of each day, but so far all he does is take more toys out. It's like having a toddler."

She walked into the kitchen with Ben right behind her, and she wondered what he thought of her place. The new paint colors were a combination of soft pastels and ivories with not an effing earth tone in sight. She'd found cream-colored slipcovers for her sofa and love seat, and they looked like brand-new pieces. You couldn't even tell that one of the cushions had a huge tear down the middle. There were now half a dozen soft and fluffy decorative pillows in robin's-egg blue and pale pinks along with a soft gray cable-knit throw blanket. The place was currently barren of wall art or knickknacks—or houseplants—but it was still a much better reflection of her just by changing the palette. Maybe that's why she was nervous about what Ben thought. Because now the house was *her*, and the codependent people pleaser inside her really wanted him to like it. To like her. Not in a romantic way, because, in spite of how attractive he was, that was a nonstarter, but just as a good neighbor. Maybe as a friend.

"Is this all new?" he asked, looking around, and after she nodded, he said, "I like it. It's very relaxing."

"Thanks. That's what I was going for. The color in here is called Tranquility Base."

Ben nodded. "That explains it. I'm suddenly feeling very tranquil."

Carli chuckled and picked her phone up from the table. "What's your cell phone number? I can just share the contact for the painters."

After they exchanged numbers, he said again, "I really like the colors in here. Do you think . . . would you be willing to come over to my place and look at the colors I'm thinking about and tell me if they look good? Honestly, I thought I'd picked out some okay shades, but Addie says the samples I brought home look like bean dip and baby poop."

"Is that what you were going for?" She quirked an eyebrow.

He chuckled. "Oddly enough, no. And I wasn't going for baby poop after eating bean dip, either. I could really use an objective opinion. And besides, don't you owe me a favor or two?"

"Well, when you put it that way. When would you like me to come look?"

"Um, can you come over right now?" His voice had that same optimistic, expectant tone as it had the night he'd wanted her to look at his new grill. It was cute and almost boyish, although little else about him was. There were a lot of overgrown man-child husbands in the neighborhood, but Ben seemed like the rare grown-up.

"Sure, just give me a couple minutes to change my clothes. I've had this dress on since five o'clock this morning, and I'm dying to take it off."

He smiled as he turned suddenly to look at her fireplace, clearing his throat. "Okay. Want to just come over after you've changed?"

"Sure. Give me fifteen minutes."

She raced upstairs as soon as he left and peeled off her dress, taking only a second to enjoy the Spanx-free moment before pulling on blue shorts and a polka-dotted top. She brushed her teeth and freshened her makeup because, yes, she was just going over there to look at paint colors for him, but she still wanted to look nice. He'd seen her looking like a mess often enough. She was just trying to balance out the ratio.

When she arrived at his place, he opened the door before she could knock. He'd changed, too, switching from basketball shorts and a plain white T-shirt with dirt smudges on it to khaki shorts and a blue shirt that made his eyes seem an even deeper sapphire. They were distractingly blue. But she'd just have to get used to them. She'd just have to get used to the fact that he was handsome, too. There were certainly worse problems to suffer through than having a good-looking next-door neighbor.

"Wow, this place looks better already," she said as she stepped inside. "There's actually sunlight in here now."

The Mortons' style had been traditional geriatric with thick, paisley-patterned curtains and big, elaborate valances on every window. All the woodwork was dark walnut, and every overhead light fixture had come straight from the bargain bin at the local lighting store. But standing inside what was now Ben's house, she saw that all the window treatments were gone, and so was the stained Berber carpet that their poor old incontinent dog had befouled in ways too numerous to list.

"And it doesn't smell," she said, then blushed with embarrassment, because that was a seriously tacky thing to say.

"What kind of dog did they have?" Ben asked, not seeming bothered by her comment about the smell. "Because judging from the carpet and pad I pulled out, this place housed a kennel of dysenteric hyenas."

Carli shook her head. "Just one little dog, but he was about a hundred years old, and once Mrs. Morton started using a walker, I'm not sure she ever brought him outside. And his name was Mr. Piddles, so that should give you some idea."

"Awesome. Well, as you can see, the carpet is gone, and the paint samples are over here."

He led her farther into the family room just off the kitchen, where a variety of legitimately awful colors had been painted on the wall in sloppy squares.

"Hmm," she said. "What kind of mood are you going for?"

"Mood?"

"Yes, like, my colors are all about relaxation and peace of mind, and to me, honestly, these colors you've got here say . . . mudslide."

"Mudslide?"

"Yes, tragic, demolishing mudslide. Lives were lost. Homes destroyed."

Ben's initial chuckle was hesitant, then built to full-on laughter. "That's terrible."

"I know, and so are these colors." She pointed to the various splotches on his wall. "Here you've got Tragic Mudslide. This one is

Puddle on a Cloudy Day. And over here you've got Michigan Road Slush in March. This must be the bean-dip color Addie was talking about. Oh, and this one is Dead Skin. I'm sorry, Ben, but these are really bad colors." Maybe she should've been a little kinder, but he had asked for her opinion. His smile suggested he could take it.

"Okay, fair enough, but in my defense, the actual names of these colors are stuff like Morning Latte and Desert Sand. None of them are called Dead Skin. Even I would've known that was a bad choice."

"Do you have any other samples?"

"Nope."

"Well, some of the shades I ended up with at my house might be a little too feminine over here, but I have about ten other samples that I brought home. Do you want to see them? There are some grays and peaches and lots of blues."

Ben stared at the wall of horror for a moment. "You really think these are that bad?"

She nodded. "I do, but you're the one who lives here, so if you like them, that's all that matters."

He shook his head. "Maybe I should try a few more colors, if you don't mind sharing your samples. I'd like to pick something that doesn't make Addie cringe."

The front door opened as he spoke, and in walked a younger, taller, skinnier version of Ben, and suddenly Carli understood why Tess was so flustered by Ethan Chase. He was movie-heartthrob cute with that teenage-boy swagger of utter nonchalance and strategically messy hair. He strolled into the kitchen and dropped his backpack on the floor.

"Hey," he said, nodding at them both before sauntering over and pulling open the refrigerator door.

"Hey, yourself, kid. How about you come back and say hello to our neighbor," Ben said, his voice not particularly stern.

Ethan turned around. "Hi, neighbor. Are you Mia's mom?"

"Yes, and you must be Ethan."

"Yep. Nice to meet you. She's really good at math. Does she ever tutor anybody?"

"Um, I don't know. She's never mentioned it."

"Oh, well, if she wants to, I could use some help." He turned back to the fridge and pulled out an apple and a package of sandwich meat. "I've got a ton of homework, Dad. Mind if I just take this upstairs and get to it?"

"No, that's fine, but before you go, what color do you want your bedroom painted?"

Ethan looked back at him as if Ben had asked if he'd rather have toast . . . or toast. As if that's how much difference it made to him. "Um, I don't know. Blue? Brown? What's wrong with the color that it is right now?"

"What color is it right now?" Ben asked. "I can't remember."

Ethan took a bite of the apple before responding, "Neither can I. I'll go check."

Carli chuckled as he walked away. "Boys are so different from girls. It took Tess an hour and a half to choose between two shades of periwinkle that were virtually the exact same color."

Ben stared back at the splotches but didn't seem to really be seeing them. "I took Addie to the furniture store, and we spent at least three hours choosing a bed and a desk, and I'm not honestly sure she likes what we ended up with. I think she just wanted to get it over with. She's not . . ." He hesitated briefly before finishing. "She's not super thrilled about bouncing between two houses. She hasn't stayed here yet." Now he glanced down at the floor.

Carli nodded, noticing his slightly dejected expression. "It's a tough adjustment. My kids have to share a bedroom when they go over to their dad's place, and you'd think he was making them share a single toothbrush and rationing out the toilet paper, but he also has a pool, so being there in the summer wasn't so bad. They have the advantage of being able to drive, so they can move back and forth a lot easier. It's just . . . it's hard. And it takes a while before it feels normal."

"Normal," he said. "What I wouldn't give for a little bit of that."

"Yeah, me too. The holidays will be . . . a challenge."

"How long have you been divorced?" he asked.

"My ex-husband moved out in January. It took until July for things to be official, but essentially, January. How about you?"

He paused for a moment, and she thought he might deflect the question, but he didn't. "I'm in the process now, and it's going to take a while. My . . . wife—technically she's still my wife, but anyway—she's currently shacking up with my business partner, so as you can imagine, there are quite a few layers to sort through before we get to any final settlement."

Carli found herself wincing sympathetically at his statement. "Ouch," she said. "That sucks."

She should have said something more compassionate and articulate, but he actually smiled at her response.

"Right? I think so, too. It sucks. For me, for my kids, for my company's employees and clients. But hey, at least my wife is happy."

The sarcasm didn't completely disguise the hurt.

"I'm sorry you're going through this," she said. "For what it's worth, I think you're holding up amazingly well. When Steve left, I spent most of my days in bed, hiding under the covers. I'd drag myself out when the kids were around, but if they were at Steve's, I'd be in bed. I didn't even turn on the TV. But it passed, and I found my way back. It does get easier."

Well, that was an embarrassing overshare. Carli wasn't in the habit of telling people she hardly knew that she'd spent almost entire weeks in bed.

But Ben nodded, seeming to understand. "Before moving here, I'd been sleeping in the guest room at my sister's house, but since it doubles as her workout room, staying in bed wasn't an option for me. Plus, she's a therapist and kept making me talk about everything, but there were definitely times I thought about driving away in my car and never turning around. I haven't thought about doing that in a while, though, so I guess it does get better. I mean, I can tell it's getting better. I just wish it would get more better, faster."

He smiled at her then, and she wondered if he realized how handsome he was when he did that.

Chapter 18

Another day, another flyer in Ben's mailbox announcing some neighborhood social event that he was either invited to or was in some way expected to participate in. He'd skipped the Fifth Annual Back to School Water Balloon Fight at the bus stop, because his kids drove and didn't go to the bus stop. If he'd gone, he'd have looked like a pervert. Just some random old guy hanging around a bus stop. No, thanks. He'd also avoided the Third Annual Choir Boosters Car Wash, because no way in hell was he letting an overly excited cluster of teenagers lather up his Lexus with dish soap and spray it with a garden hose. Nor had he attended the Autumn Fest. So chances were pretty good he'd skip whatever event this one was, too.

"You can't skip it," Carli told him later that evening. She'd been taking Gus for a walk, but the dog had decided to drop an enormous load of poop right in front of his house. Good thing he and Carli were on friendly terms now or he might have thought she'd gotten the dog to do the doo-doo on purpose.

"When I bought this house, no one told me I was moving onto the set of a Disney movie," he complained.

"What do you mean, a Disney movie?"

He unfolded the orange sheet of paper that he'd stuffed into the pocket of his jeans. It was cut into the shape of a pumpkin, and across the top it read, Tenth Annual Monroe Circle Halloween Hayride. He held it up and waved it a little.

"This. It says there's a hayride through the neighborhood on the Saturday before Halloween and that I'm *strongly encouraged* to put up decorations, but I have neither the time nor the inclination to clutter up my yard with ghosts or goblins or tombstones or whatever the hell else they think I'm supposed to do. Who is in charge of all this stuff, anyway?"

"We have a neighborhood social committee."

"Well, it's excessive."

Carli frowned at him. "Way to put the F-U in *fun*, Ben. Why are you so crabby?"

He was crabby because mediation had come to a halt thanks to Sophia's refusal to complete a discovery questionnaire about all the purchases she'd made since Ben had moved out, and Doug was being an entire bag of dicks about the valuation of their company as they negotiated Ben's buyout settlement. To top it all off, his mother had set him up on a date with an old friend of the family, and he was in no mood to make idle chitchat with some woman he hadn't seen in twenty years. Especially one who'd been thoroughly vetted by his mother.

"I just have a lot of shit going on, and none of it includes me carving pumpkins."

"But the hayride goes right by our houses, and then it stops at the end of the street so everyone can have cider and doughnuts at Renee's house. All the little kids wear their costumes, and they're all so ridiculously adorable you won't even be able to stand it."

"I already can't stand it. That's what I'm trying to tell you. No part of that sounds appealing to me."

Her eyes narrowed, and he felt himself being thoroughly judged. This was not unusual with Carli. He'd learned that as she'd helped him choose his paint colors. She'd also helped him pick out some area rugs and even some artwork for Addie's room, because, according to Carli, he must be colorblind and possibly regular blind, too.

"When the Mortons lived in that house, they put up a ton of stuff, and it was very impressive. All the kids are going to expect you to do *something*. Mr. Piddles even had a little skeleton costume." Her judgmental squint was replaced with a teasing grin.

"You are killing me with this right now," he said, shaking the orange paper pumpkin again, but she laughed at his discomfort, and he found his mood lifting ever so slightly. She seemed to have that impact on him.

"At least get one of those big inflatable things or something," Carli said. "Those take like ten minutes to set up. Are you always this much of a Halloween grinch, or is it just this year?"

Ben scoffed and folded the paper back up to put in his pocket. "I'm not a Halloween grinch. I always helped hand out the candy in my old neighborhood. Isn't that enough? Just handing out candy on the actual night of Halloween?"

"Well, of course you'll need to hand out candy on Halloween night," she said as if her point were so obvious she could hardly believe she even had to say it out loud. "And here's a tip, since you're new to Monroe Circle. Give out full-size candy bars or cans of pop. The kids love that, and then they'll remember to leave your house alone the next time they feel like egging somebody. Trust me, it's worth the investment."

"Full-size candy bars? How many kids are we talking about?" The real estate agent had told him there were almost 150 houses in this subdivision, and assuming the average American family had 2.5 kids, that meant . . . a lot of candy bars. Carli must be joking.

"Plan on around two hundred."

"Two hundred? Two hundred kids are going to ring my frickin' doorbell? That's insane. We had, like, fifty kids in my old neighborhood."

His head hurt already. Maybe he'd just leave his house dark and go to a bar that evening.

Carli smiled at him brightly as if to counterbalance his lousy attitude. "What can I say? It's a very fertile neighborhood. You'll score some points with the parents if you also have wine coolers or beers on hand, too. For the ones walking around with the trick-or-treaters. It's not mandatory, of course, but always appreciated."

"Now I know you're joking."

"I'm totally not joking, but listen, it occurs to me that I have a ton of decorations and I was planning to weed through them this weekend and probably get rid of a bunch of stuff. If you want, you can have whatever I'm done with. I'll trade you for it. If you'll help me hang my big spider on the front of my house, I'll give you some decorations."

He wanted to say no. He didn't want to be coerced into decorating his house, and he didn't want to waste the time, either. But Carli was standing there with a big, silly smile on her face, all but daring him to say yes. And God damn it, that woman was getting under his skin.

"Oh, come on, Ben," she teased. "Don't be a hallo-*weenie*." Then she burst out laughing at her own inane joke, and he knew right then that he'd give in. She was very convincing, and there was something irresistible about the way she looked in her tattered jeans and an oversize sweater, her hair fluttering from the gentle wind. She was the walking embodiment of the girl next door. And she laughed a lot, which was nice to hear, even when it was at his expense.

"You're not amusing," he said, his tone purposefully dry. He pointed to the dog, who was gazing around, droll as an old monk. "Look," Ben said, pointing at him, "even your dog thinks you're not funny."

❦

"You think I'm hilarious, don't you, Gus," Carli said later that night as her now eighty-pound dog snuggled up against her. She never should've let him start sleeping in the bed. When he'd only been forty, and then fifty, and then sixty pounds, it had been bad enough, but now he took up one entire side of her king-size bed. He should be done growing, at least, and it was nice to have him there to guard her. Especially on a night like tonight, when she was home alone and the wind was blowing, making howling sounds as it curved around the eaves. It was comforting to have another warm, lovable creature in the house. And in the event that anyone ever tried to break in—which was about a 0.000001 percent chance, given the neighborhood she lived in—Gus would certainly deter any criminal. He'd probably want to lick them to death, but no robber would wait around to find out if a dog this big was friendly before hightailing it the hell out of there.

Gus pressed a little closer, doing his very best impression of a lapdog as Carli adjusted the pillows behind her head. It was nearly eleven and she had to work in the morning, but for some reason she was feeling antsy and restless. And it wasn't because her room wasn't relaxing now. The walls were now that nice pale pink, and her fluffy new comforter was on the bed, along with her fresh and floral sheets. All remnants of Steve were gone. She'd even splurged on a new mattress, because it just seemed like the right thing to do, and Renee had painted and antiqued her dark cherry dresser, giving it a shabby-chic vibe that Carli loved. Pictures of her and the kids were in new, shiny silver frames. Everything in the room now was about her and her kids and their new life. It still wasn't perfect, but it was hers.

She reached over and turned off her lamp just as a car pulled into the driveway next door. From habit, Carli peeked outside to see what Ben was up to. She watched from the darkness of her room as he got out and then walked around to the other side. He opened the passenger door, and a strange, hollow feeling filled Carli's stomach as she watched a woman get out and lean against him. Well, not so much lean against him as fall against him. She was either a little drunk or very familiar with him and his body. Or both. He caught her arm, and Carli could hear the faint sounds of feminine laughter.

It would seem Ben Chase was entertaining a lady friend. And that was certainly his business and none of hers, so the faint heaviness filling her limbs made no sense. He was her neighbor, not her boyfriend. Good Lord, they were just barely friends. Sure, they'd had a handful of conversations over the past few weeks about the bittersweet burden of raising kids and a few generalized, global exchanges about the horrors of divorce, but mostly they'd talked about inconsequential things and helped each other with paint choices and furniture moving. It was all just neighbor stuff. She couldn't even say they'd flirted with each other, although there had been a moment here or there when she'd caught an appreciative glint in his eye. Or so she'd thought. Maybe not, though.

She tried to shake off whatever emotion was weighing her down. Because it was actually good that Ben had a woman in his life. Good for him. She continued watching out the window as the woman stumbled on the front step and Ben looped an arm around her waist, helping her to the door. They disappeared inside, and a moment later, the kitchen lights went on, and Carli realized it was time to stop spying on her neighbor and his date.

Yep. Good for Ben.

Chapter 19

"Do I really have to be here, Mom? I could be studying right now."

Mia was no fan of sports. Or crowds. Or school spirit. So sitting in the Glenville High School gymnasium at a volleyball game was akin to cruel and inhumane treatment as far as she was concerned. Every time the announcer announced or the buzzer buzzed, she'd jump like someone had poked her with a cattle prod.

"Yes, you have to be here. It's your sister's very first game, and she deserves our support." Even if the team was terrible. Maybe that was all the more reason to cheer her on, although Carli didn't particularly want to be there, either. She was still getting used to being back at work full-time, and the early-morning schedule was harsh. The gym was hot and had that uniquely icky gymnasium smell of funky shoes and stinky boys and concession-stand popcorn. The bleachers were hard, and Carli's back was already stiff after just fifteen minutes of sitting there. At least it wasn't crowded. Girls' volleyball didn't bring in much of a crowd. In fact, it was pretty much just parents of the players, a few dedicated grandparents, and a smattering of sullen siblings who'd been dragged here against their will like Mia.

"Do you want something to eat?" Carli said. "You could go get a pretzel or something." The only thing worse than bored Mia was hungry, bored Mia.

"Um . . . there's Dad," Mia said in response, and Carli's stiff back was suddenly the least of her problems.

"Oh, that was nice of him to come," Carli said, in much the same way one might say it was nice of the coroner to come examine the dead body. "I'm sure Tess will be glad to see him."

Her eyes scanned the entrance, and she caught sight of Steve quickly as he came in through the double doors. She lifted her hand to give him a wave, but her arm stopped midway and then dropped to her side.

That fucker had brought a date.

He'd brought a date to Tess's very first volleyball game.

Steve spotted them and smiled broadly, almost jovially, because why wouldn't he? He gave a quick wave and then that hand moved to the small of the woman's back as he guided her up the steps of the bleachers. So . . . this was how he was going to do it? Introduce his ex-wife to the new woman in his life at a school event? He couldn't have mentioned something about her during their *fourteen-hour* car ride when they'd visited Fairfield College? Or maybe shot Carli a text before the game to say, "Oh, by the way . . ." Nope, instead he was going to do it this way. In front of all these people.

Okay, so technically there weren't that many people because . . . *girls' volleyball*, but the people sitting on the bleachers *knew* them. They knew Steve and Carli were divorced. And they'd certainly be eyeing them all to see how this situation went down. Her heart sped up, and she wished she'd worn something nicer than a Glenville Raiders sweatshirt. Honestly, what was he thinking? He should've warned her. Then again, anticipating or caring about how his actions might impact other people wasn't really his style. And even if he had suspected this might be a bit uncomfortable for Carli, he knew she wouldn't cause a scene. Carli never caused a scene. It was both a blessing and a curse. She was able to keep her calm under almost any circumstances, and yet, maybe if she had caused a scene once in a while, Steve would've been more motivated to be a better husband. Probably not, but maybe.

As they approached, Carli took a breath, and Mia reached over and squeezed her hand.

"Hi, Dad," Mia said, remaining seated and causing Steve to lean in for a clumsy hug.

"Hey, peanut. I didn't expect to see you here. I figured you'd be studying."

"Well, it's Tess's first volleyball game, so I thought it was important to come and support her," Mia answered, mimicking Carli's earlier words.

Carli squeezed her hand back, a silent promise to keep that little lie between them as if Mia hadn't just been bitching about having to be here.

"Right. Of course. Well, that's why we're here. To support our girl."

Carli could feel the eyes on them and hear the slight murmurs. Steve's voice was loud and always traveled. Another of the many things she did not miss about him on a long and substantial list. "This is Jade, by the way," he said. "Jade, this is my oldest daughter, Mia."

Jade? Really?

Jade was tall, with reddish-brown hair that turned to nearly blonde at the tips. Some might call that style ombré, but Carli just called it a bad dye job. She was reed thin (*aren't they always?*) and had a hawkish nose accentuated by a pair of thick-framed, ultra-hipster glasses. Wide-legged jeans over chunky ankle boots, and a scarf so long it circled her throat and still hung down past her waist on either side. She was maybe thirty. If there'd been ten women in a lineup, this one would've been the last one Carli would've thought Steve might choose. She was not remotely his type, and Carli knew his type. She'd been married to the man for almost twenty years. He liked curvy blondes with big breasts. Basically, the opposite of Carli, and yet also the opposite of this myopic stick figure, too.

"Hi," Mia said to the woman. "Can you guys scooch a little? I can't see the game."

"Sure," Steve answered while glancing at Carli. She eyed him back, offering a slow, bland blink, as if daring him to introduce her, but there was really no avoiding it.

"Jade, this is Carli."

"Hi," the woman said, looking neither friendly nor threatened nor in any way interested in adding to her greeting. Good call.

"Hi," Carli said in return. It was on the tip of her tongue to say, "Nice to meet you," because that's what you always said when meeting someone new, except it wasn't nice to meet her. And yet Carli really had to tamp down the urge to say it anyway. Just to be polite. She didn't smile, either. She was a rock.

Steve and his date sat down two rows in front of them, and the woman, *Jade*, promptly pulled a phone from her beaded fabric purse and started texting someone. Mia stole a glance Carli's way. She just shrugged and shook her head, but on the inside all her organs were turning to lava. Not because she was jealous—not really—but because it was so very disrespectful to just show up with some woman that neither she nor her kids knew anything about. How was Tess supposed to feel? How was Mia supposed to feel? She breathed in through her nose, deep and slow, and kept her eyes straight ahead, because certainly there were other eyes trained on her.

She thought about texting him a barrage of nasty messages, but to what end? She didn't want him to know she was seething inside. She wouldn't give him the satisfaction of knowing she was upset. Because he'd just call her hysterical and irrational and say something patently stupid, like, "We're divorced. This is none of your business."

And maybe it wasn't. They were divorced. And it wasn't her business whom he spent his time with. But there was still a matter of being respectful, and of being sensitive to how the kids might feel about him having a new woman in his life. A woman significant enough to bring to a school function.

"Why? Why would he do that?" she said to Erin and DeeDee later that evening. She'd called a Wine Emergency, and they'd met over at DeeDee's house. "And why am I crying? I don't want to waste tears on him."

In the months after Steve had left, she'd cried buckets. Not because she'd lost something wonderful but because the end of a marriage was *sad*. Even the end of a crappy one. She'd felt overwhelmed and scared and isolated and unlovable. She'd felt angry and wounded and helpless and doomed. Those days when the kids were gone and she'd hidden under her covers, she'd wondered if she'd ever, ever feel better. But slowly, so slowly, she'd emerged from the fog. She took showers and made lunches for the kids and got her nails done and watched funny movies. She drank wine with her girlfriends, analyzing every aspect of the marriage and its subsequent failure, until all the details had been hashed and rehashed and there was simply nothing more to say. After months of looking back and wondering *what if this* or *what if that*, she'd finally said goodbye to the past and vowed to face the future. She didn't care that he'd found someone else, so why did it feel as if she did?

DeeDee patted her arm. "If it makes you feel any better, honey, my ex-husband brought a date to my father's funeral, but you go ahead and cry if you want to. You've earned it. The first of the new girlfriends is always the hardest to take. It's a shock to the system, but eventually you'll realize those women are just like cold sores, popping up at the most inconvenient times. And making you feel kind of ugly."

Carli snuffled into a fresh tissue. "She's not even his type. She's not pretty or glamorous, and the whole time we were at the game, she was texting someone on her phone. She never even acknowledged Tess, and they left before it was over." She took a gulp of wine and plucked another tissue from the now nearly empty box that DeeDee had provided.

"What did the kids say when you got home?" Erin asked.

"Not much. They didn't seem to want to talk about it, but I think they were more worried about me than themselves."

"This is uncharted territory for everyone," Erin said. "But you'll all get through it. You know that him dating was inevitable, because they all seem to do it. Men can't stand the idea of being alone."

Carli thought about Ben and his date the other night but knew if she mentioned it right now, Erin and DeeDee would get the wrong impression.

"Mom!" a gruff voice called from upstairs. It was DeeDee's oldest son. "Where's my football uniform? We have team photos tomorrow."

"Did you put it in the hamper or is it wadded up on the floor of your room?" she shouted back. "'Cause if you don't put it in the hamper, Momma ain't puttin' it in the washer."

There was a pause and the sounds of shuffling and doors creaking and hampers thumping before he called back down. "It's in the hamper now. Will you come wash it so I can have it tomorrow?" Another pause. "Please?"

DeeDee looked at Carli and Erin. "See? It's this. This is why men can't be alone. It's because mommas like me do laundry at their beck and call. And we feed them, and we buy them socks and underwear. Am I officially part of the problem if I go wash his football uniform right now?"

"Probably," Erin said. "But I absolve you, because if you don't wash it, then he'll just wear it anyway and he'll stink to high heaven."

"I should head home anyway," Carli said. "I have to work in the morning, and this 7:00 a.m. start time is a bitch."

"That's the price of celebrity, I guess," DeeDee said, standing up from her chair. "But you've been amazing in the show, and I'm still all a-tingle that you're actually on TV. Hey, speaking of tingles, is Troy Buckman single right now? I would totally tap that."

Carli smiled for the first time all evening. "You do not want any piece of Troy Buckman. I promise. But I'll give him your number, just in case."

"Would you? Tell him I could rock his world," DeeDee answered.

"I will definitely include that in the message," Carli said, walking to the front door with Erin right behind her.

"I'm sorry about Steve," Erin said as they left DeeDee's driveway and started walking down the street toward their own houses.

"I know. It just hurts so much more than I thought it would, you know? This process is not at all linear. I'll have days and weeks where everything is great and I feel fine, but then some dumb thing will set me off and it's back to square one. I was at the mall the other day and I saw a shirt that Steve would've really liked, and I was thinking, *Oh, I should buy that for him for Christmas*. But then I realized I won't be getting him gifts anymore. It's just . . . weird."

"I get it. You have all those habits that married people have, and it's hard to recalibrate."

"Right? And it's not that I want him back. God, I so do not want him back. It's just . . . I don't know. They were so comfortable with each other, and he made it seem like him being there with her was easy and normal and no big deal. Like he had all the parts of his new life all lined up, and any of the stuff we'd shared between us was just . . . dust. And since he's dating and I'm not, it makes it look like he's totally capable of relationships, which means *I'm* the reason our marriage failed."

Erin rubbed her back for the briefest moment as they walked. "I get that it feels that way, Carli, but it's simply not true. I know how hard you worked to keep that marriage going. I watched what you put up with, and as much as divorce sucks, I believe you are better off without him."

Carli shuffled her feet along the road like a kid. "I know. I guess I'm just a little humiliated. I thought he'd miss me longer than that."

"Oh, don't kid yourself. He does miss you. That's why he had to go find another warm body to make himself feel better. What's that saying? Women grieve and men replace? And just because he's got some woman, don't assume this is some fairy-tale romance he's got brewing. Steve is the same guy he's always been. He's found somebody willing to put up with his fragile ego for a little while, but it won't last. He'll jump from one superficial relationship to the next because they're nonthreatening, and since he has no capacity to grow emotionally, he'll never make a deeper connection with someone. He's just not wired that way. You are, and you deserve a man who can meet you at your level."

"Oh yeah. And those guys are all over the place."

Erin nodded slowly as they reached the end of Carli's driveway. "They are unicorns. I got very lucky when I found Rick, but we still have to work on stuff. We put up with each other's crap, but at the end of the day, he's always got my back and I trust him."

Carli let out a great big sigh. "Someday maybe I'll find a Rick, but honestly, if one showed up right now, I wouldn't be ready. The idea of dating makes me woozy. I can't imagine going through all that work of getting to know someone new. And even if I did go on a date, what would they expect? Because I'm not the kind to jump right into bed, not to mention the fact that no one except Steve has seen me naked since I was in college. Nothing on me is where it used to be."

Erin chuckled. "I'm sure the important stuff is still pretty close to where it's supposed to be, and I've told you a million times that you look fabulous. We've all shifted by this age, but you're still a catch. Any guy would be lucky to have you. Maybe you ought to take that new neighbor of yours out for a test drive." Erin tilted her chin toward Ben's house.

His kitchen lights were on, and Carli could see the silhouette of him sitting at his kitchen table. She laughed in between her leftover sniffles.

"Oh sure. That would be a great idea. Test-drive some guy who's in the throes of his own shitstorm of a divorce. And then have to live next to him for goodness knows how long. What could possibly go wrong?"

"Maybe it would go just right."

Carli shook her head. "It's too complicated. He's too close. I mean, physically close. It's not like we can have some fling and then just go back to saying hello to each other at the mailbox. That would be way too awkward for me. Besides, I'm pretty sure he had a date the other night."

"He did?"

"I think so. She seemed kind of drunk when they got back here."

"Maybe it was his sister."

"I hope not, given the way she was groping him."

"Hm," Erin said. "Well, I wouldn't write him off entirely. Rick talked to him for a while at the barbecue and seems to think he's a pretty okay guy."

"Duly noted, but I'm still not ready to start dating, and even if I was, I think he's a little too close for comfort."

Erin shrugged. "Okay, if you say so. But keep in mind, if you don't go after him, DeeDee might get there first."

Chapter 20

"Katrina Hogan is our digital content producer," Marlow told Carli as they waited in the Channel 7 conference room. "She's the one who handles all the station's social media stuff and is responsible for keeping the rest of us up-to-date on the latest trends. She's only twenty-six, so half the stuff she says makes no sense to me, and she finds most of us woefully out of touch. It's a bit insulting, but I guess that's why we need her. She can be a little snarky and pretentious. You remember being in your twenties, right? Back when we knew everything about everything and thought no one over forty could be trusted?"

Carli nodded.

"Okay, well, that's Katrina. She's kind of obnoxious, but she knows her stuff, and Jessica trusts her."

"Got it," Carli said. "So what do they want to talk to me about?"

Marlow shrugged. "Not sure, but here they come, so we're about to find out."

Jessica came into the room holding a laptop computer under her arm and a thermal coffee mug in her hand that said Boss Lady, followed by a petite young woman with perfectly straight auburn hair wearing a high-waisted black pencil skirt and a sheer black silk blouse with a camisole underneath. Her makeup was bold but flattering. She also had a laptop and a coffee mug. Hers said Bitch, please. Her smile was tight, and Carli got the sense this meeting wouldn't be that fun. Jessica made the introductions, and Katrina got right to the point.

"So, yeeeeaaaah, we need to talk about your social media presence, for starters," Katrina said without preamble.

"What about my social media presence?" Carli asked.

"You don't have any," Katrina replied. "Recipes and quips about funny things your kids say is not a platform. It's not even a Christmas letter. You need a brand. We're hoping to set you up as a kind of influencer for the over-forty set, even aside from what you do on the show. It's actually a good thing, so don't feel bad."

She hadn't felt bad . . . until Katrina said that. Because it felt very much as if Katrina thought she actually should *feel bad* about something.

"I mean, this whole meeting is actually a compliment, because early data shows you score high in likability and trustworthiness, so Jessica and I were thinking we really need to amp up your online presence. You know, Facebook, Snapchat, Instagram, Twitter."

Carli wasn't thrilled to hear that. She had no aptitude for that stuff. Instagram was a complete mystery, and Twitter was like walking into a party where everyone was talking at once about topics she wasn't familiar with. And Snapchat, with all those damn filters? She'd once accidentally sent a photo of herself looking like a caveman to Steve, and she had yet to live that down. He'd had the image put on her birthday cake that year. But hey, at least he'd remembered to get her a cake.

"We can help you with all that if you don't know how to utilize the apps," Katrina said. "I know they don't make sense if you didn't grow up with them like I did. But hey, I just found out what a rotary phone was, so it all balances out, right?" She laughed, but Carli just nodded.

"We were also thinking"—she said each word slowly as if to build the suspense—"we would have you try some of the things we feature on the show, like some of the cutting-edge beauty treatments, because if viewers see you trying it, they'll be less intimidated. Plus, it'll be fun to watch."

"Beauty treatments?"

"Yeah, you know. Like CoolSculpting, vampire facials, vaginal rejuvenation."

"Vaginal . . . Excuse me?" Carli's voice crackled with disbelief. They wanted her to try what now?

Katrina rolled her eyes and tossed her thick auburn hair over her shoulder. "It's a thing. You know, for when you've had your kids and you've gotten older and, I don't know, I guess your va-jay can age just like the rest of your skin, so this treatment tightens it back up. Or something. I don't have that issue, so I haven't really done the research, but I do know that we've got the owners of Divine Goddess Day Spa coming on the show next month, and I think it would be an awesome segment if you got some of the treatments done. Then you can be the before and after client."

"You want pictures . . . of my vagina?"

Katrina's eyes went wide before she burst out laughing. "Oh my God, no. That would be so gross! Not to mention that we'd never get it on the air. No, we'd film you getting stuff done to your face and maybe your stomach ahead of time, and *then* show your before and after photos on the show." Katrina's head wobbling and snickering continued as she muttered under her breath, "Seriously? Your vagina on TV."

Carli looked over at Jessica to see what her take was on this. She must be in her mid- to late forties, if not even a little bit older. Her skin was still flawlessly youthful, but she had to be at least as old as Carli. As usual, the news director's face was impassive and impossible to read, but she did place a hand on Katrina's wrist.

"Kat, this meeting is supposed to be about broad strokes, not the finer details. Let's just give Carli more of a general idea of what we have in mind."

If any part of what they had in mind included her vagina, Carli was going to have to take a hard pass, but Katrina nodded, her fingers flying over the keyboard of the laptop in front of her, and seconds later an image popped up on the presentation screen against the wall of the conference room. It was a Facebook page with one of Carli's promotional photos as the profile picture and underneath it had her full legal name—Carlisle Holmes Lancaster.

"So, yeah, back to your social media platform. We think you should drop your last name. Lancaster is your married name, right? That's easy to undo, and *Carlisle Holmes* has a nice ring to it. I already talked to the marketing department, and they think they can make the switch without too much trouble. The show has only been on for a couple of weeks, and no one really knows your name yet. The public will understand."

"You want me to change my name?" That was only slightly less intrusive than asking her to polish up her vagina.

Katrina gave a minimal shake of her head. "Not change it. Just tweak it. We could make a story of that, too. Showing how women of gray divorce are reclaiming their identities."

"Gray . . . gray divorce?"

"Yeah, you're part of the latest trend. People in their fifties getting divorced and starting their third act, so to speak. It's the retired empty nesters who still have maybe twenty years to go before they're too old to have any fun. They want to go out and enjoy the time they have left instead of spending it in a stale marriage. Like what you did. Another trend is older people moving in with friends rather than going to live in retirement communities. You're not thinking about that yet, are you?"

"Jesus, Katrina. I'm forty-two. Not seventy-two." Carli was starting to sweat, but heaven knew if she fanned herself, Katrina would want to pitch it as a segment about hot flashes. She wasn't having a hot flash. She wasn't in menopause or even perimenopause, and she wasn't ready to retire or move into an old folks' home, either. And she didn't want to change her name! She'd been Carli Lancaster for almost as long as she'd been Carli Holmes, and her married name was the one she shared with her kids.

"Jessica, where do you stand on all this?" Carli asked, her tone all but demanding. Every muscle in her body was tense. "And are you guys asking Troy to do this kind of stuff, too? Are we filming him getting a prostate exam or trying out a sample of Viagra?"

"Katrina, can you give us a minute, please?" Jessica said in her typical unflappable way.

"But I have a bunch of slides to show you. Some potential Instagram photos and some fun Snapchat ideas," Katrina said.

"Give us a minute," Jessica replied, calmly but firmly, and once again at an office meeting, Carli felt the urge to cry. No, not cry. Yell. Yelling would be infinitely more satisfying. Her frustration was about to bubble over. She was not some guinea pig for them to experiment with. She was not going to show off her belly or point out her crow's-feet on television. She gripped the arms of the chair, preparing for battle. So what if Jessica still intimidated the hell out of her? She wasn't going to let them humiliate her for the sake of ratings.

After Katrina left the conference room, Jessica sighed and gave Carli the first genuine smile she'd ever seen from the news director. "Oh my goodness, that girl is rough around the edges, isn't she? I'll talk to her about that later, but first I wanted to explain to you what our goals are."

"Do they have anything to do with my vagina?" she shot back.

Jessica actually laughed out loud, and Carli felt a seismic shift in the universe at the sound.

"No, they do not. What Katrina was trying so inexpertly to say is that our viewers *like* you, and we want to capitalize on that. Not by making you do anything you don't want to do, but by building up a fan base of loyal followers who relate to you and who trust your word who might be influenced to buy products or visit businesses simply because you've recommended them. It's our way of increasing advertising revenue. That's really what all this is about."

"That's not what that sounded like. It sounds like you want me to be a science experiment for the sake of ratings." She wasn't opposed to some of the stuff—the facials and such—but she wasn't interested in having needles poked into her face or ending up looking like a human Barbie doll.

"No, that's not what we want at all, and I will very much have a conversation with Katrina about her presentation skills. Sometimes her enthusiasm blinds her judgment, and she's definitely better online than she is in person. Anyway, we plan to build up the social media presence of all the Channel 7 on-air talent, but we're finding that your demographic tends to be the ones who follow the most closely. Troy and Allie already have a following, but since you're new, now is the time to start developing that. How does that sound?"

"It sounds a hell of a lot better than a vampire facial."

Chapter 21

"Are you sure you don't mind if I use some of this stuff?" Ben asked as Carli brought out yet another plastic bin full of Halloween decorations. The pile of bright orange storage tubs in her front yard was embarrassingly large, but now that they were all out of her garage, she was determined to unload it all and only put back the stuff she actually liked. As in most things, she and Steve had very different tastes when it came to holiday decorations. She liked themes, while he was more about volume.

"Not at all," Carli answered. "You'd be doing me a favor by taking some. As you can see, I've got way more than I need. My kids are supposed to be out here to help us. I'll have them take a look and tell me if there's anything they're particularly attached to, but my guess is that they won't care much about any of it."

Carli pulled her phone from her pocket to text them, even though they were right inside the house. It was the most efficient means of communication and typically resulted in less sassy backtalk, because they were too lazy to text their snarky responses.

You're supposed to be outside helping me put up the Halloween decorations.

Three dots instantly appeared, and then Mia's response filled her screen.

Are we seriously putting up decorations? You know we're in high school, right?

Carli responded.

I'm not doing it for you, darling daughter. I'm doing it for the little kids in the neighborhood. Butts outside. Now.

And then she couldn't resist adding,

Once we're done, I will take you out for sushi.

It was cool outside, with the October sun playing hide-and-seek with the clouds. A perfect autumn day. Carli was wearing a Glenville High School sweatshirt that she'd swiped from Mia, while Ben seemed to be fine in just a long-sleeved T-shirt. She was glad he wasn't wearing a jacket, because it gave her the chance to appreciate his shoulders. Just because he'd gone on a date recently didn't mean she had to stop ogling him. Not as long as she was discreet about it.

"I should get my kids out here helping, too," Ben said as he pulled out his own phone and tapped against the screen. Addie appeared almost immediately, while a few minutes later, an unenthusiastic Ethan appeared in plaid flannel pajama bottoms and an oversize MSU hoodie. With the hood up, and his hair sticking out around the edges, he looked like a raggedy lion, and when an enormous yawn nearly split his face, Carli couldn't hold back a chuckle at his silent roar. They put him to work dumping out all the bins so she could start sorting the piles into similar items.

"Why do we have so much stuff?" Mia grumbled as she made her appearance shortly after Ethan. They nodded at each other and mumbled some indifferent grumpy-teen greetings. Tess arrived a full ten minutes after that, her mascara and lip gloss confirming to Carli that her daughter had spotted Ethan before heading outside. The two of them had spoken only a handful of times, mostly just saying hi from their respective driveways, but Tess hadn't given up hope that one of these days, Ethan would *really* notice her.

"Oh hey, Ethan," she said in that *Oh, do you live right next door to me? I had no idea* voice that was only clever enough to fool him, but no one else. Ben cast a glance at Carli, and she smiled back.

With six of them working, the decorations were quickly sorted into categories of keep, toss, and donate, and Ben got to choose his stuff from the latter two piles.

"Are we actually putting this stuff up, like, outside our house? Where people can see it?" Ethan said and then yawned again.

"That's exactly what I said," Mia added, looking pointedly at Carli.

"Yep, that's the idea," Ben answered Ethan with a shrug. "Honestly, I don't really get it, either, but it's pretty much mandated by the neighborhood association, so suck it up, buttercup."

"I like it," Addie said. "I think it's fun."

"That's because you're fourteen," Ethan chided, causing her to blush.

"When you take the hayride around the neighborhood and see everybody else's decorations, you'll realize that all the cool houses have them," Carli said, although these teens did not seem convinced. She had no street cred with them, if that was even a thing anymore.

"What hayride is that?" Ethan asked.

"The Saturday afternoon before Halloween," Ben answered.

"That's my birthday," Ethan said. "I'm turning eighteen." His chest puffed up, as the comment was clearly meant to impress.

"I can't wait to turn eighteen," Tess responded, smiling at him. All day she'd tried to be closest to him, and although he'd been nice enough, he wasn't quite *noticing* her, and that gave Carli a little ache.

"Turning eighteen is a little anticlimactic, to be honest," Mia said. "Although now I can go get a tattoo without asking."

"Um, no, you can't," Carli said.

"Well, I won't, but I could. Legally, anyway."

"Maybe I should get a tattoo," Ethan said, smiling at Ben. "What do you think, Dad? Maybe a nice sleeve that covers my whole arm? Something with lots of skulls?"

"Not a chance."

"Okay, how about a party, then? I was thinking maybe I could have a bonfire in the backyard. Just have a few friends over to chill and whatever?"

Ben paused for a moment, a black plastic raven in his hands. "Sure, I guess that would be okay. The firepit is all set up, so you can use that. But I'll be here all night making sure you don't have too much or the wrong kind of fun." Ben pointed at his own eyes, and then at Ethan's in an *I'll be watching you* fashion.

Ethan nodded, the picture of chill. "Awesome. Thanks, Dad. I'll keep it small. Just like a couple hundred kids or so."

"Or maybe like twenty?" Ben said.

Ethan smiled. "Okay, thirty. Thirty should be good."

Carli stole a glance at Tess, who was all but crackling with eagerness to be invited. But Ethan was a boy and not the type to notice something like that, either. It was two hours later, after all the decorations were hung, propped, wired, or otherwise displayed in either Carli's yard or Ben's that Ethan finally thought to mention it to her daughters.

"So I don't know exactly what that hayride thing is, but if you guys want to come over here afterward for my party, that would be cool," he said, and Carli wondered if maybe he'd just been too shy to ask them earlier. This Ethan didn't seem to be nearly the player that her girls had painted him to be. And other than that one comment about Addie being *just fourteen*, he was pretty nice to his little sister. Of course, nice, friendly, polite-to-the-neighbor-mom boys could get a girl into every bit as much trouble as the wild ones could. Maybe even more.

As Ethan posed the invitation, Mia stared at him as if he were a perplexing and unsolvable math problem, but Tess was smooth under the pressure.

"That could be cool," she said, twisting a strand of her hair. "I might be hanging out with some friends that night, but we don't have anything solid planned yet."

"Are they cool friends?" he asked.

"Pretty cool." She nodded.

"You could bring them, I guess. Hey, aren't you friends with Becca Sturgis? She can come if she wants to."

And just like that, Carli saw the bubble of hope bursting all around Tess and knew her daughter's heart was doing the same. It was never a good sign when the boy you were crushing on asked you to bring another girl to his party. Kind of like how Carli felt when realizing that the attractive man from next door had entertained a sleepover date.

∽

"All right. I hate to admit this, but the decorations are kind of . . . entertaining," Ben said reluctantly after they'd packed up what was left of Carli's monstrous pile of stuff to donate to charity. They'd loaded the boxes of leftovers into the back of her SUV, and now the two of them were standing in the road staring back at their respective houses. Addie had left for a sleepover at a friend's house, Ethan was off playing basketball with a kid who lived down the street, and Carli's kids had passed on her offer of sushi to go to the movies with friends instead.

"We'll make a Monroe Circle–ite out of you yet," Carli answered. "I agree it's all a little much, but honestly, when my kids were little, this stuff was the best. So many great memories. That's probably why I wanted to keep this house instead of selling it, although the repair bills are killing me."

"Are you hungry?" he asked, suddenly feeling his stomach rumble and realizing it was dinnertime. And who was he kidding? He didn't want to eat alone again, and Carli was excellent company. It had nothing to do with how enticing she managed to make that sweatshirt and jeans look.

Her face flushed. "I've got plenty of money for food. I didn't mean that."

It took him a second to understand, then he burst out laughing at her response. "Oh my gosh, that's not why I asked if you were hungry. I asked because I'm starving. Do you want to go grab something to eat?"

Her cheeks went a shade darker, and she brushed away a strand of dark hair that the wind kept blowing around her head. "Um, sure. Where are you thinking?"

"I don't care. Is that Woodfire Grill any good? I keep driving past it and it always looks busy, so I'm guessing it has decent food."

"It does. We can go there if you want to."

"Okay, unless you had other plans. I don't want to keep you." He did want to keep her, actually. The more he thought about dinner with her, the more the idea appealed to him, and it wasn't just because he was hungry.

"Sadly, putting up Halloween decorations for the enjoyment of other people's kids was the only thing on my schedule today, so dinner sounds good. Let me run inside and change. Meet you out front in fifteen minutes?"

"Sounds good."

Apparently, Carli could do a lot with fifteen minutes, and when she emerged from her house, Ben's breath caught in his throat. She'd changed into tight jeans and those short little boots that women seemed to be wearing these days. The kind with tall, pencil-thin heels. Her sweater was black, and she wore a brightly patterned scarf around her neck. She'd even put on a bit of makeup, although not nearly as much as she wore on the days that he saw her after work. She had the whole cute-but-sexy thing going, and he realized that the twist in his gut he got every time he saw her was becoming a constant companion.

Today had been fun, not because he cared about Halloween decorations, but because hanging out with her made him laugh. It made him forget about all the crap going on in other areas of his life. It made him forget about Sophia. *Carli* made him forget about Sophia. A fact that he was determined not to overanalyze.

The restaurant was crowded, so they ordered a drink at the bar. Carli sat on a stool, and Ben stood next to her. Probably closer than he needed to. It was easy to press close and blame it on the crowd, and it gave him a chance to breathe in her perfume, a subtle but appealing scent of flowers and spice.

"Did you know you have a branch nearly touching you?" he found himself asking, which was not at all what he wanted to talk about, but her thigh had just accidentally brushed against his and the jolt went straight to his groin. Served him right for standing so close. "I mean, a branch nearly touching your roof."

Carli nodded and took a sip of her lemon drop martini. "Yes, that stupid branch has been like that for a while now. Every single time the wind blows, I'm convinced it's going to crash through my ceiling and pin me to the bed." She blushed immediately at her awkward word choice, prompting Ben to have a vision of himself doing just that—pinning her to the bed. He lost himself for a second, then cleared his throat.

"I've got an arborist coming to look at a couple of my trees. I can have them take a look at that one if you'd like." *Jesus, Ben. Way to smooth talk a lady.* A lady who'd just mentioned being pinned to the bed! What a lost opportunity. If not for her crimson cheeks, he might have thought she was flirting. Was she flirting? Damn it, he'd been married for too frickin' long. He had zero game. Not that he needed game with Carli. They were just neighbors having a neighborly dinner at the local neighborhood watering hole, but that didn't mean they couldn't engage in a little harmless flirting. If he could just remember how.

"I should probably do something about that," she said, obviously referring to the branch. "So, yeah, if you don't mind asking your tree guys to check out my trees, too, that would be great."

He nodded, allowing a moment of awkwardness to pass before adding, "Um, how about some details on this hayride thing?"

They moved from the bar to their table when the hostess said it was ready and continued chatting—about house painters, and landscapers, and their kids and school. She told him about her new job and how the dog training was progressing. He talked about his family and the stuff he was doing to his house. All topics mundane enough to distract him from noticing the rich color of her eyes, the lush fullness of her lips, or the way a tendril of her hair kept brushing against her cheek. Except that those topics didn't distract him. The only thing distracting him tonight was her.

And that was super inconvenient.

They ordered another drink as they waited for their meals to arrive, and Carli had only taken a few sips before saying, "Okay, so, I don't want you to think I'm spying on you or anything, but I couldn't help but notice you seemed to have had a date the other night."

Her words and coy delivery caught him off guard, not because she'd offended him, but because he'd so thoroughly and entirely blocked that event from his mind. And for some reason, he didn't want her to think it was a date, exactly. Because while it had started as a date, it most definitely had not ended like one.

"Uh, if you want to call it that."

She shook her head and blushed. "I'm sorry. I guess it's none of my business. We don't have to talk about it if you don't want to."

Ben laughed. "No, it's not that. Not at all. It's just that only in the loosest terms imaginable would I categorize that evening as a date."

She set down her martini glass. "Okay. Now you have me intrigued."

"Veronica DeMarco," he said and took a hearty gulp of his micro-brew, because this story required liquid sustenance. "An old friend of the family who I'd pretty much forgotten about. Our parents had cottages next door to each other on Lake Michigan, and Roni and I used to run around and hunt for frogs and grasshoppers and beach glass together. Then the summer before eighth grade she, um . . . developed, and suddenly I wasn't cool enough for her anymore."

He chuckled at the memory, because if there was anything he did remember about Veronica DeMarco, it was that seeing her in a bikini that June made him realize just how difficult it was to hide a hard-on in a swimsuit. He'd spent almost that entire summer standing in cold, waist-deep lake water while she'd frolicked on the sand.

"She dumped me for Braden Buckley because he was two years older than us. And he had a chest hair."

Carli burst out laughing. "A chest hair? Singular?"

"Yep. Just the one, but it was enough to impress her."

"Naturally," Carli said.

"Anyway, my mother sent her my way recently because Veronica comes from good stock. And of course, by good stock I mean lots of old money and minimal family scandals. But as it turned out, it wasn't so much a date as it was an impromptu intervention. She drank two bottles of merlot and then proceeded to tell me all the reasons why she hated men. It was super entertaining."

"Sounds awesome."

"Right? And then when I suggested that maybe she should eat some of the food we'd ordered and maybe not have another drink, she informed me in no uncertain terms that I was every bit as controlling as her ex-husband. Who is currently on trial for tax fraud."

"So much for minimal family scandals."

"Yeah, not sure how that one got by my mother. Anyway, after that, I'd planned to drive her home, but she said she absolutely had to *tinkle*. She actually used the word *tinkle* and said she couldn't possibly last the whole drive to her place and could we just go to my place. It actually got worse from there."

"Worse?" Carli's big, dark eyes grew bigger still.

"Yep. She passed out on my bathroom floor." He didn't add the part about how her skirt had been pulled up to her waist and her panties were down around her ankles. He kind of wanted to, because he was sure Carli would get a kick out of that. But it just wasn't fair to Veronica. He could joke about someone drinking a bit too much or being generally obnoxious, but that last part was pretty damned humiliating.

"Oh my gosh. So what did you do?"

"Well, I couldn't very well drive her home. For one thing, she was in no condition to be left alone, and for another thing, I had no idea where she lived. I just put her to bed in my guest room and let her sleep it off. Man, was she grumpy the next morning."

He'd actually sat in a chair next to the bed for a while to make sure she didn't puke, less from concern about her and more because he had brand-new carpeting. It was a great night, made even greater by his having to pull her panties up and her skirt down while trying not to look at anything between her waist and her knees. Not only was he a gentleman that way, but he just kept imagining how embarrassed she was going to feel the next morning. Oddly enough, she was less horrified than she probably should've been. Mostly she was pissed that he'd suggested she take an Uber home.

"I'm guessing she had a bit of a headache," Carli said, her tone equal parts amusement and sympathy. "I hate wine hangovers. They're the worst. I'm glad to say I haven't had one in ages." She knocked on the wooden table.

"You are very lucky. I've had several hangovers during the past few months, compliments of my divorce." He raised his glass in a toast. "But here's to not having one tomorrow."

"I'll drink to that."

She clinked the rim of his hearty beer mug with her delicate martini glass and then took a sip, and he tried not to think about her lips pressing against the edge of that glass, or the tiny dimple that appeared near the corner of her mouth when her smile was wide, because these thoughts of his were getting out of hand. What was wrong with him tonight? Why the fixation on her? It's not as if she was the most remarkably gorgeous woman he'd ever met, or the most scintillating conversationalist. She didn't flaunt her sexuality or pretend that he was anything other than a friend. So what was it? He had no interest in Veronica DeMarco or any of the other women who'd contacted him over the past several weeks, but he was going to have to take somebody up on an offer soon, if only to blunt the irrational and inconvenient feelings he had brewing for his next-door neighbor.

"It's not really that surprising," Ben's sister said to him the next day, as she helped him shop for new light fixtures and window treatments. "Carli is sweet and nonthreatening. She's like a touchstone and represents everything you thought you had with Sophia. A wife, a mother, a friend. And to be honest, you guys have kind of been playing house."

"We haven't been playing house," Ben replied, thinking that meant sex. There'd been no sex. Not even a hint of it.

"I mean playing house like helping each other with chores and things. Decorating for Halloween, talking about parenting, playing with her dog. Stuff like that creates intimacy. Maybe not physical intimacy, but certainly emotional intimacy."

"Emotional intimacy sounds very complicated," he said. "I'm not really up for that. I just need some straight-up . . . transactional intimacy."

"Then I'd suggest Tinder," she said dryly, tossing two zigzag-patterned curtain panels into the shopping cart.

"Tinder? Seriously? Is that a therapeutic recommendation?" He took the curtains from the cart and put them back on the shelf. He didn't like the colors.

Kenzie put them back in the cart. "Those panels are for me, and no, it's not my therapeutic recommendation. As a therapist, I'd encourage you to spend some time alone to get comfortable with your own company. Or if you can't handle that, go out with some buddies, get lots of exercise, maybe volunteer at an animal shelter or something, and wait at least a year before getting into a new relationship."

"A year?" That seemed like a long time.

"Yes, that's the clinical recommendation, but in the real world, I realize life gets lonely and that this is a time when you want some . . . fun to distract you. So . . . Tinder. Someone else looking for a casual hookup. Not your next-door neighbor. You are not in a good space for something significant, and she doesn't seem like the transactional-intimacy type. I don't think that would be fair to her, so I suggest you look elsewhere."

Okay. So he'd look elsewhere.

But Tinder? *God.*

Chapter 22

The Tenth Annual Monroe Circle Halloween Hayride was its usual rousing success, and even Ben seemed to enjoy watching cartload after cartload of kids roll by on their way to Renee's house. Gus had participated, wearing a set of moose antlers, which made every kid that rode by wave and laugh. And since the hay wagon was pulled by a tractor instead of horses, the dog retained his privilege of being the biggest animal in the neighborhood.

"See, I told you it would be fun," Carli said to Ben as they walked down the street to the posthayride party. Gus was now safely tucked inside his crate with a chew toy the size of a brontosaurus femur, and she and Ben were going to get their obligatory cider and cinnamon sugar doughnut. Mia and Tess were already there, having been coerced into riding with some of the little kids.

"Hey, you two," Renee called out as Ben and Carli arrived. "If you need a little splash of Captain Morgan in your cider, let me know."

"I definitely need that," Ben said. "Where are the cups?"

"I'll get you some," Carli answered, following Renee into her house. As she'd suspected, Renee pounced the minute they were inside her kitchen.

"Sooo, what's going on with you and the delectable Mr. Chase?" she asked, pulling two red Solo cups from a stack and filling them with ice from the refrigerator. "I know you keep saying there's nothing there, but Lynette said you two are constantly hanging out in your yards and that sometimes you disappear into each other's houses for suspiciously long periods of time. Why do I have to hear this from Lynette? Why haven't you told me yourself?"

Carli laughed as she leaned against the quartz countertop. "First of all, are you really getting your intelligence briefings from Lynette? Shame on you. And second, I haven't told you anything because there's nothing to tell. We're just friends. I should have that printed on a T-shirt." Carli picked up the fifth of spiced rum from the counter and opened it.

"Friends who go out to dinner at the Woodfire Grill? You didn't think anyone would see you there?" Renee set the cups down next to the sink and took the bottle from Carli.

"Totally platonic. We were hungry after putting up the Halloween decorations. And if there was something going on, do you think we'd show up at the Woodfire Grill?"

Renee rolled her eyes. "If things are totally platonic between you two, then you're dumb, because he's a catch."

Carli laughed again and felt her cheeks heating up. "I'm not dumb. I'm the opposite of dumb, in fact. He's a good guy and a good neighbor and a good . . . friend. Listen, I'm not going to pretend that I haven't thought about it because, come on. Who wouldn't? There's even been a moment or two when I thought he might be thinking less than platonic thoughts, but we're in different spots in our lives and neither of us is ready for any kind of . . . romantic entanglement. I'm too busy with my kids and work and the dog, and he's busy with his divorce and his company and all that crap. Trust me. He's a high-risk candidate, and I am a low-risk kind of gal."

Renee crooked a dark brow. "High risk, high reward. Honestly, even if it ended in disaster, what a delicious disaster it could be. You deserve a little fun." Renee poured a generous splash of rum into each cup. "And then you could tell me all the scandalous details and I could live vicariously through you. Rob and I are having a bit of a dry spell, and I need something to spice it up."

"Maybe you need a vaginal rejuvenation. I hear it's all the rage."

Renee's movements paused even as her eyes went wide. "A what now?"

"Oh, just something I learned about at work. From what I've gathered, it's like a facial for your hoo-ha."

Surprise turned to skepticism. "Yeah, I'm not going to do that, but I am willing to hear all about your escapades, especially if you decide to get a little crazy with Mr. Right Next Door." She topped off the cups with apple cider.

"I will be of no help to you there, I'm afraid. You know me and my vanilla sex life. Steve's idea of wild and crazy was to do it in the living room instead of our bedroom."

"Sure, Steve was boring, but I'll bet that sexy neighbor of yours has some tricks up his sleeve. Or down his pants. Whichever."

"Ah, great," said Carli, accepting the cup Renee offered. "Now I'm going to spend the rest of the afternoon thinking about what's in Ben's pants."

"You and me both, honey. You and me both."

They were laughing as they walked out the front door to find Ben standing with a group of husbands, who were also laughing. It was hard to be too serious when surrounded by little kids in Avenger and Frozen costumes. Carli approached the cluster and handed him his drink.

"Renee's a heavy-handed bartender, so consider yourself warned."

Ben took the cup with a smile. "Thanks."

"So that's the second weekend of December," Rob said to the group, continuing on with their conversation.

"What is?" Carli asked.

"This year's Holly Trolley."

The Third Annual Monroe Circle Holly Trolley Pub Crawl was a newer event created by the dads in the neighborhood who felt their needs had been underrepresented by the social committee. This night of revelry included a party bus that took them all around Glenville, stopping at various pubs and microbreweries before ending the evening at an all-night bowling alley. Carli had gone on this a handful of times but never made it past the third or fourth bar before having to call it a night and get the babysitter home. Steve always managed to last until the very end and typically came home with outlandish stories of what went on after she'd left. True stories, but outlandish nonetheless. One year DeeDee's second ex-husband (before he was her ex-husband) had come home wearing a stinky Santa costume that he'd bought right off the back of some equally stinky guy at the bowling alley—a mall Santa who'd just stopped by the alley for a (another?) drink before heading home.

"Holly Trolley, huh?" Ben said. "That sounds pretty fun. Count me in on that one. Even better if I don't have to bring a dish to pass."

∽

"Mom, where's our Ouija board?" Tess shouted from beneath Carli's deck, where Carli was sitting with Ben, Erin, and Erin's husband, Rick. They were surreptitiously monitoring the activities of Ethan's backyard bonfire while giving the illusion of not actually acting as chaperones. At one point, there'd been upward of forty kids, but as the midnight hour approached, most of them had left, and now only a handful of Ethan's closest friends were there, along with Mia, Tess, and three of her girlfriends. Oddly enough, Becca Sturgis was a no-show, and Carli had to wonder if she'd actually gotten the invitation.

Carli stood up and leaned over the railing to see her daughter. "I have no idea where the Ouija board is. Somewhere in the basement, probably. Why?"

"If I find it, can I take it over to Ethan's? A couple of us want to go in the woods behind his house and give it a try."

"That sounds terrifying to me. Ben, are you okay with them doing that?" She looked back over her shoulder at him.

"Where do they want to go?"

"Back behind your house." The wooded area along the rim of their backyards was about fifty yards deep and ended at the property line of a grouchy old neighbor who'd lived there forever. He liked to wander into Carli's yard and complain about people having parties, traffic near his house, moles, rabbits, deer, power lines, water towers, government conspiracy theories—pretty much every word that came out of his mouth was a complaint of some sort.

"I haven't really looked around back there. Is it safe?" Ben asked. "Any quicksand or werewolves or things that go bump in the night?"

"As long as they don't get poison ivy or run into skunks, I guess it's safe," Carli answered. "Except for the part about going into the dark woods to summon spirits and get advice from all sorts of underworld demons."

He shrugged. "Okay, then. Sounds like fun to me."

Carli turned back and called down to Tess. "That's fine, but if you turn in the wrong direction and end up in Mr. VanderBrink's yard, all his floodlights will go on and he'll probably start waving a shotgun at you, so how about if you don't go too far away from Ben's yard. You'll need some light to see anyway, right?"

"Sure, Mom. Thanks." Tess ducked under the deck, and Carli could hear her opening the sliding glass door that led to the basement. She was back out in minutes and ran over to Ben's yard.

"They're totally taking that thing deep into the woods. You know that, right?" Ben said as soon as Tess had left Carli's yard.

Carli nodded. "Probably, but at least I did my part in warning them. And Mia's over there. She's usually the voice of reason, and maybe she'll keep them from wandering too far."

"Well," Rick said, standing up and stretching. "I think that's our cue to leave. You know, before they conjure up something evil? I'd like to get home before the ghosts start appearing."

Erin stood, too. "I think seeing a ghost would be kind of exciting. As long as it was, like, a friendly ghost."

"A friendly ghost?" Ben asked.

"Yeah, you know. Like Casper or the Ghost of Christmas Present, or something like that. None of those scary ones who moan and rattle chains and shit like that." She shuddered. "Damn it, now I'm going to be thinking about scary ghosts, and we have to walk all the way down the street past everyone's Halloween decorations."

"I'll protect you, honey," Rick said, wrapping an arm around her shoulders.

She kissed his cheek. "I know you think that, but if you saw an actual ghost, you would run so stinking fast, you'd be nothing but a blur as you left me in your dust."

"Well, that may be true, but let's hope we never find out."

Rick and Erin were what Tess would call *relationship goals*, and they were the one couple who gave Carli the slightest hope that one day she might, maybe, possibly, perhaps find a man to share the rest of her life with. Not now, of course. But later. Sometime much later. When she was ready.

She hugged her friends as they said their goodbyes and watched as Rick and Erin walked down the steps of the deck, vanishing into the darkness. Seconds later Rick let out an evil-sounding mwah-hah-hah, and Erin's laughter floated out along with it.

"Are you ready to call it a night?" Ben asked. "I can chaperone the kids from my own porch if you'd like."

"That's okay. There are two of mine out there, so I'm happy to sit here a bit longer. Unless you wanted to go back to your house." She didn't want him to go to his house. She wanted to stay outside on her deck, where the chilly night air made everything feel crisp and fresh and invigorating. She'd left her outdoor lights off, so they were sitting in the shadows with only the house lights to illuminate the area around them, and the glow of the bonfire from his yard next door made everything feel cozy and private.

She was enjoying his company. Probably more than she should. It was a risky game she'd been letting herself play tonight, imagining that she and Ben had something starting. They didn't, of course, because Carli knew that even though she found Ben intriguing and thoughtful and sincere, the timing was wrong. There was a big difference between being divorced and *getting* divorced, and Ben had yet to cross that threshold. Carli wasn't even certain if *she'd* crossed it. One of them had to be sensible, and she knew that right now what both of them needed most was a friend, not a romance.

But maybe more than that, more than any of the other reasons, Carli was afraid that even if he said he was interested in her, it really wouldn't be about *her* so much as it would be just another lonely guy trying to fill an empty space. Someone to comfort a wounded ego, or to handle the minutiae of his life so he could focus on bigger, better things. She didn't want that. She was working hard enough taking care of Mia and Tess and Gus. She just didn't have the emotional bandwidth to take on more. Her hands were full. So as much as she might like to take those hands and squeeze Ben's ass with them . . . it just wasn't going to happen.

"No, I'm good out here for a while longer," Ben said, tucking the corner of her blanket in around her feet as she sat back down. She'd grabbed the throw an hour ago as the temperature dipped. "How long do you suppose it'll be before those kids come flying back in from the woods screaming their fool heads off, anyway?" Ben asked with a chuckle.

"I'm guessing about fifteen minutes, which is about fourteen more minutes than I could take."

"Not a fan of ghosts, I take it?"

"I'm happy to say I've never met one, and I'd like to keep it that way."

His laughter was soft, and they sat for a moment in companionable silence as faint voices of the kids tromping into the woods wafted through the air along with the sweet, earthy smell of autumn foliage and fallen leaves.

"What else did you do for Ethan's birthday?" Carli asked after another moment had passed. "I didn't see him around earlier today."

"He and I are officially celebrating tomorrow, because he was with his mom last night and this morning. He showed up at my place right before his party started, and he was spitting mad."

"About what?"

"Apparently, he told his mother that now he's eighteen, he wants to live with me full-time, and she took it about as well as you might expect. But in his defense, her boyfriend is around all the time, and Ethan's pissed. I've asked him to give me some time to work on all this, but eighteen-year-old boys are not the most patient creatures."

Carli smiled wistfully into the darkness. "Neither are girls at that age. For what it's worth, I can totally relate. Steve has a shiny new girlfriend, and I'm not sure what my kids think of her. They don't say much, but I think that's because they worry it'll upset me."

"Does it?" he asked. His voice was soft, as if he was hesitant to ask the question.

Carli paused with her answer. "Yes, but not because I'm jealous or want him back. It's just kind of . . . weird, and it puts the kids in an awkward place."

He nodded slowly. "Yep. I get that. I guess at least your ex was out of the house before he started dating. Sophia started her next relationship before I even knew ours was over."

"That's very rude."

Ben chuckled and then sighed. "Right?"

"Maybe you need to give that Veronica De-what's-her-name another shot." She wasn't sure why she'd said that. She didn't want to think about him spending time with some other woman, but maybe she'd secretly wanted to see his reaction.

He shook his head more vigorously and took a sip from his bottle of beer. "No, thanks. She had her chance."

That was a relief. "Too bad for her. I guess timing is everything."

Another silence descended, this one less comfortable than the last because of things that *weren't* being said. In moments they were back to discussing innocuous things, like home improvement and funny stories from their own teen years. And when Mia came back from the woods half an hour later and climbed the steps to the deck, Carli realized it was time to call it a night.

"Not interested in Ouija boarding?" Carli asked.

"I save all my important questions for the Magic Eight Ball," Mia answered. "And you didn't hear it from me, but hypothetically, if some of the kids out there were drinking, would you want to know about it?"

Ben sighed. "Yep. I would. I guess Ethan's party is over."

"Tess isn't drinking, is she?" Carli asked.

Mia shrugged. "It's pretty dark out there. Very hard to see. And anyway, it was a hypothetical question, remember?"

Ben and Carli exchanged a look, the one that said *parenting is hard*, and then he stood up.

"Hypothetically, in that case, I think I'll go see what the kids are up to in the woods," he said.

"Will you tell Tess she has to come home?" Carli asked.

"Of course, and I'm sorry about this," he said. "Ethan should know better."

"For what it's worth," Mia added, "Ethan's not the one who brought the bottle."

"I guess I'm glad to hear that, but did you see him drink from it?"

"Did I mention it was super dark?"

Ben chuckled. "Yes, you did. Thanks, Mia."

"Sure. Good night, Mr. Chase. Night, Mom."

Mia went inside, closing the door firmly behind her, and Carli stood up, next to Ben. This was an abrupt ending to the evening, but maybe it was a good thing. Not the teen-drinking part, but the part where they each went into their respective homes before she said something she shouldn't. Like how she liked the way his hair touched his collar or the way his smile made her happy.

"Well, I hope you enjoyed your first Monroe Circle Hayride," she said.

"I did. Thanks for hanging out with me tonight and helping me do a piss-poor job of chaperoning my kid's birthday party."

They were standing close and saying goodbye, so the hug came as naturally as a leaf falling from a tree, easy and gentle. His arms around her were solid and warm, and it took all her willpower not to lean in closer and make it last longer. It was over almost as soon as it started, but Carli's torso tingled long after he was gone.

Yes, Ben Chase would be so easy to fall for and care for, and then she'd lose herself again. Just when she was starting to embrace her independence. She just couldn't go down that road again. Even if that road led to a handsome man with a warm laugh and sapphire-blue eyes.

Chapter 23

The 5:30 a.m. alarm was never a welcome sound, but after a few weeks of live broadcasts and several on-location segments, Carli was finally starting to feel as if this was *her* life. She'd get up, reluctantly, and drag Gus from the bed, because even *he* thought that was way too early to start the day. They'd take a quick walk so he could handle his morning business, and then her lazy-ass dog would get back into bed while she showered and got ready to go into the station. On the days her daughters were home and not at Steve's, she'd leave them notes reminding them to take their lunch or to remember they had an appointment after school. Or sometimes she'd just leave notes with smiley faces and an *I love you*. Maybe they thought the notes were silly, or that she was too nostalgic, but she didn't care. Someday, hopefully, they'd have kids of their own, and then they'd understand.

This morning, Gus was particularly uninterested in getting up, and she couldn't blame him. It was the middle of November and still dark outside, and chilly, too. She pulled her coat on over her robe and pajamas and hooked the leash to his collar before heading out the front door. He was completely trained to stay within the boundaries of the electric fence now, but she'd learned that if she took him out of the yard on his leash, he was apt to get to business pretty quickly. Sometimes she didn't have to walk him any farther than the edge of the yard before he was ready to go back in.

Today, his head lifted as they paused on the front porch, and he sniffed at the air before easing down the two steps and meandering over into the grass toward Ben's house. She gazed around, noting only a smattering of lights on at neighbors' houses. Ben's place was dark, but a lamppost near his mailbox shed light on his driveway, and Carli suddenly felt a squishy sort of thwack in her chest, like a paintball hitting, as she noticed a cheerful yellow Volkswagen Beetle parked there. It wasn't Ethan's. He drove a small black car, like a Camry or an old Impala or something like that. A teenage-boy kind of car with rust and more than a few dents. Ben's car was a black Lexus, and she couldn't in any way, shape, or form imagine him driving this girly little vehicle.

Which left only a handful of options. It was an early birthday gift for Addie, who wouldn't turn sixteen for another year and a half. That was a highly unlikely scenario. Perhaps it belonged to Ben's sister, Kenzie, although Kenzie had been over a few times since Ben had moved in, and never once had Carli spotted such a car. Or, this option she liked least of all, Ben had an overnight visitor. Maybe Veronica DeMarco had sobered up and come to her senses and was back for another date. Or maybe this was another friend of the family or woman from his past. Or maybe it was someone completely new, and Carli didn't like that idea at all.

Sure, it was technically none of her business. There wasn't any romantic understanding between them. Since the night of the hayride, they'd chatted a handful of times, usually when she was outside with the dog or while they'd both handed out the candy to the trick-or-treaters. Then they'd watched from her front porch, drinking coffee, as Tess and Ethan took down all the Halloween decorations as a punishment for drinking out in the woods. Carli had taken Ben a plastic container full of chili because she'd made too much, and he'd coordinated a time for the tree guy to come over and remove that branch that scraped her roof. It was casual. And friendly. And neighborly. Because they were casual. And friends. And neighbors.

The problem was that Ben was also funny and thoughtful and kind. And terribly sexy. Because he was funny and thoughtful and kind. And terribly handsome. On a whim, Carli had gone online last week and looked for photos of him. You know, just for fun and to satisfy her curiosity. Being a Chase meant being in the Glenville public eye, and she discovered no shortage of pictures. There were some of him alone or with his siblings or his parents. He came from a long line of organically attractive people, and Ben Chase was there to represent. There were shots of him standing with his family on the front porch of the governor's mansion up on Wenniway Island and cutting a ribbon in front of the Wallace-Chase Arena. There were pictures of various galas and events around town as the Chase clan rubbed elbows with the area's movers and shakers. And, of course, there were also pictures of Ben's soon-to-be ex-wife. She was no slouch, either. A statuesque blonde with sharp cheekbones and a model's pout. Basically the average woman's worst nightmare, and the opposite of Carli in virtually every way.

And because she was already cyberstalking, Carli had unblocked Steve's Facebook page just long enough to see a dozen posts about him and the new girlfriend. They'd gone to a wine tasting and a concert, and there was even a picture of them carving pumpkins. With Mia and Tess. That one was tough to take. Although Carli had sufficiently recovered from seeing her ex with another woman, seeing that same woman with her arm around Mia's shoulders and everyone smiling for the camera was a gut punch she hadn't expected. The kids hadn't mentioned anything about this. And she guessed they weren't obligated to. It's not as if they were smoking a joint together or doing anything remotely out of the ordinary. It was just the cozy familyness of it that got under her skin. DeeDee had assured Carli her feelings were typical and understandable, and that she'd get used to this kind of thing, but that hadn't stopped Carli from eating an entire pint of Ben & Jerry's. And reblocking Steve's page with a vow to never look again. But somehow, seeing a cheerful, girly car in Ben's driveway bothered her more than seeing a photo of Steve and Jade at a University of Michigan football game.

Gus woofed at the air, and the wind rustled the leaves that remained on the trees. Carli paused for another moment, staring at the car. She thought about traipsing into Ben's yard to get a better look inside it, because surely other people in the neighborhood would notice it, and then they'd ask her all sorts of questions. Ben should realize by now that there was a fast and proficient grapevine around here, keeping tabs on his every move. But it was cold, and she was in her coat and robe, and Gus had already taken care of his own business, so she had no excuse for loitering around outside at that time of the morning. The last thing she wanted was to be caught snooping. Lynette probably had her binoculars trained on Carli right this minute.

And it wasn't any of her business anyway, she reminded herself again. Ben's social life was his to manage. So what if they'd shared one hug? Just because it had left her tingly and breathless, it was just a friendly gesture that she had obviously read too much into. All her friends kept telling her to get back into the dating world, as if a new relationship would somehow erase the scars of the last one. She knew that wasn't true, but maybe there was something to be said for seeking out some companionship. Ben obviously had, so what the hell was she waiting for?

❧

Ben stared at his bedroom ceiling, feeling much as he had the first morning he'd woken up in this new house. Mind spinning. Ready to move forward with his future but not certain where to start. One thing he knew for sure, though? His future wasn't going to have Patricia Harrison in it. And somehow, he didn't think she'd mind.

Last night had been a disaster. Not quite as bad as having Roni DeMarco passed out on his bathroom floor, but dinner and too many drinks with his old college girlfriend Patty had gone only slightly better. He'd thought sex with someone he knew from the past would make it . . . easier? Better? More passionately satisfying? God, was he that guy now? The kind of guy who thought good sex required emotional connection? Is that what twenty years of marriage had done to him?

Patricia gave up a soft, snorty kind of snore next to him, and it was all he could do not to oh-so-accidentally elbow her in the shoulder so she'd wake up and go home. No surprise she was tired, having put a lot of energy and enthusiasm into their encounter. Maybe she was trying to make up for his lack of enthusiasm.

Damn it all to hell. What was wrong with him? He'd wanted to have sex. In fact, he'd been thinking about it *a lot* lately, but when push came to shove, as it were, he ended up literally just going through the motions until his body finally took over and finished what his brain had started. The five minutes of postcoital satisfaction were far too quickly replaced with postcoital regret. Well, maybe *regret* was too strong of a word. It was *sex*, after all, and even lousy sex was still . . . *sex*. So maybe it was just postcoital indifference, because Patty could have been anyone. There were at least seven women who'd asked him out in the past few months. He'd chosen Patty because he'd been crazy about her in college, for about four months, but now he couldn't remember anything about her, other than the fact that she had an annoying laugh. That may have been why he'd dumped her in the first place. Or perhaps it was the way she held up her pinkie as she sipped from a cocktail straw? Or maybe he'd dumped her because he'd met Sophia.

Ah. Yes. Sophia. She'd crept into his brain last night, somewhere after the fourth glass of wine and right before Patty started pulling off his shirt. Maybe that wasn't such a strange thing, given the circumstances, but it sure as hell was annoying. And worse even than that? Not only was Sophia messing with his head, but Doug had been in there, too. Picturing your wife with her new lover was not the best way to maintain an erection. And Patty must have noticed, because she'd slapped his ass right about then and said, "Giddyup, cowboy."

That hadn't helped, either. The only thing that had—the crazy brain game that nudged his body over the edge—was the image of Carli in that damn pink T-shirt from the Monroe Circle barbecue. And the memory of hugging her that night after the hayride. She'd felt so good in his arms, comfortable and *right*, yet leaving him completely off-kilter. But thinking about her set into motion a whole other host of issues for him to stress about. Thoughts he was trying to suppress.

He'd helped her take down the big Halloween spider after Ethan and Tess had nearly destroyed it with their clumsy attempts, and Ben had once again found himself with his face mere inches from her ass while she climbed a ladder. Such a temptation. And days later, he couldn't help but notice how nice her hair smelled when she'd leaned over to look at his computer screen while helping him pick out some lamps online. She'd brought him chili, and he'd eaten it. In some countries, that was considered a marriage proposal, wasn't it? The woman was a walking trigger for him, and he needed to tamp that shit down. It's the only reason he'd returned Patricia Harrison's phone call in the first place. So she could distract him from Carli. Only she hadn't. But that wasn't her fault. It was his. And Sophia's. And Doug's. And Carli's. Mostly Carli's.

As Ben stared listlessly up at the ceiling of his bedroom, he wondered how many people he could have ambling around in his brain before he was certifiably certifiable. It was getting pretty crowded in there, and clearly no one was in charge. All he knew for certain was that Carli Lancaster wasn't just living next door. She'd all but taken up residence in his mind, and he needed to evict her somehow.

Chapter 24

Troy Buckman in a fluffy white robe was something Carli had never, in the breadth of her imagination, anticipated seeing, and yet there he was, sitting across from her in the tastefully decorated private waiting room of the Divine Goddess salon. Thanks to Katrina's machinations, they were taping various segments of spa treatments and beauty procedures. Allie had somehow escaped this adventure, and Carli had gotten Jessica's sworn promise that she'd have final veto power over any video footage before she'd agreed to try this—while Troy was fully on board with whatever the lovely technicians wanted to do to him. Carli suspected he thought this place was more like a happy-ending kind of spa. Boy, was he in for a rude awakening when he found out that a Manzilian Sugaring was not at all what he was expecting.

He shifted in the plush blue velvet chair, adjusting the lapel of his robe. Carli looked away as his knees went a little too wide for her to handle, but she laughed as he said, "I can sense you dressing me with your eyes."

"Sorry, Captain Manspreader. I'm just not used to seeing you without . . . clothes."

"The human body is a beautiful thing. Nothing to be ashamed of here. I'll show you mine if you show me yours. But only in a completely consensual and equitable exchange." Troy still had some reprogramming to do before he was fully evolved, but at least he was trying.

"I'm going to take a hard pass on that, Troy."

"Meh. Your loss."

"Uh-huh."

He shifted in the chair again. "So when they sugar my nethers, it won't hurt, right? Anything with sugar seems like it should be pretty comfortable."

Carli decided this was a voyage of discovery Troy needed to take on his own. "I'm sure you can handle it," she said. "In all honesty, I've never sugared, so I don't really know."

"You've never sugared? Do you mean, like, you're in your . . . natural state?" She'd never seen Troy blush before. The moment was worth the embarrassment.

"I've waxed. I've never sugared."

"Ah, so this is your first time, too? I think that makes us sugar virgins. I think we're really bonding now."

"Uh-huh," Carli said again. "Sure." And while there were few things she wanted to think about less than Troy Buckman's *nethers*, she *was* tempted to listen outside the door just to hear him yelp when he realized that sugaring wasn't all that sweet.

This was their fourth pretaped segment this week. Yesterday they'd tried out the new Glenville ropes course, and Carli had discovered she was even more afraid of heights than she'd realized. She'd powered through, and Hannah had gotten some great footage. Thank goodness, because she was never doing that again. The day before, she and Troy had visited the new penguin exhibit at the zoo, where he wore a tuxedo so the *fancy little birds*, as he called them, wouldn't make him feel underdressed. And before that, they'd visited a podiatrist to learn all about good foot health. That segment sort of veered off course when Troy kept referring to the doctor as Paul Bunion.

The past few weeks had been a whirlwind of job stuff and dog stuff and school stuff, and she'd been glad for all the things that occupied her mind and helped her not think about Ben and the fact that he'd had an overnight guest. She'd spent Thanksgiving Day with Allie Winters, hosting the Glenville Turkey Trot 5-K run, and then had dinner with Erin's family because Mia and Tess were with their father and his "size-four whore" (as DeeDee had dubbed her). And now it was the first week of December, and she'd decided to enjoy and embrace the spa treatments. She'd earned them. Jessica had even said as much to her yesterday at the postshow wrap-up meeting.

"Viewers are really responding to you, Carli," she'd said to the entire group. "Social media posts include words like *genuine*, *adorable*, *vivacious*, and *sincere*. One viewer even said, 'I feel like I've found a new best friend who tells me where all the fun things will be happening this weekend.' And that is exactly what we were hoping for. Well done!"

Getting a *well done* from Jessica Jackson was like getting a Pulitzer wrapped in an Oscar sitting on top of an Emmy. Carli felt warm all over again, sitting in the spa's lounge, remembering how it had felt to earn Jessica's praise. What felt even better was starting to believe she was earning Jessica's respect, too. She desperately wanted to do a good job, and her performance was hard to measure. There wasn't a grade that could be assigned, or a specific task to complete. Viewer feedback and new advertisers were among the few ways that the station could evaluate her success. But so far, so good.

"Dad, I need you to take me to the store." Addie was standing in Ben's bedroom door, wearing baggy black sweatpants and an oversize T-shirt. Her blue eyes were wide, and her tone decisive.

"The store? Addie, it's almost eleven o'clock at night."

She shifted from one fuzzy-socked foot to the other. "I know, but . . . I just really need you to take me to the store. It won't take long. If you can just drive me, I can go in by myself."

It was Saturday night, and Ben had worked on the house all day. He was tired and had just gotten into bed, planning to watch the news before (hopefully) falling asleep and not being kept awake by random Carli thoughts. "That's ridiculous, Addie. Whatever you need, we can get tomorrow. Go to bed."

Her cheeks flushed to crimson, and her feet shifted again. She may have stomped, but the sound was muffled between her socks and the plush carpet. "Dad! When a girl says she needs to go to the store, she needs to go to the store. It's a girl thing. I need . . . girl supplies."

"What the hell are girl supplies? Lip gloss?"

"Oh my God, Dad. You know. Girl supplies. And there's nothing here."

What was she— *Oh! Girl supplies!* Ben finally caught on and felt like a caveman for not understanding sooner. When she said *girl supplies*, she wasn't talking about lip gloss and bubble gum. She was talking about, God help him, woman stuff. This wasn't her first period. At least he knew that much, but it hadn't occurred to him to stock the house with any of that stuff. He wouldn't even know what to buy.

"Ah, I see. Okay, then." He pulled the covers off and swung his feet to the floor. The last thing he wanted to do right now was get dressed and drive over to the nearest twenty-four-hour convenience store, but this wasn't optional. "Just write down what you need, and I'll go pick it up."

She shook her head, her ponytail swaying. "I'll come with you."

"Addie, it's eleven o'clock. You get ready for bed, and I'll be back as fast as I can. It shouldn't take too long."

Her adamant voice dropped to a murmur. "God, Dad. That's too embarrassing. Just let me come with you."

"There's nothing to be embarrassed about. It's all totally natural." He was evolved. He could handle this.

"It's not natural to have your dad buying you . . . tampons." She whispered the last word, and Ben fought to keep his smile under wraps. If he laughed, she'd think he was teasing her.

He lowered his voice in return. "I won't tell anyone they're for you."

"Oh. My. God. Dad, that's even creepier. Who else would you be buying them for? God!" she said again and flounced from the room. He wasn't sure where she was headed, but he got up and pulled on a pair of jeans. He was buttoning his shirt when she came back into his bedroom.

"Forget it. I've got it all under control," she said.

"You do? How?"

"I texted Mia, and she's going to bring me some stuff. She'll be here in a minute."

"Are you sure? I'm totally willing to go to the store for you, you know. I'm a very modern kind of dad, and I can totally handle this sort of thing."

The hint of a smile twitched in the corner of her mouth, and Ben could see her struggling against it. It was the part of her that he questioned the most. Her absolute determination to avoid displays of happiness. She worked so hard to be so somber.

"Yes. I have everything under control. You can go back to bed, and please never mention this again."

"You mean the fact that I almost went to the store to buy you maxi pads?"

"Oh my God, you're so gross."

"And tampons?"

"Please stop talking."

"Because you're menstruating?"

"I'm leaving now because you're being a jerk," she said, but the smile at the corner of her mouth tugged again. She nearly had his bedroom door shut before she poked her head back into his room. "You know I'm just kidding about the jerk thing, right?"

He smiled at her. "Of course you were, because I'm awesome."

"Oh my God," she muttered again and closed his door.

Ten minutes later the doorbell rang. "I've got it!" Addie called, but Ben heard the front door open before Addie's feet had hit the landing, then Ethan's voice said, "Hey, Mia. What's up?"

"Oh my God, Ethan. I said I've got this," Addie exclaimed.

Ben stuck his head out of his bedroom door just in time to see his daughter nearly body slam her brother out of the way before grabbing the paper bag from Mia's outstretched hand.

"Thank you so much, Mia. You saved my life."

"Hey, no problem. I've been there. This should get you through a couple of days." Mia offered up an understanding nod at Addie and a shy smile at Ethan, who was standing there looking utterly confused.

"What's in the bag?" he asked.

"Nothing," Addie snapped. "Mind your own business."

"What did you think of that physics quiz yesterday?" Mia asked, deftly distracting him.

"I thought it sucked ass," Ethan answered. "But you probably crushed it, right?"

She shrugged. "Not sure, but the next assignment looks kind of rough."

He ran a hand through his shaggy hair. "Uh-oh. If it looks rough to you, then I'm in trouble. Any chance you want to coach me through it? I could use some help."

Ben saw her cheeks pinken, even from his view from the top of the stairs.

"Sure. Are you working on it right now?"

Ethan chuckled. "Not on a Saturday night. I'm watching a movie right now. I was thinking tomorrow? Would that work?"

Mia nodded. "Sure. I have to head over to my dad's house around dinnertime, but I'm around all day before that."

"Sweet. Thanks. I'll text you."

"Okay. Hey, do you know how to put air in car tires?" she asked.

"Doesn't everybody?"

"Um, no, not really, and I think my tires are getting kind of flat."

"Okay. I'll check 'em for you tomorrow then. Even trade."

She smiled again. "Cool. See you tomorrow. See you later, Addie," she said almost as an afterthought as she turned to leave, and Ben found himself smiling as Addie trotted upstairs and waved the paper bag at him.

"Crisis averted. Nothing to see here," his daughter said, leaning over to kiss his cheek. A sweet, tender gesture that meant more to him than she could comprehend. Then Ben watched as Ethan opened the front door again.

"Hey, Mia," he called out.

"Yeah?" Her voice was distant.

"Want to watch a movie? I just started it."

"Um . . . I should ask my mom. I'll text you in, like, two minutes."

Ethan nodded and shut the door, then turned to look up at Ben. "That's okay, isn't it, Dad? Can Mia and I watch a movie?"

That was a surprise turn of events. Mia Lancaster was about as far from Ethan's type as Ben had ever seen, but if she could help him pass a class, he was all for it. And since Ben knew Mia was not the drinking sort, she'd be a good influence on him, too.

"Sure, if it's okay with her mom."

Ben smiled to himself as he went back into his room. Addie was finally starting to relax around here, and Ethan was clearly feeling right at home. Life was beginning to feel just a little bit . . . normal. His chest went *whump* just a moment later as he received a text from Carli.

Is Addie all set?

Ben typed his response.

I think so. I'm forbidden from asking too many questions. Is Mia coming back for a movie?

There was a long pause before Carli's answer popped up on his phone's screen.

I guess so. I assume that's okay with you?

Yep.

He thought about adding something more. Something along the lines of, "Hey, you should come over, too, and you and I can have a drink." He typed the words. Deleted them, and then typed them again. His attempts to purge her from his mind had only made it that much harder to not think about her. Maybe he was creating drama where none existed? Maybe they should explore whatever there was between them? Why fight it?

Want to come over for a nightcap?

God, could he be any cheesier? His heart rate doubled as he waited for a response. After the debacle with Patty, he'd tried going out with Alicia Newhaven, a woman he knew from . . . somewhere, but their conversation had been stilted and awkward and he'd called it a night when she'd started talking about her loom and using terms like *weft* and *woof* and *heddles*. And then he'd had lunch with Candice Collins, the general manager of the Wallace-Chase Arena, but it was clear she'd thought it was more of a meeting than a social excursion, judging by the fact that she'd brought her laptop with a slide presentation all about the shows they'd be hosting the next year. He hadn't given in and fallen into the Tinder trap yet, but times were getting tough. Just one glass of wine with Carli would be relaxing and fine. And if it led to more? Better still.

Sorry. No nightcap for me.

His gut turned sour at the clipped response. That was it. Kind of abrupt. No *Sorry, I can't, because I'm tired* or *maybe another time*. Not even an *enjoy your evening*. Just . . . no. And no emojis. They'd texted often enough for him to know with certainty that Carli was a rampant abuser of emojis. She must be in the middle of something, or maybe she was already in bed. It was eleven o'clock, and she was used to getting up very early. Was it strange that he knew so much about her schedule? Was it strange and stalkerish that he peeked out his own bedroom window right then to see if the light was on in hers?

He texted another quick note.

Okay. Another time then. G'nite.

He waited for a response, but the light in her room turned off, and he wondered how long it was going to take him to fall asleep now that he was actively thinking about the fact that she was over there in her bed with her dark hair curling against the pink pillows. He knew she had pink pillows and pink walls because he'd changed out a light fixture for her last month, right after she'd had the room painted. He'd noticed then that the family picture above the bed, the one with her jughead of an ex-husband and their kids, was no longer there, replaced by a painting of a big flower. When Ben closed his eyes, he could barely picture his own room, but Carli's was imprinted in his memory. Maybe he should get his extension ladder out and go break in through her window . . .

Chapter 25

There was always a bit of a reentry period when Mia and Tess came home from Steve's, and Carli had learned to give them some space before asking how their time with him had been, but today they were both oddly quiet and, quite frankly, more than a little pissy. Tess had snapped at Mia about leaving her shoes in front of the door, and Mia had snapped back about a sweatshirt Tess had borrowed without asking. They weren't immune to the typical sister bickering, but Carli's maternal instincts were telling her it was something bigger than the usual squabble.

"So . . . how was it at Dad's? Did you do anything fun?" she asked once they'd sat down for dinner.

Mia glanced over at Tess, who suddenly seemed very interested in the rice pilaf on her plate.

"Dad's was fine," Mia finally said. "We didn't do much together. He was kind of busy, and we both had a lot of homework."

"He decorated the tree without us," Tess blurted out.

"The tree?" Carli said.

"Yes. He and Jade went out and got a Christmas tree and decorated the whole thing without even asking me and Mia about it. It was decorated when we got there."

Like most families, decorating for the holiday, especially trimming the tree, had always been a big event, and although Carli had

anticipated this first Christmas apart would be new and strange and that
parts of it would be difficult, this was a twist she hadn't seen coming.

"Do you think maybe he did that because he wanted to surprise
you?"

Mia scoffed. "He said that's why, after he realized we were upset,
but I don't buy it. He and Jade are having a Christmas party this weekend, and I think he wanted his place decorated for that, so they put up
all kinds of stuff. His whole condo is decorated, but it just looks weird
and ugly. It's all like glittery twigs and wreaths made from feathers. And
all the balls on the tree are white. Who the heck wants an all-white
Christmas tree? It's like Jade can only handle monochrome décor."

Carli's heart squeezed inside her chest, and she felt a little light-
headed. Just the verbiage alone was enough to give her vertigo. Steve
and Jade were now a *they*. *They* had decorated. Not two separate individuals, but a couple. A unit. A unit that didn't include his children,
who were visibly upset about it. And why wouldn't they be? Christmas
was all about family, and Jade was not family. She was just some woman
in *his* life.

"Well, I guess the good news is we won't have to sit around in that
gross, ugly décor over Christmas break," Tess said, flicking at the pilaf
with her fork, indicating she thought it was exactly the opposite of
good news.

"What do you mean?" Carli asked, heart squeezing tighter still.

Tess glanced over at Mia, and the long pause hung heavy in the air,
until Mia finally said, "Dad's not going to be home over Christmas. He
and Jade are going to Aruba."

That one really knocked the wind out of Carli. She'd thought his
ability to shock her or hurt her feelings was past. But this one got to her.

"They're going to . . . Aruba? For Christmas?" Every word stuck in
her mouth like bitter taffy that she was struggling to spit out—because
Aruba was the one place where she and Steve had always talked about
going, but they never managed to make it happen because he was always

working or because he thought it would cost too much. *Now* he was going? With Jade?

Mia nodded, her eyes clouding with emotions that Carli couldn't name. Probably because her own eyes fogged with a disbelief/ rage/wounded-heart mixture that made her blink fast and all but hyperventilate.

"He told us not to tell you, but I'd feel like I was lying if we didn't. And he is going to tell you. He just hasn't had a chance yet," Mia added.

But he'd had time to tell them? And put them in the position of keeping a secret from her? *Not cool, Steve.* And he'd had time to buy decorations and a tree and decorate his place for a party but not include them? *Also not cool, Steve.* She wondered if breathing into her napkin would be the same as breathing into a paper bag. Maybe. But it would also freak out her daughters.

"So when are you guys supposed to celebrate Christmas with him? He's still planning to do *something*, isn't he?" Her voice was tense, and she knew she should be asking Steve about this, not them, but the question came out before she could stop it, in a voice she didn't recognize.

"He wants to talk to you about that, too," Mia said. "He wants us with him over New Year's Eve. He was, like, really insistent about it, and I told him we'd probably have plans with our friends, but he said it wasn't optional. He said that since we'd be with you for all of Christmas, we should be with him for New Year's Eve."

Tess was staring down at her plate, hands in her lap, but Carli saw her dash away a tear, so although she wanted very much to have a tantrum of her own, at the moment, she had to hold her shit together and try to clean up the emotional shrapnel left behind by Steve's actions. It certainly wasn't the first time she'd done that, and she was technically the adult in the room, after all. She could have her own meltdown later, in private.

"Well . . . I'm sure Dad didn't mean to hurt your feelings with any of this. Maybe he figured we'd be doing some special stuff over here and so his tree didn't matter so much. I'm not really sure about the vacation."

"One family, two houses," Tess murmured.

"What?"

"That's what you guys promised us when you said you were getting divorced. You said we'd still be one family but with two houses, but it doesn't feel like that. I mean, I know you kept things around here the same for a long time just for our sakes, but honestly, you could've changed everything the day Dad moved out, because even if it looked the same, it still felt totally different. I'm honestly kind of relieved that you finally painted the walls and got some new stuff, but over at Dad's, everything is new and different and it's like when we're there, we're just visiting. We don't actually *live* there."

Carli reached over and squeezed her daughter's wrist, but Tess wasn't finished.

"And ever since Dad started seeing Jade, he's been super distracted. She's nice enough, I guess, but she acts like it's her condo. She told us we had to keep our coats in our bedroom because there wasn't room for them in the entryway closet. And the other day she told me I couldn't make microwave popcorn because it stank too much, and Dad just stood there, like she was in charge. And when we tried to talk to him about it, he said we were being selfish."

"He said that?" She couldn't keep the screech of surprise from her tone. For all Steve's faults, he did love his daughters. In his own way. And accusing them of being selfish seemed heavy-handed, even from him.

Tess dashed away another tear as Mia nodded and said, "Yes, he did say that. He also said that we needed to listen to Jade, because if we didn't, she'd think we didn't like her and that would hurt her feelings."

Her feelings? That's what he was worried about? Jade's feelings, rather than those of his own daughters?

Where to keep their coats and when to make popcorn weren't really the issues, but Carli could read between the lines, and what she saw was two girls longing for some attention from their father. His priorities had shifted, and as always, the rest of them just had to adjust.

"I'm sorry, you guys," she said. "This is new territory for all of us, and I wish I could make it easier for everyone. I'm just not sure how. But what I can promise you is that you are not selfish. I'm super proud of both of you, especially for the way you've handled all the changes. I'll talk to your dad about this."

Tess's chin jutted forward even as she sniffled. "Don't bother. I'm over it. I hope he gets sunburned in Aruba."

So did Carli. In fact, she kind of hoped he'd get eaten by a shark. One limb at a time.

Chapter 26

"What's Steve's email address?" DeeDee asked Carli as they sipped peppermint martinis at the first stop of the Third Annual Monroe Circle Holly Trolley Pub Crawl. "I'll sign him up for every digital newsletter on the internet."

Carli was surrounded by her girlfriends and had filled them in on Steve's holiday vacation plans, which sent DeeDee into overdrive, plotting out a suitable revenge strategy. It wasn't that DeeDee was so convinced he was doing something insensitive—she just really loved tormenting people in untraceable ways. If there were ever any suspicious deaths in the neighborhood, her browser history could undoubtedly land her in jail.

"I'll forward his address to you," Carli said. "And all the passwords I still have. He's too lazy to change any of them."

DeeDee rubbed her hands together with glee. "Excellent. Time to do some shopping. I love messing with my ex's Amazon accounts. Last week I put a bunch of men's underwear in Greg's cart, but not, like, regular underwear. I loaded it with pink jockstraps and lime-green banana hammocks and all sorts of see-through and mesh stuff. He must not have noticed, because when I checked his orders yesterday, he'd actually purchased them all!"

Erin, Renee, and Lynette laughed along with Carli.

"Maybe he saw them in the cart and thought you were trying to send him a message," Erin said, signaling the waiter to bring them another round.

DeeDee shook her head, her reindeer antlers wiggling. "I doubt it. That guy couldn't interpret a message properly with a team of cryptologists helping him. I just wish I could see his face when he opens those boxes and finds the leopard-spotted thong."

"Well, now!" said Erin's husband as he came up behind DeeDee. "What's this about a leopard-spotted thong?"

"I'm getting you one for Christmas," Erin answered.

"What a coincidence," he replied smoothly. "That's just what I was planning to get you."

The evening was rolling along, with a dozen Monroe Circle couples plus Ben and Carli enjoying drinks and conversation. They'd started at Renee's, where she served them homemade eggnog in glasses rimmed with nutmeg before everyone boarded a party bus decorated to look like Santa's workshop on wheels. The mood was merry and bright, and even though Carli was frustrated with her ex and feeling slightly worried about her kids, she was primed and ready for a night out. Work had kept her busy lately, and she hadn't gone out with friends in ages. Tonight was a welcome and much-needed boost, and she'd put some extra effort into her appearance—because it was a party, and not at all because Ben was there. Hovering. She'd only spoken to him once or twice since seeing the yellow Volkswagen in his driveway. Not because she was upset with him, but because it was just easier to avoid the whole situation and all the messy feelings. Being near him felt . . . *big*. Confusing in a way that was, well . . . confusing. She didn't want to waste energy thinking about him, and the only way to really do that was to stay away. So she'd done her best, walking her dog in the opposite direction so she wouldn't pass Ben's yard and turning down his invite for a late-night cocktail. She'd even passed on the chance to go over to his place and watch a football game when Tess and Mia had been invited by Ethan, saying she had to take care of some things at home. She'd focused on work instead. And her kids, and training the dog, and dealing with Steve, and heaven knew that was enough to fill her mind.

But it was impossible to avoid Ben tonight, because he kept ending up in her path, almost as if he was doing it on purpose. Was he doing it on purpose?

"You look really nice tonight," he said as they boarded the bus to go to the second pub. And then he squeezed in right beside her when he could've just as easily, and more comfortably, sat on the other side. His thigh pressed against hers as the bus lurched into motion, jostling its rowdy passengers, and she wondered how she'd get through the evening without asking him about the overnight guest. Because it was none of her business, even if it felt like it was.

He was wearing a dark blue sweater over gray pants and somehow managed to make that look just a little sexier than it would've looked on any other guy. Maybe it was the way the blue enhanced his eye color, or the way the cashmere accentuated his nicely broad shoulders. Of course, most of the other guys were wearing ugly Christmas sweaters, but even if they'd all been dressed in their Sunday best, somehow, Carli knew Ben would still look better than any of them. It was a problem.

By the third pub, and her third martini, she stopped trying to avoid him. She stopped wondering if he kept seeking her out simply because she was the only single woman in the group and he was the only single guy, because even if that was the reason, she was okay with that. At least for tonight. Because she missed him. She missed talking to him. They were friends, and she liked him, even if the idea that he was probably screwing some woman who drove a yellow Volkswagen did make her want to kick him in the shin. Tonight she was full of Christmas cheer, and vodka, so all was forgiven.

"I just wish I could do something really special for my kids this Christmas," she told Ben as they sat at the end of the bar, away from the rest of their group. "You know, something to make up for the fact that Steve is literally going to be phoning it in this year."

"Like what?" he asked, leaning in closer as if to hear her better. As if they were sharing something private. His cologne was nice. She'd noticed it once before, when she was leaning over his shoulder looking at lamps online, but tonight, her nose practically craved it. Their knees had bumped once or twice, and some might even say he was sitting closer than necessary. None of her friends would say that, of course. DeeDee had been telling Carli for weeks that she should just forget about the damn Volkswagen and plant herself on Ben's lap. Even Erin had suggested that maybe it was time for Carli to get some action and that maybe Ben wasn't such a bad option, in spite of him being a neighbor. That was easy for them to say, though. Carli would be the one who had to deal with the repercussions. So tonight, she'd stick to talking about benign stuff, like what to get their kids for Christmas.

"I don't know. I have the sneaking suspicion my furnace is about to give out, so it can't be anything terribly expensive, but I'm trying to come up with something really memorable. Something unique, because this Christmas is a tough one. I know Tess really wants to go to the Nolan Hart concert in January, but the only tickets left are either in the nosebleed section, where we'll need oxygen masks just to breathe, or the ones that cost about five hundred dollars apiece. I may suck it up and get some of the cheap seats. Hopefully she'll think that's better than not seeing him at all."

"Nolan Hart? Why does that name sound familiar?" Ben asked.

"You've probably heard Addie talk about him. He's a singer, obviously, and according to Tess, he's the hottest of all the hotness that ever was. He started out on some Disney Channel show, but then he had what Mia calls a *glow-up*. That's when puberty hits and all of a sudden a dorky preteen scarecrow blossoms into a Grammy-winning heartthrob."

"Well, now I've got to google this kid. He sounds dreamy." Ben smiled and pulled out his phone and tapped at the screen until a myriad of images popped up. "Well, I'll be damned. He is dreamy. Where's the concert?"

"At the Wallace-Chase Arena. Perhaps you've heard of it."

"It sounds vaguely familiar."

"Hey, buddy!" Mike Barker gave Ben's back a hearty wallop and listed toward them. His cheeks were ruddy, his forehead beaded with perspiration. By the looks of it, Lynette's husband was tipping back quite a few drinks tonight. But who could blame him? If Carli were married to Lynette, she'd be drunk all the time.

"I heard you've got something to celebrate tonight," Mike all but shouted, and his beer-addled tongue made him say it like *thumb-thing to thell-a-brate.*

"Celebrate?" Carli asked, but Ben's smile had gone a little dim.

"Yep, I guess," Ben said, his glance darting at Carli before his expression turned sheepish.

Mike thwacked him on the back again. "You might want to put on a little lipstick, Carli, because this here is a single man."

Ben looked back at her. "Divorce is final, as of noon today."

Ohhh, she remembered that feeling. The day the divorce was final. It was like walking into a pitch-black room that you'd never been in before and not knowing if it was full of scary monsters or if someone would flip on the lights and yell, "Surprise! Welcome to the future!" What she'd learned over the past year was that the room would slowly brighten, but most days it was still dark enough for you to trip over random shit that you didn't realize was there. She also knew that celebrating Divorce Day was kind of like finding out the doctors had removed all the cancer. That clean bill of health still had a shadow cast over it.

"Lemme buy you a drink!" Mike said, listing to the other side and whacking Ben on the back again.

"How about you let me get you a glass of water instead?" Ben asked.

"Sure. Okay." Mike nodded like a bobblehead and then turned and teetered aimlessly back into the crowd.

"Now you know why we hire a bus for this event," Carli said.

"I suspected as much."

She took a sip from her drink while Ben continued staring at Mike's retreating back.

"Do you want to talk about it?" she asked.

"Not really," he said, returning his gaze to hers. "I mean, I feel like I've said everything that needs to be said about it. I tried my best. Sophia wanted something different. Now it's time for everyone to move on."

His eyes locked with hers when he said *time for everyone to move on*, and she wondered if he was simply trying to prove how very *recovered* he was from what he'd been through or if he thought that the moving-on part in any way involved her.

"Moving on is good," she said lamely.

Ben nodded. "I think so, too." More staring.

She wanted to ask him about the yellow Volkswagen and if he hoped to scrub away the icky divorce feelings with a steady stream of one-night stands, because that wasn't for her. She didn't want to be his growth and recovery girlfriend. His divorce was literally hours old, and she wasn't a convenience. She wasn't there just to soothe his wounds so he could leave her behind when the next woman came along. She wasn't Jade. But he was staring at her, still, as if there were more he wanted to say. Something meaningful.

∽

He should just tell her. He should tell her that he'd been thinking about her. A lot. He'd thought about her today at noon when he'd signed those papers. And he'd thought about her basically every day since . . . well, ever since her damn dog had stolen his steak. Of course, it would be complicated. Of course, there were a dozen things to consider, but he knew how he *felt*, and that wasn't something he could ignore. He should just tell her all that. Right now. But his phone vibrated on the bar where he'd set it after looking up pictures of the singer. He picked it up to slide it back into his pocket without answering it, but it was Ethan. Ethan never called him. He texted, and even then, only if it was something really important.

"Um . . . sorry. It's Ethan. I think I should answer."

"Of course," Carli responded. She was a mom. She understood.

He pressed the phone to his ear and plugged the other with his finger. It was loud in there and hard to hear.

"Hey, buddy. What's up?"

"Dad. Are you with Mrs. Lancaster?"

"Yes." That was a strange question, and Ben's nerves began to tingle.

"Okay," Ethan sighed on the other end of the call. "Good. I guess. Um, Mia's been in an accident."

Ben slid from his chair and turned his back to Carli so she couldn't see his face. He didn't want to alarm her until he had more information.

"What kind?"

"A car accident. She hit a deer. We're okay, but the car's a mess, and Mia's pretty freaked out."

"Were you with her?"

"Yeah, we were watching a movie, but then Brenden needed a ride home and she offered to drive because I don't have any gas in my car, and I swear to God, Dad, she was driving really careful and we were wearing our seat belts, but that deer just came flying out of nowhere."

Ben took a breath. "Okay. Okay. You're sure everyone is okay?"

"Yeah. I mean, there's glass everywhere because the deer flew up over the hood and cracked the windshield, but we're okay. What should I do now?"

Ben prided himself on thinking fast on his feet, but suddenly his capacity for decision-making seemed to be moving in slow motion. Still, his mouth asked questions, and somewhere in the recesses of his mind, he thought they were logical.

"Can you give me an address of where you are?"

"Um, we're not really by any houses right now. Brenden lives out in the sticks, but we're on Canfield Road between Linden and Parkway. I think. Can you just track my phone?"

"Yeah, I can try that. In the meantime, call the police and sit tight. We'll be there as soon as we can. Okay?"

"Yep. Okay. Thanks, Dad." Ethan sounded calm but uncertain, and Ben's gut churned. So not how he'd expected this night to go. So not what any parent wanted to experience. And now he had to tell Carli. He took another deep breath before turning back around to face her.

"Everything okay?" she asked, her face registering concern almost instantly. Apparently he didn't have much of a poker face.

"Not exactly. Mia and Ethan were driving a friend home, and it seems she hit a deer. Ethan says they're both fine," he added quickly as Carli popped off the barstool at full attention.

"They're fine? Are you sure?"

"Ethan seemed pretty steady, but I told him to call the police." He tapped at his phone to activate the phone finder. "They're on Canfield Road. I told him we were on our way."

"We don't have cars," Carli said, her voice rising with tension. "How are we supposed to reach them?"

A vision of the collection of drunken Monroe Circle neighbors piling into the party bus to go rescue the children nearly made him laugh, but that was more from the stress than from humor.

"I guess we call an Uber," he said. "You grab our coats from the bus. I'll get us a ride."

The ten minutes while waiting for the car had been the longest of Ben's life, and now he and Carli were in the back seat speeding along toward Ethan and Mia. Carli had taken her phone out of her purse to discover three missed calls from Mia.

"She tried to get ahold of me, and I didn't answer," Carli said. He could hear the guilt in her voice where there should be none. She quickly dialed, and Ben could hear both sides of the conversation.

"Mom?"

"Honey, are you okay? What happened?"

Mia's voice warbled with distress. "I'm fine. Just scared. I swear I was watching the road, but that deer came from out of nowhere. I'm so sorry."

"I know, honey. You don't need to apologize. It was an accident, and deer do that sometimes. All that matters is that you and Ethan aren't hurt."

"We're not hurt, except for a couple little cuts from the glass flying all over, but Dad's going to be super mad about the car. The front hood is all crunched up and the windshield is shattered, and the deer . . ." Ben heard Mia burst into tears and felt Carli trembling next to him. He put his arm around her shoulders and pulled her close. And she let him. She talked to Mia for another few minutes, uttering words of reassurance that he knew she didn't feel, and then she ended the call so her daughter could preserve her phone battery.

"I think . . . I might be having a panic attack," Carli said quietly, breathing erratically next to him.

Ben pulled her closer still. "This will be fine. I promise, this will be fine."

"How can you promise that?" she asked.

"Because the police are on their way, and both kids are coherent and capable of talking on the phone. And we'll be there in"—he glanced at the app on his phone—"thirteen minutes."

"I make my kids keep blankets in the car, even during the summer. And twenty dollars in cash and a first aid kit. And jumper cables. I try to keep them safe, but then this happens."

Her voice broke, and Ben started to feel as much worry for her as for the kids. She was trembling, and whether that was from the cold or her agitation, an overwhelming sense of protectiveness engulfed him. He wanted to fix this, somehow.

"I'm sure I'm overreacting," she said, as if to convince herself.

"I'm certain that they'll be okay, but I think you're entitled to some overreacting. Do you want to talk, or would you rather be quiet? I could tell you a story about the time my brothers and I challenged each other to a unicycle race."

She let out a chuff of laughter and dashed a tear away from her eye. "I think I'd like to hear about that."

For the next ten minutes, Ben managed to completely fabricate a story about him and his brothers getting unicycles for Christmas and having a race that ended with Terrance getting a black eye and Bill breaking his wrist. None of it was true, but the more elaborate the story became, the more he felt Carli relaxing in his arms, and the more his need to engulf her in security grew. Someday he'd tell her how he made it all up, but for tonight, it seemed a suitable distraction.

Flashing lights from the police cruiser let them know they'd arrived, and Carli was out of the car and halfway to Mia before he even had his door open.

"This is the strangest place I've ever dropped anybody off," the driver said. "Do you want me to stick around in case you folks need a ride back home? I don't think that minivan is going anyplace without a tow truck."

"Would you?" Ben asked. "That would be so great."

The driver nodded. "No problem. Got kids myself."

"Thanks," Ben said. He exited the car and walked across the street, shattered glass crunching under his feet. It was dark and windy with a few meager streetlights illuminating the area, along with the flashers, making everything appear as surreal as it felt. The hood of the minivan was crumpled like an accordion, the windshield gone except for shards around the edges. A shiver ran through Ben as he acknowledged how lucky they were to have been wearing their seat belts, and as he spotted

Ethan, relief poured over him like a hot shower. He realized then he'd been all but holding his breath since the moment they'd gotten off the phone.

"Hey, Dad," Ethan said casually, but then he hugged him tightly, dipping his head down to Ben's shoulders. Damn, the kid was tall. And he was fine. Everybody was fine. Except for the deer. That poor thing was done for.

Mia stood next to the police car, wrapped in a fleece blanket and Carli's arms, while two officers were inspecting the minivan with flashlights. A light drizzle had started to fall, mixed with minuscule snowflakes.

"You hanging in there?" he asked a sniffling Mia. She nodded.

"You hanging in there, too?" he asked Carli, who gave him a weak smile and a tiny nod of her head. If he'd had another blanket, he might've wrapped *her* up in it, but there wasn't one, and for the moment, the kids were the top priority. He talked to the police and confirmed that the car was going nowhere without some roadside assistance. They all gave their names, and both Mia and Ethan explained their version of events, which was basically the same as they'd told Ben and Carli. A policeman with a bushy mustache and wire-rimmed glasses took some notes on a small pad of paper, took Mia's license, and then got back into his car while the other officer shined a flashlight at the carcass of Bambi's mother.

"You folks like venison?" he asked, his tone light, and Mia burst into tears once more.

"No, I don't like venison. I'm a vegan," she wailed. Carli looked toward Ben, and he was relieved to see a tiny, indulgent smile at the corner of her mouth as she rubbed her hands up and down Mia's back.

Chapter 27

The ride home in the Uber was mostly silent, with Mia tucked in between Ben and Carli in the back seat and her head on Carli's shoulder, and tall, lanky Ethan in the front. It was raining in earnest now, the sound of it drumming upon the roof of the car, and Carli was grateful that it had held off until they were on their way home. The only thing that might have made the last half an hour more miserable would've been an icy-cold rain. She was grateful for Ben, too. He'd talked to the police and dealt with getting a tow truck arranged. He'd helped her get Mia's belongings from the demolished minivan and load them into the trunk of the Uber, and he'd reassured Mia that there was nothing she could've done differently to have avoided hitting the deer. Ethan backed him up on that.

"You were just doing your thing, Mia," Ethan had said. "One minute the road was clear and the next minute, bam, there he was. Like a Patronus."

"If he was a Patronus, I could've driven right through him," she'd responded, but his words had seemed to soothe the remorse she felt over her involuntary deer-slaughter. His Harry Potter reference even made her smile, and Carli had smiled, too, at the unlikely friendship blossoming between them. At one point she might've thought there was more to it—something romantic—except she'd overheard them the other day, talking about a different boy and a different girl, and vowing to help each other *get with them*. So they were allies as much as friends. Either way, Ethan brought out something in Mia that Carli liked to see. A buoyancy that had been missing since Steve left.

Oh damn. Steve. She needed to let him know what was happening. He had a right to know, of course, but involving him always made the simplest of things more complicated. She hadn't realized until he was gone just how much energy she expended trying to manage his expectations and his reactions to things. Maybe she'd call him tomorrow, once the drama had settled. Then again, if the situation were reversed, she'd want to know immediately. She opted to send a quick text.

Everything is handled but Mia hit a deer. She's fine. The van not so much. I'll call you tomorrow.

After a short ride, the Uber dropped them off in Carli's driveway, and the kids went inside their respective houses while Carli stood outside, waiting as Ben quietly insisted that the driver accept some money.

"I told you. I've got kids of my own, so this ride was just a favor, parent to parent," the guy said.

"Well, if you've got kids, then I know how much you can use this cash. Thanks for helping us out tonight," Ben said.

In the end, the driver relented, accepting graciously. "Okay, then. I'll give this to the wife. I'm sure she'll have it spent before it even touches her hand. You folks enjoy the rest of your night. What's left of it, anyway." He put the car in reverse, and they watched him back out and drive away, his red taillights glowing like cinders in the darkness.

Then Ben turned to look at her, and she looked up at him, her heart tumbling around inside her rib cage, spurred on by adrenaline and too many emotions to categorize.

"Well," he said after a moment. "That was quite a night."

"Yes. It certainly was. Thanks for your help with everything," she answered. "Not sure I could've managed without you."

The rain had changed back to a light snow, and the streetlamps in their neighborhood were far brighter than those near the accident, so she could see him clearly, although she couldn't quite make out the expression on his face.

"I'm sure you would've managed just fine. I didn't do much." He shrugged.

"Of course you did. You called the tow truck and got the Uber and talked to the police. And kept me from losing my mind during the drive. That was a big one." She let out a nervous chuckle and was suddenly overcome with fatigue and the need to sit down for a nice long cry, which turned that chuckle into a bit of a catch in her throat. Ben stepped forward and wrapped her in his arms. And how she needed that—his solidness, his warmth, his support. She leaned in, wrapping her arms around his waist. Her cheek was pressed against the damp wool of his jacket, and she wondered, if she looked up at him, would he kiss her? She wanted him to. And she kind of thought he wanted to kiss her, too. But then her phone growled like Chewbacca, her ringtone for Steve.

"Shit," she muttered against Ben's lapel. "I texted Steve about the accident. I told him I'd call tomorrow, but I should probably talk to him now."

"Hm," Ben said, not moving his arms. She stayed where she was for another fifteen seconds, the best fifteen seconds she'd had in a very long time, then she reluctantly stepped back.

"I suppose you should call him," he said. "I'm sure he's worried."

"Fifty bucks says the first thing he'll ask about is the car."

"I think I'll pass on that bet, but let's hope you're wrong."

"Yeah, let's hope." Her phone started to roar again, and she pulled it from her purse. "Really have to take this call. Good night, Ben. And thanks again."

"Good night, Carli." He turned and walked slowly toward his house.

∽

Well, that was disappointing. The whole night had been a clusterfuck, in fact. First, she'd avoided him at the first two bars, although why, he had no idea. And when he finally did corner her, Ethan had called. The accident was no one's fault, of course, and that would've been enough to derail any evening, but Steve calling just now? That was just plain bad luck. Ben had been enjoying the hug. He'd wanted it to last longer, and truth be told, some kissing would've been nice.

Three more dates over the past two weeks had proven to Ben that there wasn't much point in trying to purge Carli from his system. The only way to deal with his infatuation with her was to face it head-on and see if it developed into something more. That would require some participation from her, of course, or at least a very firm rejection. But life had gotten busy for the both of them, and even though they lived next door to each other, she seemed more elusive than ever. She'd been doing lots of on-location segments lately. He knew that because he watched her show every morning, and because he saw her car coming and going at all hours.

Next week, he'd be back to work at Chase Industries as the new vice president of green technologies. Along with today's divorce settlement, he'd also made all the final arrangements to sell his shares of his company to Doug. It was a momentous step, and Ben had thought he'd feel a crushing sense of failure or disappointment when he signed all those legal documents—ending his marriage, relinquishing his company ownership, and effectively ending his relationships with both Sophia and Doug—but oddly enough, he hadn't felt anything at all. Not doom or sadness or regret. Not joy or relief, either. Just a mild sense of . . . freedom, like waking up on a Sunday morning with literally nothing to do and wondering how you might best fill your day. Not that he could ever remember a Sunday like that, but he could imagine.

"Well, that sucked," Ethan said as Ben walked into the kitchen. He was standing next to the refrigerator, drinking orange juice from the container, which he wasn't supposed to do. But given the events of the evening, Ben would let it go.

"Yes, it did." Ben was pretty sure they were thinking about two different things. "I'm just glad it wasn't worse. I'm proud of you for handling it so well." He took off his coat and hung it on a chair.

Ethan shrugged. "Thanks. I thought we did okay, but Mia was freaking out about what her dad was going to say, so thanks for not being *that* guy."

Ben had heard enough stories about Steve to be very glad he wasn't *that* guy, and he wondered how Carli was faring with him on the phone right now. That pesky need to protect her engulfed him once more, and he wondered where it came from. He'd never really felt that with Sophia, but for Carli? Well, he did, and it was ironic, because Carli could handle most stuff by herself. Except for maybe when she lost her keys.

Chapter 28

"Nolan Hart? Are you serious?" Tess's elation was palpable, convincing Carli that, although the pile of gifts under the tree didn't have quite the bulk that her kids were used to, she'd still managed to pull off a pretty good Christmas. The house was decorated from the rugs to the rafters, including a hefty-size tree that she and the girls had managed to put up themselves. There were gingerbread men and presents and carols playing softly in the background. And for the concert tickets, their one big present, she'd done the whole gift-wrapped box inside another gift-wrapped box in order to make this one take longer to open, and from the reaction she was getting, the suspense was worth the end result.

"I'm sorry I couldn't get us seats closer to the stage," Carli said. "There weren't many tickets to begin with, and the resale ones for the decent seats are crazy expensive."

"These are awesome, Mom," Tess said immediately, hopping up from her spot next to the tree and giving her a rib-crushing hug, her eyes bright with excitement, her cheeks flushed. "These seats are perfect. Just being at the concert at all is going to be amazing, and I know how hard tickets are to get. Most of his shows sell out in like five minutes."

Mia's smile was equally bright. "The only thing I'm bummed about is that it's not until January. I wish it was tomorrow."

"Oh my gosh! Me too!" Tess said. "What are we going to wear?"

Carli laughed and said, "If you open up the rest of the packages, maybe you'll find something."

"Maybe you should look under the tree, Mom," Mia said. "There are a couple things for you, too."

"For me?" She'd secretly wanted some presents, because honestly, who didn't? But she hadn't expected anything, because the kids had always gone shopping with their dad to get her something. But he'd been *too busy* to take them this year, and then he'd left for vacation in frickin' Aruba with that stick figure of a girlfriend. *Whoops. So much for Christmas spirit!*

Tess handed her a gift bag with a big red bow stuck to the side. "Open this one. It's from me, and it's something we can share."

Carli chuckled, because only a teenage girl would give you something that she wanted half of and consider it a present. Inside the bag was a set of key chains shaped like llamas. One said MOMMA LLAMA on the side—the other said DRAMA LLAMA.

"Guess which one is for me and which one is for you?" Tess asked with a giggle.

"I think either would suit me, but I guess I'll use the Momma Llama one. Thank you, honey." She leaned over and kissed Tess's cheek.

"I got us something to share, too," Mia said, handing her another bag. This one was silver with gold ribbons that Mia had taken the time to twist into intricate loops. "And it's a two-part present. Open it and then I'll tell you what it's for." Mia sat down on the arm of Carli's chair.

Carli untwisted the ribbons to open the bag and found two burgundy-colored, leather-bound journals along with some stickers and a handful of markers.

"Journals," Carli said with a smile. "They're beautiful. And pretty self-explanatory. I think I can figure out how to use them."

"These aren't just any journals, though. I read this article about a mom and a daughter who each had a journal," Mia said. "And they'd each write stuff in one, and then they'd swap and write in the other one.

Kind of like a conversation but not exactly, and I was thinking that, you know, since I'll be going away to school next year, maybe we could use the journals to keep in touch. I mean, when we can't just talk on the phone, of course."

Carli felt her eyes well up at the thoughtfulness of the gift. "Oh, I love this idea!"

"Do you? Oh, I'm so glad. This mom and daughter that I read about, they did this for, like, decades. The daughter, like, lived in Paris or something, and so they'd have to mail it back and forth, and the mom said she'd read it whenever she was missing her."

That tugged at Carli's heart, because she would miss Mia next year. She'd gotten acceptance letters from virtually all the colleges she'd applied to, even the University of Michigan, and with each one, Carli felt a wave of pride quickly followed by a wave of inevitability. Her baby birds would have to leave the nest, and she'd just have to deal with it. But not today. Today was for celebrating their family Christmas.

"Now here's the next part." Mia handed her an unmarked envelope, but before Carli could even break the seal, Mia exclaimed, "Guess who got a full-ride scholarship to Fairfield College? This girl!"

"A full ride—" How was that even possible? "I didn't even know you'd applied for a scholarship."

"Well, I did. And I got it. It's based on your grades, and I had to write, like, four different essays and get letters from my teachers, but they must've all said nice stuff about me, because I got it. I've known for a while now, but I was keeping it a secret until today so I could surprise you. Merry Christmas. Looks like I'll get to go to college!"

Mia leaned over and hugged Carli around the neck, and she almost couldn't breathe, but she wasn't sure if that was from the angle of the squeeze or because Fairfield College was six hours away.

"I'm so proud of you, Mia," Carli said, gasping a little from lack of oxygen until Mia let her loose. "Have you decided that Fairfield is where you want to go?"

"Maybe? I like that it's all paid for, don't you?"

"I just want you to go wherever you'll be the happiest." Now the gift of the journals made even more sense. And if that's where Mia wanted to go, Carli wouldn't dissuade her, but damn, that was far away. Maybe Carli should've listened to Steve and pushed Mia toward U of M, since it was only half an hour from where they lived. And she had been accepted there, too.

Mia shrugged. "I don't have to decide today. It's just fun knowing I could go someplace for free."

After opening presents and having an enormous brunch that ended with candy from their stockings, Mia and Tess modeled their new outfits, then they all spent the day watching Christmas movies and giggling over silly things. Carli wanted to soak up every moment. She was filled with nostalgia, and although it was strange celebrating without Steve, it wasn't awful. She suspected the girls were working hard to keep their focus on all that they had rather than the things they were missing, and she was proud of them both.

Late in the afternoon, Carli texted her dad a simple Happy Holidays, and he responded a few hours later with a basic Same to you, kiddo, but from Ben she got a Merry Christmas followed by no fewer than two dozen emojis from snowmen to Santa to presents to angels. He'd taken Addie and Ethan to Colorado for a big Chase-family Christmas with their extended relatives, and she couldn't deny she missed him. They hadn't had any time to connect since the night of the deer incident, because he'd gone to work at Chase Industries and she was preoccupied with other things. There'd been a friendly text here and there, but nothing that hinted at anything significant, and she wondered if all the feelings she'd had brewing since the Holly Trolley were just her imagination trying to create romance where none existed.

Regardless, she was looking forward to him getting back to Michigan. And maybe if she played her cards right, she could get him under the mistletoe.

Chapter 29

New Year's Eve had never been Carli's favorite. There was too much pressure to have the *best night ever*. Sometimes it happened and then it was great, but more often than not either she or Steve, or both of them, drank too much and suffered through the next day in cotton-mouthed misery. A brutal hangover was no way to kick off a new year, and she had no intentions of overimbibing tonight, even though she did have a lot to celebrate. Getting through the past twelve months was a major victory, a year full of deep lows but also high achievements, and she'd decided to focus on the latter.

Now it was December 31, the eve of the new year, and it felt as if she was on the eve of a new self, too. Not just a new job, but a new career. A new attitude. She was learning and growing, and if nothing else, she knew the coming year couldn't possibly be as emotionally draining as the last. And if it was, somehow? Well, she'd manage.

She put on her sparkly red top and dangly earrings and looked into the mirror, feeling pretty damn good. The only cloud over the evening was the fact that Ben was still in Colorado, so there was no chance of a kiss at midnight. Not even from her kids, who were begrudgingly spending the weekend with Steve and Jade, no doubt tanned and relaxed from their tropical vacation. Too bad for them, because they were about to miss a very fun evening.

The Fifteenth Annual Monroe Circle Progressive New Year's Eve Party would start at DeeDee's at 8:00 p.m. before moving on to Renee's at 9:00 p.m. and end up at 11:00 p.m. at Erin's, where they could all watch the ball drop. Carli planned to go, mix, mingle, have one or two drinks, and be back home in bed by 12:05 a.m., and when the rest of her friends felt miserable tomorrow, she'd be feeling fantastic.

That was the plan, anyway. DeeDee greeted her at the door with an effusive hug that nearly knocked Carli right off the front step.

"Oh, I'm so glad you're here. I wasn't sure we'd see you tonight."

Carli's general lack of enthusiasm for this particular night of forced revelry was well-known, and there had been a few times she'd skipped it altogether.

"Yep, here I am." She took off her coat and hung it up in the front hall closet. "Do you need help with anything?"

"No, I'm just taking care of a few things in the kitchen that still need setting up. You sure you're good?" DeeDee squeezed her shoulder.

"Yeah, I'm fine. Totally fine. You do what you need to do, and I'll get myself a drink."

"Is that Carli?" Renee came around the corner and gathered her into a hug that rivaled DeeDee's. Girlfriends were feeling the love tonight. Maybe they'd already started drinking, which was a bad sign. If ever there was a night to pace yourself, it was New Year's Eve.

"I'm so glad you're here," Renee said, squeezing her a second time. "What a day, huh? Kind of a rough one, I guess. How are you holding up?" Renee's voice was full of compassion, and Carli wondered if her low opinion of New Year's Eve was really *that* obvious.

"I'm hanging in there," Carli said, smiling.

Erin came from the kitchen next, and Carli got another warm hug. So much love. So much. She felt a rush of gratitude for her friends. They were really coming through for her today, and it was a good feeling.

"How are the kids handling everything?" Renee asked.

"They're okay. Christmas was really nice for us, even though, you know, Steve took Jade on that big vacation, and now they're sort of bummed to be stuck at his place this weekend. They didn't want to go, but he was pretty adamant about it. Typical Steve. You'd think he'd understand that sixteen- and eighteen-year-old girls have better things to do than spend New Year's Eve with their dad, but you know him. World revolves around his needs, and all that."

Renee and Erin exchanged glances, and Carli felt a flutter of unease. She made a mental note to be more positive. It was a party, after all, and her new year's resolution was going to be to focus on the positive. DeeDee came back from the kitchen, and they caught her eye, waving her over. Kind of insistently, in fact. Wow, it was just one little comment. They'd all said worse about her ex, but suddenly they were all gazing at her with various levels of concern on their faces, and her stomach took a nosedive into the deepest pit of the deepest pit.

"What?" she asked. Good grief. *Please don't have this be some kind of an intervention.* She just wanted to have a couple of drinks and a nice evening.

"Let's go in the den," Erin said, weaving her arm around Carli's shoulders. Once in the smaller room, they gathered around her, and whatever was on their collective minds, it didn't seem good.

"You guys are freaking me out. What the fuck?" Carli said as DeeDee closed the door behind them.

"Maybe you should sit down," Renee said, laying a hand on her shoulder.

"Or maybe I should stand and you guys can tell me what's up. Why are you all looking at me like that?"

"Do you not know why Steve wanted the girls with him this weekend?" Renee asked.

"Um, yeah, I know why he wanted them. It's because he's been gone for two weeks and he missed Christmas, so now he wants to celebrate with them." *Not that complicated.*

They exchanged more emotionally charged glances, and Carli's gut took another dive.

"Seriously, you guys need to tell me what the hell is going on. You're all looking at me like you've got my terminal test results or something."

DeeDee had pulled her phone from her pocket and tapped on the screen while Carli was talking, then slowly handed it over to her. Carli noticed her own hand trembling, although she didn't know why, and when she looked at the picture on the phone, the rest of her started trembling, too. All the air left her lungs. And the room. And the planet. It was a photo of Steve in his favorite black suit. And Jade in a short white dress. And a veil. A veil? Her vision was suddenly too blurry to read the caption, and her stomach filled with hot lava that very much wanted to erupt up and out.

She stared back at the concerned faces of her friends. "Did he . . . did he marry her?"

Erin nodded. "I'm so sorry, honey. Apparently, they got married in Aruba, but they posted this picture about an hour ago. There are a bunch more of the wedding and a couple from tonight. It looks like they planned a New Year's Eve party and then surprised everyone when they arrived and told them it was a reception. None of us knew about this, though. It must just be her friends who got invited."

Where was the oxygen? Seriously? Where was it?

"He's only been dating her for, like, two months. What the hell is he thinking? He can't marry her. Oh good Lord, when do you think my kids found out?" The floor started to wobble, or maybe that was her legs. She really had no idea, and she fell down into the chair.

There were so many questions and emotions erupting all at once, Carli thought her head would explode, but above all else, she wondered how Mia and Tess were handling this news. This was big! And there was no way they could've known before tonight. He must have sprung it on them as a *surprise. Surprise!* You have a new stepmom. *Surprise!* I know you don't know her at all, but she's going to be in our lives now. *Surprise!* I'm an insensitive asshole. Oh, wait. That last part was no surprise at all.

"For what it's worth," DeeDee said, "you're way prettier."

"And way smarter," Renee added.

"And much stronger," Erin chimed in. "And better off."

Carli was better off. She knew that, deep down, but there was a lot to unpack from this situation. How was she supposed to feel? She didn't even know. She was sweaty and cold and confused and incredulous. Steve's life was Steve's life, but this impacted her kids, and they deserved better. And it was all so spontaneous and impulsive and stupid.

"I need to text my kids," she said breathlessly. "Can someone get my purse?"

DeeDee was back with it in a flash, or maybe it had taken her an hour. Carli couldn't really tell, because time was frozen and meaningless. Her heart ached, but she wasn't sure why. Her thumbs were clumsy, but she managed to send a message to Mia and Tess. It simply said, I've heard the news about Dad and Jade. I love you both very much. Call me if you need to.

"So what do you want to do now?" Renee asked gently. "You can stay here and get royally shitfaced, which I think is your best option. Or if you want, I'll go back to your place with you and we can eat ice cream and call Steve every vile thing we can think of. What do you need?"

"Shitfaced," Carli answered emphatically. "I definitely need to get shitfaced."

⁓

"Thanks for bringing me back a few days early, Dad," Ethan said as Ben left the airport parking structure and eased their way into the evening

Glenville traffic. Addie was still in Colorado and would fly home with his parents the day after tomorrow, but he and Ethan had traveled home today because, at eighteen years old, his son had a *major party* to go to. Ben let him think it was a generous offer, coming home sooner than expected, but the truth was, Ben wanted to return to Glenville, too.

Maybe his neighbors had made a Monroe Circle–ite out of him after all, because he'd chosen to leave his family vacation early just so he could go to something called a progressive, and if he understood things correctly, that meant his neighbors would travel from house to house throughout the evening, drinking and partying. That seemed like a poor choice for December in Michigan, but whatever. It's where Carli was. So it's where he wanted to be as well.

He took a fast shower at home and dressed in record time, noting from his watch it was already almost 10:00 p.m. According to the red flyer with sparkly gold lettering sitting on his kitchen counter, they should all be at Renee's house right now. Perfect. That was just down the street.

Carli was just this side of tipsy by the time he arrived, and she greeted him with a tight, full-body hug that lasted long enough to leave him feeling both breathless and restless. It took all his willpower not to keep his arms around her and just kiss her then and there. But according to the rules of New Year's Eve, he'd have to wait until midnight and the strains of "Auld Lang Syne." She was wearing a silky red top that had a shimmer to it, and when she leaned forward toward him, he could see her lacy bra. He felt like a fifteen-year-old boy, thoroughly captivated by something so innocent and yet so dangerously alluring at the same time. This was going to be a long night, even if it was already ten o'clock.

He needed a drink. A strong one. He made the rounds, saying hi to various neighbors who'd become his friends, and poured himself a tidy vodka tonic, all the while keeping Carli in his line of vision. Her cheeks were flushed, and she was laughing very hard at something Erin had said. It made him warm all over, and he wondered if by some miraculous chance they'd finally have a moment tonight. It was crowded, and everyone in this group knew virtually everyone else, so catching her privately was going to require some strategy, but he was up for the challenge.

He got his chance about fifteen minutes later, when she walked into the empty living room, where all the coats were piled high on top of a sofa.

"Hi," he said, coming up behind her as she stared out the front window.

She turned too quickly, and her drink splashed. She didn't seem to notice, though, and he wondered how many of those she'd had. No judgment. It was New Year's Eve, after all.

"Hi," she said a bit too loudly. Then her voice lowered as she leaned toward him and tapped her chest with her index finger. "Guess what?"

"What?" he asked while thinking that sloppy Carli was kind of cute. She moved closer still, and he dipped his head to hear her better.

"Steve got married in a Roomba."

"What?"

"A Roomba. I mean, he got married in Aruba."

She said Aruba like *ah-rooooooo-bah*, tilting as she spoke, and Ben realized Carli wasn't a little drunk. Carli was very, very drunk. And no wonder. When he'd found out about Sophia and Doug, he'd drunk an entire barrel of whisky.

"Steve? As in your Steve?"

She shook her head and took a gulp of her drink, tilting back to the other side. "Not my Steve anymore. That's for sure."

"Wow. That's . . . wow. I'm not even sure what to say about that." Other than, *what a douchebag*. Ben knew from Carli that Steve had just met that woman a few months ago. Or was it weeks? Either way, not long enough to marry.

She leaned forward again. "Do you know what I say about that?"

"What?" He smiled, because she really was adorable this way, but his heart twisted, too, because he knew she was upset. Who wouldn't be?

Carli gave a big, overly animated nod of her head and poked him in the chest again. "I say that you and I should go back to my place."

His smile froze. *Fuuuuuuuuuuuck. Fuck, fuck, fuck.* This was his moment. His chance to kiss her and see where it led. To touch her skin and taste her mouth and do all the things he'd been thinking about doing since the first time he'd seen her standing in his yard with her dog. But . . . she was drunk. As in *very, very*, and there were very specific rules about such things. Yes, he wanted to kiss her, and yes, he wanted to take her to bed, but if she'd just heard that her ex had eloped, she probably wasn't thinking all that clearly. He didn't want to be somebody's drunken mistake. Especially not Carli's.

Or did he? The devil on his shoulder poked a searing pitchfork into his brain as Ben contemplated his answer. Take her home and rock her world? Or take her home and put her to bed, alone, while she slept this one off? This was not a dilemma he wanted to face, especially since every nerve in his body wanted to agree with her. Damn his moral compass.

Carli sensed his hesitation and straightened her shoulders so abruptly that she spilled her drink again. Her sassy grin evaporated as a slightly horrified expression took hold.

"Or not. Just kidding." She tried to smile, but it didn't take. She'd misunderstood his delayed response, thinking he didn't want to because he didn't want *her*, but nothing could be further from the truth. He did want her. He just wanted her clear minded when she made the offer, because if they took that step, and she regretted it in the morning, he'd never forgive himself. Could he tell her to go have a cup of coffee and sober up a bit and ask him again in an hour?

He reached out to take her arm, but she twisted to the side with an uncomfortable laugh.

"Carli," he said quietly. "I would. Honestly, there's nothing I would like more than to go to your place, but I'm not sure you really mean it right now."

"You're right. I didn't really mean it. I just figured, you know? What the hell? Two consenting adults on New Year's Eve? But that's okay. I get it."

But she didn't get it. Not at all. He was doing the right thing here, so why did he feel like such a shithead for turning her down?

"No, you don't get it, Carli. It's not that I don't want to. It's just that—" He was going to say it was just that she wasn't thinking clearly because of the alcohol, but drunk people rarely realize that they're drunk, and he doubted his explanation would erase the embarrassment on her face. She interrupted him by holding up her hand.

"Hey, no means no, you know? It's okay. Maybe you should go party with yellow Volkswagen girl. Do you want another drink? I think I'm going to get another drink."

The Volkswagen comment surprised him, and Carli moved away before he could stop her, but he decided right then and there that this was not how their night was going to end. He followed a few paces behind and caught hold of her wrist, stopping her as she entered the dining room. She looked back, her frown turning to uncertainty as he took the glass from her unresisting hand and set it on the table. Fortunately, there was no one there to see them.

"Follow me," he said quietly, tugging her along down the hall as if he knew what he was doing. As if his heart weren't hammering in his chest and all the blood in his body weren't crackling through his veins like electrical currents.

The layout of this house was nearly the same as his, and if he was lucky, then there should be a laundry room through the second door on the left. He twisted the knob, and no, not a laundry room. More like an office, but it was empty, so he pulled her in behind him and shut the door. She fell against it and looked up at him. A night-light in the corner gave the room a bluish glow, and her eyes were dark and mysterious, her lips lush and begging for a kiss.

He cupped her jaw in his hands, and she sighed, putting her hands on his waist.

"God, you're pretty," he said. Then he kissed her, and his world fell away.

○⊃

Carli was pretty sure it wasn't midnight, pretty sure there'd been no countdown, and pretty sure she was in Renee's craft room right now. But what she knew for certain was that she was, at this very minute, being wonderfully and thoroughly kissed by Ben in a way that made her knees turn to water and her heart turn to fire. His hair was as soft as she'd imagined, but everything else about him was firm, from the muscles under his shirt to the determined way he wrapped his arms around her body. She melted against him as his mouth captured hers, and she tried to remember what they'd just been talking about. Not that it really mattered. All that mattered was the feel of him, the heat and the urgency. She wanted more. Lots more.

Fuck Steve and his young, skinny bride and their surprise wedding. Fuck him and his fancy, low-maintenance condo and his monochrome décor and his dog-free life. Carli had everything she needed right here. She had Ben. She reached down between them, rubbing her hand against his zipper, and he groaned deep in his throat. Her senses reeled, because Renee had been right. Ben Chase had some big tricks in those pants of his. And Carli wanted to know more. With her other hand, she reached down and tugged at the waistband of his jeans, trying to undo the button, but he stopped kissing her and looked down at her face.

"Not here," he whispered, his voice raspy and seductive.

"Yes, here."

"Seriously?"

Why was he arguing with her?

She pulled at the tab of his zipper, and Ben gave up another sexy growl of surprise.

"Yes. Seriously," she said. "Right here. Right now."

Chapter 30

Carli had long believed that waking up with a hangover was the worst way to greet a new year. Now she realized there was something even worse. Waking up covered in shame. And embarrassment. Oh, holy hell, the embarrassment! She'd thrown herself at Ben like some desperate, horny sorority girl at her first kegger. He hadn't even wanted to at first. She'd had to *convince* him. Her stomach roiled, and her head throbbed. She should never, ever drink tequila. She *knew* that, but she'd drunk it anyway. Her mouth tasted so bad she wanted to shower in Listerine. Had she eaten the worm from the tequila? She must have. And all because Steve went to Aruba and got married.

Now it was *sometime* in the morning, judging by the wintry light coming in the window of her room, and she was bent like a pretzel, perched on the farthest edge of her bed, immobilized by the twisted sheets and something even worse. Her arm was numb, and she couldn't straighten out her legs because something, or *someone*, was pressed up against her and lying almost diagonally across the bed. It was time to pray to whatever patron saint was in charge of regrettable actions that the immovable object was Gus and not Ben. Of course, she wasn't Catholic, so her prayers might not make it to the right saint, but it was worth a shot because she desperately needed Ben to be gone. She simply couldn't face him. Not yet. Maybe not ever.

She tried in vain to nudge the obstacle with her foot, hoping she might hear the jangle of Gus's dog tags, but no. Against all instincts of self-preservation, she slowly opened one eye, and a fresh wave of humiliation flooded over her. Because her worst fears were confirmed. Ben Chase was in bed next to her, and Gus was sprawled on the other side of the bed, his long doggie legs stretched out to their full length, all but pushing Ben in her direction. That damn dog was seriously going to have to start sleeping in his crate.

How had this happened? What on earth had she done? Chunks of the night were missing from her memory. There'd been the news of Steve's elopement, of course, and then some drinks. And a few more drinks. There'd been shots of peppermint schnapps and shots of Fireball whisky, all of which were currently churning in her gut. She remembered seeing Ben arrive, and then . . . Her skin heated up as visions cascaded through her mind. She remembered inviting him to her place, running her hands through his hair and tugging at his clothes in—oh God!—in Renee's craft room. Holy hell. If Renee ever found out that Carli and Ben had fooled around in her beloved craft room, it would be the end of their friendship. But had they? That part was foggy in her mind. There'd been kissing, after she'd all but begged him, and she had a vague memory of him pressing her against a wall, and she may have stuck her hand down his pants . . . but she might have just imagined that part, too, because she distinctly recalled him telling her no.

That was humiliating. Throwing herself at a man only to have him turn her down. But . . . if he'd turned her down, why was he next to her in the bed? And why was she wearing her sexy-time nightgown? The one she used to wear when she still cared if Steve noticed her? The one that had been jammed into the back corner of a drawer for the past ten years? Her heart started skipping every other beat as anxiety took hold. She remembered being in the cold and Ben walking beside her, back to her house. He'd kissed her in the doorway of her room. She remembered that clearly, because he'd said something about the dog being in the bed. And then . . . nothing. She couldn't remember what happened after that. All she knew for sure was that Ben was lying next to her. And she needed him to leave. He had to get out of her house and back to his own without Lynette from across the street spotting him. And she needed to call Mia and Tess and see how they were doing this morning because they'd started off their new year with a stepmother.

First things first. She needed to wake up Ben and used the only means available.

"Hey," she said softly, gently tapping him with her elbow. He was flat on his back and didn't stir. If she hadn't been so consumed with confusion and regret, she might have taken a moment to appreciate the muscles of his chest. She had a vague memory of running her hands over them at some point, and she'd liked it. Her bare skin flushed, and she shoved the thoughts away.

"Hey," she said more loudly, not-so-gently jabbing him with that same elbow. That time it worked. His eyes opened, and he scrubbed a hand across his face as Gus lifted his head.

"Hi," he said, his voice raspy, his lips tilting into an awkward smile.

"Hi," she said, avoiding his eyes and pulling at the sheets as if that would miraculously make her less vulnerable.

"Um . . . happy New Year," he said, the awkward smile turning into a full-on grin. She did not have time for that. Not right now.

"Sure. Um, listen, I don't mean to be rude or anything, but you've got to get the hell out of here."

"Why? I happen to know you have zero plans today."

"How do you know that?"

"Because you told me, along with a lot of other stuff. You're a very chatty drunk."

"Oh God. Could you just please go home?"

He rolled over to his side, but at least the dog moved, too, so Carli could straighten her legs. They began to prickle all over as the blood started to circulate once more, but the discomfort in her limbs was nothing compared to the discomfort in her chest.

"*Now* you want me to go home?" he said.

"Yes."

"You sure didn't want me to go home last night." He was obviously teasing her, but she was in no mood for it. Once the booze cleared her system, she'd certainly remember all the grisly, gory details from last night, and that suited her just fine. She didn't need him taunting her.

"Well . . . last night was last night and now is now, and right now I need you to leave."

"Okay," he said slowly, "but I'm not sure if I can find my pants. I think you threw them somewhere over there." He gestured to the corner of the room, and her cheeks burned.

There was no part of her brain that remembered that. She didn't remember either of them getting undressed, or what happened after that. Just her luck. Carli may have gotten laid for the first time in over a year, and she couldn't even remember it.

"Gus," he said, pushing at the dog. "Get up, lazy hound."

The dog moved in slow motion, relocating to the end of the bed and curling up into a ball with a big, doggie sigh, as if they were really interrupting his twenty-two hours of sleep. Ben rose from the bed, and she felt a molecule of relief that he was wearing underwear. The stretchy knit kind that did wonders for his ass. He walked a few feet from the bed and picked up his pants before turning to face her. His hair was messy, making him look more like Ethan than ever, but the stubble on his face was all Ben. Mature, sexy, attractive. No wonder she'd thrown herself at him.

He put one leg into his jeans and said, "So about last night—" But his words were cut off by a rattling sound, and Carli's life flashed before her eyes in the span of a split second before her bedroom door swung open . . . and there stood Mia and Tess.

"Mom?" Mia exclaimed, eyes going wide.

"Mr. Chase?" Tess gasped, eyes going even wider before she clapped a hand over them and squeaked in dismay.

The moment hung suspended as Carli looked to Mia, to Tess, to Ben, and then back to Mia. Her older daughter's expression turned from shock to a scowl before she spun around on her heel and shouted, "Jesus H. Christ! What the fuck is wrong with all the grown-ups these days?"

Chapter 31

He hadn't meant to take it that far. Ben had thought he could just kiss her in that room at the party and that would be that. Maybe they'd go back to her place for a bit more *kissing*, because she was in no frame of mind to be making any sort of decisions, but then Carli had kissed him back and his heart nearly stopped in his chest. And then she'd wrapped her leg around his and unzipped his pants, and he'd been lost. And now, just what he feared would happen had happened. They'd landed in bed and now she regretted it.

Of course, they hadn't actually *done* anything.

She'd wanted to. That much was crystal clear, and he should receive some kind of medal of valor or something for being able to resist, because he'd wanted her, too. Hot damn, he'd wanted her, but she was drunk and he wasn't, and he also wasn't willing to ruin his long-term chance with her by taking advantage of the situation.

After kissing at Renee's, they'd left the room only to discover that everyone else had already gone to the next house, so his honorable intention was to walk her home and leave her at her front doorstep. Or maybe tuck her into bed just to make sure she got there, but Gus had needed to go out to pee. So he took her dog for a walk, and by the time he got back, she was wearing a flimsy nightgown and invited him to stay.

Seriously, the biggest medal of honor. That's what he deserved. And some kind of honorary priesthood, because the nightgown was sheer and silky and merely seeing her in it had just about pushed him over the edge. But she was still tilting back and forth and talking about Steve and his wedding and her kids and her impending empty nest. So even if her body was saying *Come and get it*, her words were every sort of buzzkill. She wasn't really looking for sex. She was looking for comfort, and as much as he was willing to accommodate her in that department, if they'd had sex, she'd have been mad at him this morning.

Then again, she was mad at him anyway. When all they'd done was *talk*. Of course, getting caught by her kids had been the worst luck imaginable. She'd jumped from the bed, put on the thickest, most grannyesque robe he'd ever seen, and started throwing his clothes at him. He'd walked home barefoot through the snow, wearing nothing but his jeans and his jacket and carrying the rest. Then he'd walked in his front door only to discover Ethan waiting. Apparently, it had taken Mia all of thirty seconds to text him.

"I'm guessing you have some questions," Ben said to his son as he dried his ice-cold feet on a dish towel before pulling on his sweater.

"A couple," Ethan said dryly. "Because it seems to me you may have been drinking irresponsibly with Mrs. Lancaster last night. I've half a mind to ground you."

Ben cast a glance at his son, who had the shittiest of shit-eating grins on his face. "Is that all you've got?"

Ethan chuckled. "What do you want me to say, Dad? Mom's been hitting it with Doug for months now. I'm glad you're finally getting even."

Ben tossed the towel toward the laundry room. "What? No. No. That's not what this is, Ethan. God, I need a cup of coffee." He walked over to the counter to fire up his espresso maker, and Ethan followed, padding behind him in slippers and a robe over his flannel pajama pants.

"So what is it then?" Ethan asked, pulling some orange juice from the fridge and drinking it straight from the carton.

"Hey. Hey, use a cup, dude. Germs, remember?"

"Yeah, speaking of germs. Did you use a condom?"

Ben turned and stared at him. He could hardly take the moral high ground at the moment, having just done the walk of shame across his own front yard.

"Dude," he said again. "This situation is not exactly what it looks like, so I'm going to need you to go easy on me this morning, okay? I'm not really up for the snarky commentary."

"Fair enough." Ethan grabbed a glass from the cupboard and sat down at the table with the jug of orange juice. "But . . . can you at least explain how the heck you ended up in bed with Mrs. Lancaster?"

Ben added coffee and water to the coffee maker and pushed the necessary buttons before turning back to Ethan. "Look, I won't deny I was in bed with Carli, but I wasn't *in bed with her*, if you know what I mean."

Ethan shook his head. "No, sorry. I don't know what you mean."

"Nothing happened," Ben said decisively. Not because it was any of Ethan's business, but because Carli deserved some defense of her honor, such as it was. "Here's what you need to know," Ben continued. "I like Carli. I like her a lot. She got a little tipsy last night, and I stayed with her, but I kept my hands to myself, okay? And this has nothing to do with anything that's happened with me and your mom, other than the fact that we're no longer together. She's moved on with her life, and so now, I want to move on with mine."

"And is that going to include Mrs. Lancaster?"

Ben sat down heavily on one of the kitchen chairs. "Honestly? I don't know. I hope so, but . . . this morning was kind of rough. She seemed pretty bummed that Tess and Mia walked in on us, so I don't think she wants to see me right now."

"But them walking in wasn't your fault."

Ben sighed and leaned his elbows on the table. "Bit of advice about women, son. It doesn't need to be your fault for them to be really pissed at you. Sometimes they get mad at you for stuff you had absolutely nothing to do with."

"That's stupid."

"Well, so are most men, so it all balances out somehow. Plus, when the girls walked in, I may have been putting on my pants."

Ethan chuckled. "You didn't have on any pants?"

"My jeans were wet from walking the dog, so I took them off." Ben recognized the defensive tone in his voice as well as the absurdity of this entire conversation.

"You do realize that if I used that excuse, you'd lock me in my room, right?"

Ben nodded. "I do, but this is my story and I'm sticking to it."

"Okay, so, what are you going to do about Mrs. Lancaster being mad? I mean, if you like her, how do you make her stop being mad?"

"No idea, but I do know I need you to promise to keep all this to yourself. You can talk to Mia and Tess if you feel you need to, but don't say anything to Addie, and don't go telling all your friends. I need to keep this under wraps until I've had a chance to sit down with Carli and figure out where we're at."

"Cool," Ethan said. "Can I go back to bed now?"

"Sure." Ben got up and poured himself a cup of coffee, but as Ethan reached the door, he turned back and smiled.

"Hey, Dad?"

"Yeah?"

"For what it's worth, I think you and Mrs. Lancaster would be kind of a cool thing. She's pretty nice, and I know Addie likes her, too."

"Good to know. Thanks."

"Sure. And happy New Year."

"Yeah, you too."

Ethan shuffled off, and Ben pulled his phone from his pocket. He was beyond certain that Carli wouldn't take his call, but hopefully she'd at least read his text.

Hey. I'm sorry about this morning. I hope everything is okay with you and the kids. And for the record, you do realize nothing happened last night, right? Just some drinks and some sleep. Text me when you feel up to it. I think we need to talk.

Chapter 32

Carli read the text and wasn't sure it made her feel any better, and she didn't really want to talk to him. Not right now. And *why* hadn't they had sex? She remembered enough to know she'd been willing. Maybe he wasn't interested. Or maybe he was just a gentleman. Either way, her kids had seen him in her bedroom with no pants on, and that called for a conversation with her girls, as did the fact that Steve had gotten remarried. So far, the new year was not getting off to a very good start!

She took off her sexy-time nightie and threw it in the trash. She wasn't sure why she even still had the thing, and she sure as hell would never wear it again. She pulled on the softest sweatpants and top she could find, because her stomach was spinning like a riptide and all those shots were threatening to escape. She drank a glass of water in her bathroom and then went to find her traumatized offspring.

"Although Ben and I didn't take things too far, my actions last night are not the message I want to send to you two. I made a terrible mistake by drinking too much and not thinking about the consequences, and I don't want you to think that anything I did last night was acceptable," Carli said once they were all sitting in the family room.

"Excellent PSA, Mom. Don't get drunk and then not have sex with the neighbors," Mia said. "I think I can remember that."

"I think the real lesson here is that you should always lock your bedroom door," Tess added. "I, for one, know that I will never walk in again without knocking first."

Were they . . . were they teasing her? Carli prided herself on being the best mother ever, and this was the conversation she was now having? Don't have sex with neighbors? Or nearly have sex? That was her take-home message? Her alcohol-dehydrated brain was having a hard time discerning their tones. But she looked at them, and Tess was smiling, and Mia was bemused, and no one seemed nearly as traumatized as she'd expected. Except for herself, maybe. Carli was traumatized by virtually every aspect of last night and this morning.

"I'm confused," she finally said. "And to be quite honest, this is the worst hangover I've ever had. My life has become a cautionary tale for the two of you, and I'm not sure what to do next."

"Relax, Mom," Mia said. "We're fine. I mean, I definitely could've lived my whole life without seeing Mr. Chase in his underwear, but it's fine."

"It's seared into my retinas," Tess added, but her grin indicated she thought most of this was pretty damn funny. Not quite the reaction Carli was anticipating.

Mia continued. "And at least he's a good guy. I mean, he was really nice the night I hit the deer, and he was pretty cool when Tess and Ethan drank in the woods. You could've done way worse. Believe me. I have friends whose moms date some real derelicts, so if you and him want to, whatever, well, I guess I'm okay with it."

"I'm cool with it, too," Tess added. "Ethan's never going to ask me out, but at least this way he can be my stepbrother."

"Wait, wait, wait," Carli said, holding up her hands. "There will be no stepbrothers. Ben and I haven't even gone out on a date, and if we ever decide to, well, no stepbrothers. I have no intention of getting remarried."

"That's probably what Dad thought, and then Jade came along," Tess said, her grin disappearing.

"About that," Carli said. "I'm not in the best frame of mind to talk about this, but how was your night? I mean, were you . . . surprised?"

Mia nodded. "Yeah, we were basically stunned. And it kind of sucks, but mostly we were worried about how you might take the news. To be honest, judging from what I saw this morning, I can't tell if you took it really hard or took it really well."

Carli's head hurt, and she was exhausted and nauseous and embarrassed and ashamed. And she hadn't even had time to categorize her feelings about Steve's marriage. But one thing she did know? It hadn't destroyed her. It's not as if the two of them were ever, ever going to reconcile. And it's not as if they weren't both better off not being married to each other. Neither of them had been happy, and at least now, they could both move on. Steve was doing what he wanted, and now, so could she.

She just needed to figure out exactly what that was.

Chapter 33

Carli spent the next two weeks focusing on her job and trying to be an exemplary role model for her children. Although they'd said they were fine with the events of New Year's Eve, she knew by subtle comments they made that Steve's elopement and her bad judgment had left a mark. It was no wonder. They considered themselves mature, but Mia and Tess were dealing with big life issues from a teenage perspective, and that was hard. So she left them homemade granola and muffins every morning to make sure they'd have something to eat for breakfast before school so they'd know she was thinking about them. She made their favorite dinners and made sure their laundry was washed and folded and put away. She took care of all the dog chores, which she did most of the time anyway, but now she didn't even pester them to help. She'd even (finally) taught Gus to put his toys away in his basket. She didn't drink wine or swear or in any way display any sort of vice around them. And it was fucking exhausting.

None of her friends knew what had happened. Or had nearly happened, and Carli suspected they thought her overzealous attempts at being the perfect mom and homemaker had something to do with Steve's marriage, or maybe just her new year's resolutions. Renee liked this version of Carli, and they'd spent an entire day creating decorative labels for her spice jars. And then alphabetizing them.

But the whole time Carli was sitting in Renee's craft room, she felt guilty and awkward and embarrassed. Everything about that night was so out of character. The blackout drinking, the throwing herself at Ben, the discovery by her kids. If word got out in the neighborhood, she'd never live it down. And everyone would think she'd gone off the deep end just because Steve got married, and she didn't want anyone to think that mattered to her.

Ironically, the one person she probably should talk to about all this was Ben. But for some reason, she just wasn't ready. Because not all of that night was blocked from her memory. She had recalled a few things here and there. She remembered putting on her nightie and doing a little dance, lifting the hem to entice him. But all he'd done was wrap her in a throw blanket from the couch and get her a glass of water. And she remembered crying on his shoulder about how Steve had never found her special. Then, when Ben had tucked her into bed, she'd cried again and asked him to sleep with her. Just sleep. And he was such a good sport, he'd done it.

He'd sent her text messages every day, asking how she was. And she'd say she was fine and that she was busy and that she hoped he was having a nice day. But every time he said he thought they should talk, she ignored him. And she wanted to ignore him when he showed up on her doorstep that Thursday, too. But she also wanted to see him. Because she missed him.

It was a dilemma. She couldn't hide from him forever, so she opened the door and saw relief ripple over his handsome features. Because he was, you know, really frickin' handsome.

"Hi," he said, his voice a little breathless, as if he'd come from much farther than just next door. It was snowing behind him, and the wind blew right into her house. She'd have to let him in or freeze.

"Hi," she said with a shiver. "Come in."

He stepped inside but stayed on the rug by the front door. "Thanks. Um, I have something for you and the girls," he said. "I think you'll like it."

"Is it a time machine? Because I could really use one of those."

Ben chuckled, and the lines of tension on his face eased up. "Not a time machine. Sorry. But still good. You know that Nolan Hart concert you're taking Tess and Mia to this weekend? The one at the arena?"

"Yes."

"Well, I managed to upgrade your tickets a little bit. I know some people."

"You didn't have to do that."

"I wanted to. In fact, as soon as you'd told me where the concert was, it got my wheels turning. Like I said, I did this a couple of weeks ago. I got tickets for me and my kids, too, and I know you're upset about . . . stuff, but I hope you'll let me do this for you. And for Mia and Tess."

That was a mean trick. Making it about her kids so she couldn't say no.

"Thank you. That's very nice of you. I accept on their behalf."

A smile lit up his face, and she wondered how she'd ever found him unfriendly. "Awesome. I'll drive. Be ready to leave by two o'clock on Saturday."

"Two o'clock? The concert doesn't start until 7:00 p.m."

"You're right. It doesn't. But I thought the kids might enjoy getting a tour of the new arena. Addie, Ethan, and I are going to do it anyway, so you may as well join us. My kids will have more fun if Tess and Mia are with them. And honestly, I'll have more fun if you come, too. Please?"

How could she resist that?

"Okay. Two o'clock. Just a couple of friends and their kids going to a concert, right?"

"Sure," he said. "See you Saturday."

Chapter 34

"I thought you guys might want to check out one of the suites," Ben said after they'd visited the executive offices and the main lobby. "It's nothing fancy, but I figured we could grab a bite to eat before we go on the rest of the tour. Sound good?" Ben asked, leading them down a wide hallway full of oversize black doors with big metal numbers on them.

"This is already so cool," Tess said, nearly skipping next to Addie. "Thank you so much for bringing us."

"My pleasure," he said, pushing open a door, and Carli was halfway inside before she realized the sign on it had said THE WILLIAM GEOFFREY CHASE SUITE. Ben's father. That was pretty swanky. She nearly joined Tess with the skipping. The older kids were playing it much cooler, but Mia's eyes sparkled as she looked at Carli.

"Right in here," he added, herding them inside before letting go of the door. It closed softly behind them. The suite was nearly as big as Carli's bedroom and decorated in various shades of creams and whites with rustic accent pieces and comfy leather seating. One full wall was made up of sliding glass panels that looked out into the arena, providing a perfect view of the stage. Outside that was another private seating area. Best seats in the house, other than the front row. The kids all rushed to the glass to peer out over the arena.

"This is awesome," Mia said, giving up on trying to be reserved.

"Right?" Ethan said. "Privilege has its privileges, I guess."

Off to the side was a table laden with mini sandwiches, cookies, bags of chips, and other assorted goodies. There was a soda machine, a coffee bar, and a refrigerator with a clear glass door to display bottles of wine and beer.

"This place is nicer than my house," Carli said, turning slowly in a circle to see everything at once.

"It's very nice here," Ben agreed. "But not nicer than your house. I like your house."

She blushed under his gaze, because it seemed as if he wasn't talking so much about the aesthetics of her house as he was referring to the cozy hominess of it. He'd been respectfully flirtatious all day, and she was starting to feel very much noticed, and very much appreciated.

"Oh my gosh," Tess murmured to Mia. "Can you imagine what it would be like to watch the concert from here?"

"Would you like to?" Ben asked.

She turned around, eyes round, and nodded as if he'd just asked if she'd like to ride a flying unicorn.

"Okay, then. Let's watch it from here." He tried to sound nonchalant, but Carli could see he was pleased with himself—as well he should be. That was a pretty amazing offer.

"Seriously?" Mia and Addie exclaimed in unison, their voices each raising an octave.

"No way," Tess added, her voice going low in disbelief.

Ben shrugged. "Sure, it's the Chase suite. We can use it whenever we want."

The three girls jumped up and down, their giggles so loud they nearly didn't hear the soft knock on the door.

୬

This was the pièce de résistance of Ben's assault of awesomeness, and he could hardly wait to open the door. All day he'd been by Carli's side, watching her enthusiasm grow and her defenses come down. He'd reveled in the sound of her laughter, and his heart sped up every time he caught her eye, reinforcing his recent realization that he was falling for her. He'd suspected it for a while now, but having her avoid him these last two weeks just made him more certain than ever that he needed her in his life. He'd missed her like crazy since the fiasco on New Year's Eve, and the more he tried to convince himself that what he felt for her was just biological, the more he realized it was oh-so-much more than that. If today went according to his plan, she'd realize that she was falling for him, too. God, he sure hoped she was.

"Hey, guys," he said, trying to calm them down for a millisecond. "There's someone you might want to meet."

Ben opened the door, and in walked an enormous hulk of a man with a bald head and a sleeve of tattoos, but right behind him stood pop sensation and infamous heartthrob Nolan Hart.

"Hi. How's everybody doing?" Nolan stepped inside with a small wave and a surprisingly shy smile. He had swoopy blond hair and a Disney-prince jawline. Honestly, Ben had to hand it to the kid. He really was dreamy.

A silence so complete you could have heard a feather falling against a cloud was followed by a collection of teen-girl squeals so high-pitched that Ben thought the bulletproof glass of the suite was going to shatter. The kids were shocked and amazed, and he was going to live off the goodwill benefits of this moment for years. He'd keep it in his pocket for times when Addie was giving him grief.

"Remember that time I introduced you to Nolan Hart? Good, now go do the dishes."

That wasn't why he'd gone to all this trouble, of course. He looked over at Carli and thought she might be on the verge of shattering, too. But she wasn't staring at Nolan Hart. She was staring at Ben with a look of such joy and disbelief, he knew he'd hit the mark. Because he'd made this happen. He'd created this moment for her, and she seemed to understand that's exactly what he'd wanted. He'd wanted to make her smile, and to make her happy.

Tess was the first to approach the singer, her voice barely a whisper. "Hi. Um, what are you doing here?"

Nolan chuckled and pointed at Ben. "I came in early for sound check, and this guy invited me. He said there were brownies in here and that I should come have lunch with you guys."

"Ohmygosh," Addie said, hopping forward. "You should totally have lunch with us. You can have all the brownies, and the cookies, too, if you want."

"Just a couple of brownies ought to do," he answered. "But thanks. So where do you guys go to school?"

Mia and Ethan stepped forward, and before long they were all asking him questions, and he volleyed back just as many. He wasn't much older than they were, and if you didn't know the circumstances, you'd think they were just a group of friends hanging out on a Saturday afternoon. In a really expensive suite.

Ben walked over to Carli, his heart racing. "So do you like the surprise?"

She beamed up at him. "Very much. Well done."

"You're welcome," said the tattooed hulk, Nolan's oversize body-guard, who was just a few feet away.

Ben laughed. "Thanks for getting him here on time, Hank."

"Sure thing. Thanks for the hundred bucks."

Carli laughed. "Is that the going rate? A hundred bucks and some free brownies?"

Hank the Hulk nodded and plucked a cookie from the table. "Yep, as long as it's for a good cause."

"Oh really? What's the good cause?"

Hank smiled and nodded toward Ben. "This guy said he's trying to impress a lady. I'm guessing that might be you."

Chapter 35

"You really didn't have to go to all this trouble just to impress me," Carli said later that evening as Nolan Hart sang an up-tempo yet ridiculously romantic love song from the stage and all the kids sat in rapt attention in their seats. Ben pulled Carli into the shadows in the back of the suite, then pulled her, unresisting, into his arms.

"It wasn't so much to impress you, although I'm certainly glad if it did. I just wanted you to know . . ." His voice faltered, and she leaned against him.

"Wanted me to know what?"

"That you're special. And special to me in particular."

"That's a really sweet thing to say."

"Well, it's true. I know that New Year's Eve was . . . not ideal, but for what it's worth, I had a lot of fun spending time with you. I always have fun spending time with you." He lifted a strand of hair from her shoulder and twirled it around his finger. "And Ethan thinks you're pretty cool, so there's that."

Carli smiled. "Oh yeah? Well, my girls have said they don't ever want to see you in your underwear again, but in spite of that, they think you're pretty cool, too. And besides, after this whole thing?" She gestured toward the suite. "I'm fairly certain you've won them over."

"I'm glad to hear that, but it's not the kids' affection I'm after. It's yours. I could say I like you, Carli, but it's so much more than that.

I've been trying to make that obvious, but either I'm really bad at this or you're really resistant."

She wondered if he could see her blush, even in the dim light. "I was resistant, but I think you might be starting to win me over." He was totally winning her over. She was halfway in love with him already.

"I hope so, because I'm not going anywhere." He sighed and moved his hands to her hips, pulling her closer.

"You mean you're not going anywhere because we're neighbors?"

"No, I'm not going anywhere because I'm crazy about you. Don't you think it's time you considered falling in love with me? I think it's time." His smile was sexy-sweet.

Laughter bubbled up inside her like champagne. His words and his smile and the feel of him in her arms made her senses tingle and her pulse race. "Oh, you do, do you?"

He nodded. "Yep, but I'm patient, and I'm willing to work for it. Think there's any chance I'll succeed?"

"In making me fall in love with you?"

"Yes." His tone was light, but his gaze was intense, and her heart filled with hope.

"I think so. I'd say you're off to a pretty good start." Such a good start!

And then she kissed him.

Epilogue

It was a beautiful sunny day in May as the neighbors gathered for the One and Only Monroe Circle Epic Ethan and Magnificent Mia Graduation Party in the yard space between houses.

"You two have the strangest arrangement," Renee said from her spot on a reclining lawn chair. "Why don't you sell one of these houses?"

"Because I like my house, and Ben likes his house, and the kids have their own rooms and it just works for us. We like bouncing back and forth. It's our normal," Carli answered.

"Any whispers of marriage?" DeeDee asked.

"Whispers," Carli laughed. "Only whispers, and that's just fine by me. I like our current routine, and honestly, I just love him so much. It's stupid how much I love him."

Erin's smile was bright. "I think it's wonderful how much you love him, and it's obvious he feels the same way. You guys practically sparkle every time you're together. I'm so happy for you. You deserve this. You found your unicorn."

"I guess I have. I'm so lucky."

"*He's* so lucky," Renee said.

Carli chuckled. "Damn right. He's so lucky." They clinked their glasses together to toast as Ben smiled at her from across the lawn, where he was cooking burgers on his big, fancy-ass grill. Her heart did that clumsy tumble that it did every time their eyes met. Yep, she was stupid in love. She blew him a kiss. He blew one back.

"Actually, you're kind of nauseating," DeeDee said. "But I like it."

"Yep," Carli said, laughing. "I like it, too."

ACKNOWLEDGMENTS

First and foremost, thank you to my devoted readers, who ask for more stories, who send notes of appreciation, and who keep me at the keyboard well into the night. I will always have more stories, so if you keep reading, I'll keep writing.

Thank you to Nalini Akolekar, who continues to support me in ways too numerous to list. I'd buy you a puppy, but you already have too many. Thank you to Melody Guy for trusting me and trusting the process, and for always, always helping me make the sausage. Thank you to Anh Schluep for giving me *just one more week* and the entire team at Montlake Publishing for continually turning my words into *real* books.

A heartfelt thanks to my writing sisters at Fiction From the Heart— Jamie Beck, Sonali Dev, Kwana Jackson, Donna Kauffman, Sally Kilpatrick, Falguni Kothari, Priscilla Oliveras, Barbara Samuel, Hope Ramsey, and Liz Talley—for teaching me things (and for making me laugh) every single day. I am better for knowing you.

To the friends and writers who have inspired me, challenged me, and occasionally talked me off a ledge: Catherine Bybee, Marina Adair, Kimberly Kincaid, Alyssa Alexander, and Elizabeth Essex. Hugs and smooches to you.

Thank you to Jane for your virtual red pen and for always being willing to talk over plot points. I'm sure I owe you more coffee.

Thank you to Terri DeBoer for the friendship and for all the great details about life at a TV station.

And finally, thank you to Webster Girl and Tenacious D, who make everything more fun, even the stuff that isn't. Without you, none of the rest matters.

AUTHOR NOTE

To learn more about the love story of meteorologist-turned–morning show cohost Allie Winters, look for my novella *Weather or Knot*.

ABOUT THE AUTHOR

Photo © 2017 Kristy Berands Photography

Tracy Brogan is the *USA Today* and *Wall Street Journal* bestselling author of the Trillium Bay series, the Bell Harbor series, and the stand-alone novels *Hold on My Heart* and *Highland Surrender*. She is a three-time finalist for the Romance Writers of America RITA Award and a two-time recipient of the Amazon Publishing Diamond Award for sales exceeding one million copies and has won several Booksellers' Best awards. Her books have been translated into dozens of languages and have hit number one on Amazon in both the United States and Germany. She lives in Michigan with her daughters, Webster Girl and Tenacious D, who credit her DNA for their inherent gifts of sarcasm and irony and her questionable parenting choices for their well-developed ability to adapt to other people's mood swings. She is a clumsy dancer, an obsessive organizer, and terrible at house-breaking puppies. For more information, visit www.tracybrogan.com.